A RIVER IN BORNEO

The Nathaniel Drinkwater Novels

An Eye of the Fleet
A King's Cutter
A Brig of War
The Bomb Vessel
The Corvette
1805
Baltic Mission
In Distant Waters
A Private Revenge
Under False Colours
The Flying Squadron
Beneath the Aurora
The Shadow of the Eagle
Ebb Tide

* * *

Also available from McBooks Press

A River in Borneo
The Darkening Sea

A River in Borneo

A Tale of the East Indies

Richard Woodman

Essex, Connecticut

McBooks
Press

An imprint of Globe Pequot, the trade division of
The Rowman & Littlefield Publishing Group, Inc.
4501 Forbes Blvd., Ste. 200
Lanham, MD 20706
www.rowman.com

Distributed by NATIONAL BOOK NETWORK

British Library Cataloguing in Publication Information available

Library of Congress Cataloging-in-Publication Data

Names: Woodman, Richard, 1944- author.
Title: A river in Borneo : a tale of the East Indies / Richard Woodman.
Description: Guilford, Connecticut : McBooks Press, [2021]
Identifiers: LCCN 2021038983 (print) | LCCN 2021038984 (ebook) | ISBN
  9781493061921 (hardback ; alk. paper) | ISBN 9781493063437 (epub) | ISBN
  9781493075164 (paperback ; alk. paper)
Subjects: LCGFT: War fiction. | Novels.
Classification: LCC PR6073.O618 R58 2021 (print) | LCC PR6073.O618
  (ebook) | DDC 823/.914—dc23
LC record available at https://lccn.loc.gov/2021038983
LC ebook record available at https://lccn.loc.gov/2021038984

♾️™ The paper used in this publication meets the minimum requirements of American National
Standard for Information Sciences—Permanence of Paper for Printed Library Materials, ANSI/
NISO Z39.48-1992.

Author's Note

This story is set in three distinct periods, the greater part of the narrative being between summer 1867 and March 1872, with a prologue and epilogue taking place in the summer of 1964 and an afterword in 2018. Both the dialogue and attitudes herein depicted are, therefore, those of these times. Consequently there is some racist dialogue along with other inter-social prejudices carried by my characters in sections of the story which are today unacceptable. I wish to make it quite clear that no offence is intended by this historical verisimilitude. However, to dismiss the past without reflecting the known—and well documented—behaviours of the time in question, would weaken both the credibility and integrity of my yarn. If nothing else, it shows that while we have a long way yet to go, some progress has been made.

I hope that the occasional use of foreign terms is generally self-explanatory, but just in case the reader finds this difficult some explanations here may help. The Malay term *orang puteh* means white man; *orang kaya,* a rich man, and *orang laut,* man of the sea—specifically herein a Bugis pirate. The title *Tuan,* as used on the Singaporean waterfront of the day, was the colloquial and contemporaneous equivalent of the English use of the word 'sir' (occasionally elevated to 'Lord') as a general term of respect, caste or rank being as important to cultures other than those of the British imperium.

Ship-board ranks were often confusing but broadly speaking the Malay nouns *Tindal* meant boatswain, and *Casab* signified the boatswain's mate (itself a rank that might also be known as lamp-trimmer —'lampy'—in colloquial English); *Jurmudi,* was a quartermaster, charged with the vessel's steering. Titles of other etymology common at sea were *Tomelo,* the ship's carpenter, and *Shawbunder,* the collector of customs and/or harbour-master. Other Malay words/phrases in common use by all races living in the Lion City were *hujan*, meaning rain, and torrential tropical rain at that; *arriah*, meaning 'lower-away there'; *makanan*, meaning 'food,' and *makan* 'eat,' so that '*saya pergi makan*' meant 'I am now going to eat,' and *bagus*, meaning 'good' as in 'it is good,' 'I am satisfied.'

Other nouns and adjectives in common use were *Crani* (a clerk, but usually a tally-clerk who checked the number of slings, bales, etc. being loaded or discharged by a cargo-vessel), *kampong* (village), *telok* (bay), *selat* (*strait*), *tanjong* (headland, point, etc), *batu* (rock), *sungei* (river), and *besar* (big, often used to denote the larger of two islands in small archipelagos, its antonym being *kechil*). Islands themselves were either *pulau* or *pulo*, while small boats—roughly the equivalent of the generic *sampan* in Chinese waters but also used by Singaporean Chinese—were *perahus*, pronouced *prau*, which is sometimes used as an alternative spelling. The Malay *kris* was a long dagger with a wavy blade, often beautifully made, and a *parang* a sword or *machete*. Such weapons were a danger in the hands of an *amok*, a man who had lost his head and who rushed about killing indiscriminately and from which we derive the expression 'run *amok*' for someone acting in a murderously uncontrolled manner.

Indian—Hindi, Urdu, etc.—words and phrases also migrated east, carried by ships and often mixed up with English, Portuguese, and so forth. Those used herein are *Nakoda*—meaning a native of the subcontinent who commands a merchant ship and the Malay equivalent of which is *Kurmudi*. Such vessels were usually termed *country-wallahs*, an Anglo-Indian compound noun meaning a merchantman, often a large one, beneficially owned in India. The vessel concerned flew a British red ensign and enjoyed the protection of the British Navy. A very large fleet of these vessels had grown-up in the Eastern Seas during the eighteenth century owing to the monopoly held until 1813 (to India) and 1834 (to China) by the East India Company, which prevented British owners in the United Kingdom from trading with places beyond the Cape of Good Hope except under licence from the Company. However, trade from India throughout the eastern seas was permitted in such ships and it was these that first conveyed opium to China in large quantities; however, after the Treaty of Nanking (1842) and the acquisition of Hong Kong, the processed opium was carried in fast British-registered ships, and it was for this reprehensible trade that the *Tethys* in my story had originally been built.

Country-wallahs were commanded by a variety of men, British, Indian, and mixed-race seamen, often being owned by Brito-Indian merchant houses of which the combination of Scotsmen and Parsis was commonplace, both ashore in their counting-houses, and also afloat. In Singapore Chinese-owned trading houses were headed by a *Towkay*, or chief merchant.

In Singapore men employed as watchmen or guards were known as *Jagas*, armed servants of private companies—what we should today call 'security officers' and, like their modern equivalents, they would wear a uniform, usually indicating the identity of their employer. For this reason the *Jagas* working for the House of the Green Dragon wore bright green turbans. Such men, at the time of which I write, were usually of Sikh extraction, domiciled in Singapore and as proud—and often as smart—as guardsmen, frequently being former soldiers of one sort or another.

Originally European vessels trading in eastern waters carried a 'supra-cargo,' or 'super-cargo,' sometimes known by the Portuguese noun *Comprador*. This individual was a merchant sailing in a merchant ship to undertake the commercial business on behalf of the ship's owner(s). In the earliest days of European trade with the east he out-ranked the Master (or Captain) but by the 1860s these tasks were usually a part of the Master's duties, allowing the Masters to accrue small fortunes on their own account.

However, to smooth commercial transactions, at the time the *Tethys* was sailing among the islands it was common to carry a *Shroff*, the Chinese synonym for which was *Chin-chew*, as a commercial agent who handled cash (itself a word that crept into the English language from the Far East), testing coin for its value, and so forth. The *chin-chew* usually handled either the universally used currency of the Spanish silver dollar (the *reale*) or pieces of silver known as *sycee* silver. He was often the ship's principal interpreter and could become a very rich man because all trade and commercial transactions were accompanied by presents/bribes/back-handers of various complexities known by a number of names. Here I have used the most common in this part of the world—*cumshaw*.

Chinese phrases were often too difficult for the white man to learn so a form of common tongue, initiated by the Portuguese as a *lingua franca* but vastly expanded by the British who, in their traditional failure to master native tongues, simply adopted terms and anglicised them, creating and augmenting 'pidgin.' Some of these adoptions linger as remnants today in our own daily discourse: 'cup of char,' for a drink of tea; 'chop-chop,' meaning 'hurry-up'; 'top-dollar' meaning 'the best' or 'of the finest quality'; 'savee,' signifying understanding/knowledge as in 'I savee' or 'you savee?'; and 'look-see,' meaning 'show me' or 'I had a look,' being a few examples. Among the thousands of men manning and servicing ships in eastern waters during these years, pidgin of one sort or another became the common tongue.

To wrap up our definitions, a brigantine of the period was a relatively small sailing vessel having two masts; the foremost, the foremast, carries yards and so-called square sails; the after or main mast bears fore-and-aft sails somewhat similar to a vintage, gaff-rigged yacht of today.

Turning to historical background, although Singapore was founded by the East India Company by treaty with the *Temenngong* (Sultan) of Johore in 1819, the nature of its rapid expansion as an *entrepôt* under the protection of the British flag made it not a Malay but an essentially Chinese city, filling with this industrious people, despite edicts by the Emperor in distant Beijing forbidding emigration from the Middle Kingdom. It remains so to this day, its adoption into greater Malaysia having failed. However, at the time in question, despite the city being dominated by Chinese, Malay formed the shared language common to many among the racially diverse inhabitants of the Lion City.

Elsewhere the political map requires some explanation. At the time in which the chief section of this story is set, the huge island of Borneo/Kalimantan was, over most of its southern territory, part of the Dutch East Indies (today's Indonesian Kalimantan). Its northern coast, however, consisted of three states. The largest was the independent territory of Sarawak, whose ruling Rajah was a white-man, Rajah Brooke, the title having been ceded—uncoerced—as a gift by the nominal overlord and last Malay ruler. At the north-eastern end of the Borneo coast another such private fiefdom, Brunei, under its own Sultan, lay next to the most easterly, a territory today known as Sabah and part of Malaysia, having been for some years known as British North Borneo and corporately owned. In the 1860s and '70s, however, it was part of the Sultanate of Sulu, and was viewed with an envious eye by the Spanish, the colonial power in the adjacent and huge archipelago of the Philippine Islands. The actual Sulu archipelago stretches from the north-eastern tip of Borneo to the Basilan Strait on the far side of which lies the Philippine port of Zamboanga on the large island of Mindanao.

At the time the Sultanate of Sulu also incorporated the now Philippine island of Palawan, making it a significant power in the region. Sunni Muslim in religion, ruled by Sultan Jamal ul-Azam, its existence as a buffer state between two European colonial empires—the Spanish and the Dutch— both of whom attempted the exclusion of others in their trade, attracted 'British' merchants, that racial mix domiciled in that extraordinary city-state of Singapore. These men exploited opportunities provided by legitimate trade and civil unrest. The major port for trade in the Sulu archipelago itself was Jolo, on the island of the same name. In the 1860s it was the centre of a slave-trade as well as a rich source of what was known as 'island produce' which included pearls, mother-of-pearl, gum copal and gum damar, camphor, rattans (from which many a Parisian *boulevardier's* Malacca cane was made), *trepang* (sea-slugs), seahorses, and bird's nests (the Chinese delicacies producing soups and medicines). In addition to these commodities, greater Sulu offered apparently limitless quantities of timber, gums, hides, shells, copra, hemp, sisal or coir, and gutta-percha (a rubber-like product and a precursor to the imminent development of latex rubber), which was used as insulation. Also, dried fish and other comestibles were often on offer to trading vessels in times of plenty. Imports included a variety of western manufactures, clothing, soap, paint, tools, nails, sheet iron, boots and shoes, oils, spirits, glassware, and guns.

In February 1867 the Spaniards (already a declining colonial power shortly to lose the Philippines to the rising Pacific imperialism of the United States of America) sent an auxiliary steam corvette to 'show the flag' off Jolo. And on 5th March 1872 thirteen Spanish men-of-war half-heartedly blockaded Jolo in an attempt to put an end to piracy, for which the place was said to act as a base. From the following year they maintained this blockade and in 1875, as part of their colonial policy, they landed 9,000 soldiers, laid siege to the place, captured it, and turned it into a walled stronghold. This ended Jolo's commercial prosperity and presaged the absorption of the Sultanate into the Philippines, and the turning of its Sultan to a puppet.

A century later, in the 1960s, the ambitious President Sukarno of Indonesia—the hero of the anti-colonial wars against first the occupying Japanese and then, post 1945, the returning old colonial power of the reinstated Dutch—announced his opposition to the formation of a greater Malaya—or Malaysia—from the old British Malayan Straits Settlements, Singapore, Sarawak, and British North Borneo, initiating a vicious and largely forgotten war in which British forces took a part in support of their own former colonies. Its nastiness was hidden behind its bland, euphemistic name: 'Confrontation.'

One final note; lest it be thought that the name Cha Lee Foo smacks of some pantomime character, I preserve in his memory (and in my mind's eye as I write), a kindly and already old Chinese Quartermaster of this name aboard the cargo-liner *Glenartney*, who was my sea-daddy on my first voyage to sea in 1960.

Otherwise this story is dedicated to:

J.C. and J.G.,
both of whom, in their different ways, conjured the flame of imagination,
and to
P.McL.
for her loyal support,
but chiefly for Arlo, who is as familiar with the Tethys *as the author.*

What shall I tell you? Tales, marvellous tales
Of ships and stars and isles where good men rest.

James Elroy Flecker, *The Golden Road to Samarkand*

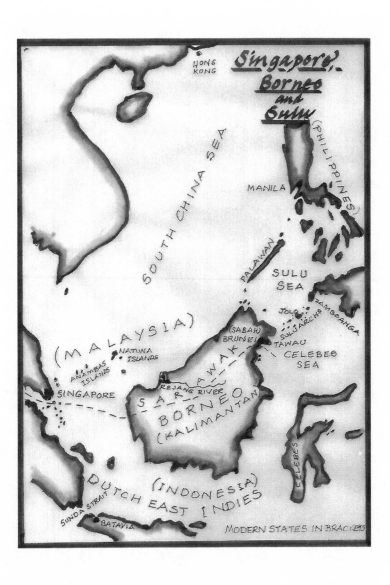

The Sultanate of Sulu

SOUTH CHINA SEA

PALAWAN

SULU SEA

SPANISH PHILIPPINES

PANAY

NEGROS

MINDANAO

ZAMBOANGA

BALABAC STRAIT

MARUDU BAY

BANGGI

MALAWALI CAGAYAN

MOUNT KINABALU

TAWAU

SIBUTU PASS

DARVEL BAY

BUMBUM

SULU ARCHIPELAGO

JOLO

SIASI

CELEBES SEA

SARAWAK

DUTCH BORNEO

TARAKAN

Somewhere hereabouts Captain Henry Kirton found his River in Borneo.

PART ONE

The Rain Forest of Kalimantan (Indonesian Borneo), Early Summer 1964

'Where's the Boss?'

'Probably gone for a shit.'

'He can't have unless he wants the Wog to wipe his arse . . .'

'Knock that off right now!' snapped Sergeant McGuigan in his thick Ulster brogue. 'The Dayak Ranger's name is Bangau, if you can remember that, Snedding. In the meantime cut the crap and get a brew on; we need to eat as soon as possible.'

Sergeant McGuigan fingered the trigger of his carbine, leant his back against a twisted mangrove, and cast his eye over the Royal Marine patrol of which he was second-in-command. They had had a hard march through near impenetrable rain forest that had changed into equally near impenetrable mangrove swamp since first light, and now the sky was darkening with the premature onset of darkness that came with a mustering of heavy rain cloud. He tried to calculate how far they had come through what had seemed at times like impassable vegetation, but Lieutenant Kirton had kept them moving as silently as their brief stint of training in jungle warfare had enabled them; and to think that only six months ago they had been on skis in Norway training in Arctic combat gear, defending NATO's northern flank! Hey-ho, McGuigan thought, after nine years in the Corps he should not have been surprised.

As for their relentless pace, that was all Charlie Kirton's idea. 'I hope to find this river by nightfall, Sar'n't,' he had said curtly, which was pretty much all the briefing he had given his second-in-command before setting out on their fourth day's march. Well, the young lieutenant certainly lived up to his name, curt he most certainly was—and he had been in theatre far longer than his men, a veteran of the armed force Britain had sent out to assist its former colonies of the new Malaysia as they fought off the ambitions of President Sukarno of Indonesia in a quiet, vicious, and deadly war that the politicos preferred to term, euphemistically— 'Confrontation.' Kirton had been on detached service for several months; he had had some hand in training the local defence forces and spoke Malay. He was also known to every marine in the Corps as a fine yachtsman and a very tough cookie. Sergeant McGuigan admired him very much, even if he was a rather too obviously practising Roman Catholic.

As the light dropped with the rapid westering of the sun and the increase of cloud Kirton had told McGuigan to make camp. 'I'm going to press on for another few hundred yards, Sar'n't, I'm damn sure that river is nearby, as is Bangau. See the men get their chow. I'll take the Dayak with me. Leave a bite for us.'

'Very good, sir,' McGuigan had responded, standing guard while the men around him hunkered down, squatting on their haunches to avoid the ants and other insects that seemed to teem in all their variety across the forest floor among the dead and rotting vegetation that stank of wet decay and oozed water under their weight. Not that he thought them much in danger of being found by an Indonesian patrol, and if they were the buggers would be upon them before they knew it if their woodcraft was any good—and it should be, it was their turf, after all.

Since they had been landed by the Royal Malaysian Navy's high-speed *perahu* that had picked them up at Tawau and dumped them just inside enemy territory they had glimpsed Indonesian aerial activity on three occasions, the last that morning when a chopper had flown fairly low above the forest canopy and suggested, to Lieutenant Kirton at least, that the river they had been sent out to find could not be far away.

McGuigan gave the men in his charge a brief over-arching scan; they were all first class soldiers, though one or two were inclined to be lippy. Snedding, an angular lad from East London with a dubious history, was keen on baiting Benjamin, a black Brummie who gave as good as he got; while Bennett, a big, powerful farm-boy from Suffolk enjoyed playing pranks on his mates, which under the present humid circumstances wore thin very quickly. But he was a strong lad, with a fine musculature under his sweating layer of blubber, so-much-so that he got to carry the patrol's 7.62 support machine gun, leaving the spare barrels, the tripod for sustained fire, and the belts of ammo to the rest of them.

Casting his eyes over the remainder of the patrol McGuigan concluded that they were a pretty impressive platoon and, catching Corporal Willis's eye, McGuigan sufficiently relaxed the bonds of discipline to wink at his fellow NCO. He and the corporal had known each other for a long time and had been delighted to re-make each other's acquaintance when they received their draft-chits for the frigate *Llandaff*.

Willis was on the point of winking back when his expression went tense and he reached instinctively for his own machine gun.

McGuigan had heard it too: the snap of rotten wood and the sudden alert it caused transmitted itself to everyone. The hiss of the small stove heating the evening's pot-mess was instantly suppressed and every man-jack had his gun in his hand and was faced-about, outwards from the small glade in which they had intended spending the night.

The light was fading fast and the chirrup of the cicadas was fading with it. McGuigan regretted not having re-anointed his blackened face with insect repellent as he felt a mozzie bite his neck. The broken wood could have been natural, the work of a monkey or gibbon, or whatever other primates hung in the dense canopy above them—and they had been told of the huge *orang utang*—the Man of the Forest—who was the dominant species in this lush and rather terrifying land. It might, McGuigan thought with a tightening of the muscles in his belly, be a tiger. But whatever had caused the noise, McGuigan concluded, it was unlikely to have been Lieutenant Kirton and his Iban Dayak scout; they were far too skilled at moving quietly through this terrain and had left their packs in the camp to make their recce easier.

And then suddenly Kirton and Bangau emerged from the vegetation and the tension eased. 'Where's supper then?' Kirton asked, half in jest, for it was clear to McGuigan that he, or Bangau, *had* caused the noise.

'Coming up, sir,' replied Snedding, reigniting the small stove.

'There's tea here, sir,' offered Meadows, a Pompey lad with a face like a boxer's but the manners of a gentleman. Meadows was after more than a sergeant's chevrons.

Kirton took the steaming mug and squatted on his haunches like his men. Silently Snedding offered a second mug to Bangau who nodded his thanks and then backed off, to hunker down on his own with his back to a tree, just clear of the close-knit group of Royal Marines. McGuigan looked quizzically at Kirton; the lieutenant was five or six years his junior and, as with Corporal Willis, McGuigan had known him previous to their present deployment. And right now, despite the streaks of camouflage 'blackening' that concealed Kirton's deep tan, he would have put money on Kirton having had a shock. He transferred his gaze to Bangau;

to his astonishment the tough little Iban warrior was visibly shaking as he quaffed his tea.

McGuigan shuffled his way across the yard or so separating himself from Kirton.

'Any luck, sir?' he asked in a low voice.

Kirton swallowed hard. There was a long pause during which the young officer took deep draughts of tea before emptying the dregs and decorously removed a tea-leaf from his tongue. Then, McGuigan noticed he swallowed hard, shot a glance at Bangau, and nodded.

'Yup. We found the river just a few hundred yards away. It runs deep and wide; I suspect we're sitting in it right now, for these mangroves cover the shore, so the approach is difficult . . .' Kirton paused again. Indeed, he seemed to have wandered off into some other place and McGuigan—a naturally impatient man—filled the void by asking:

'No immediate sign of the sort of place we are looking for then, sir . . . without making a look-see upstream, that is?', adding '*ulu*' with a jerk of his head and inordinately proud of his knowledge of the Malay word for upriver.

'Eh, what?' McGuigan's words seemed to recall Kirton from somewhere else; an unusual circumstance for this focussed officer, McGuigan thought, with a twinge of anxiety as to what the hell was going on. Something was, though.

Then Kirton seemed to gather his wits. 'No, no. I've found the perfect place, Sar'n't, perfect in every—well most—respects.' Kirton paused a moment before continuing, his voice low but, to the sergeant's infinite relief, full of its usual confidence. 'Actually it pretty much found us. About twenty minutes after leaving you here our friend,' Kirton nodded perfunctorily towards Bangau who remained clutching his mug of tea and staring at the ground before him, 'refused to go any further; said the place was full of spirits. I have to confess that what with his reluctance to proceed and the onset of twilight, I was having second thoughts about the wisdom of my decision to scout out a bit further . . . then I saw what Bangau had already seen, only feet away . . .' Kirton broke off, shaking his head, as if he could still not quite believe it, then he resumed his tale. 'Rearing above us was the bow of a small ship, a very old ship with a bow like the clipper *Cutty Sark* at Greenwich and a long bowsprit that disappeared into the branches overhead. She's surrounded by the growth of years of vegetation and while my companion would venture no further, I . . . I scrambled aboard.'

Kirton ceased speaking as Snedding shuffled towards them on his knees with two mess-tins full of an unappetising brown concoction of rehydrated protein. 'Supper, gents,' he said briefly, handing the pot-mess over to his two seniors. After Kirton had taken a few mouthfuls he resumed his account, his voice low and confidential.

'She's pretty much perfect for our purposes, with a few little modifications. God knows how she got there but long ago she was rammed into the river's bank, if you can call it that; she's almost totally over-grown but she has a long counter stern which is no more than ten or twelve feet inside the outer growth; we can mount the M.G. there and command the entire reach of the river . . .'

'Will an old wreck stand the stresses of the recoil of a 7.62, sir?' McGuigan, ever the practical NCO, asked.

'Oh. Yes,' Kirton nodded. 'There's very little paint left on her and although there's evidence of a small fire, even in the failing light I could see she was built of teak; it's practically indestructible.'

'And she's got accommodation too, I suppose, such as a bunch of rough-necks as we are can live in . . . ?'

'Yes . . .' Kirton's voice had become uncertain again.

'Then where's the problem, sir? I just fancy operating from a house-boat.'

'Well, precisely *there* is the problem, Sergeant,' Kirton responded with uncharacteristic formality, 'in the accommodation . . . though we will have to clear a bit of vegetation to provide arcs of fire from the stern . . .'

'But there's another modification we've got to make?' McGuigan queried, thinking that this was like trying to get blood out of a fucking stone. 'In the accommodation?' he prompted.

'Yes. There *are* spirits there, as Bangau sensed . . .' Both men looked across at the Dayak Ranger who was tucking in to his supper and looked up as he felt the scrutiny of the two *orang puteh* fall across him. Kirton smiled reassuringly but McGuigan's eyes were narrowed. Bangau did not like the Ulsterman and McGuigan knew it. Although he had been selected for this mission in part because of his command of English, the Dayak could not understand the big man's Ulster brogue. He lowered his eyes and continued his meal. He was deeply unhappy that the British officer was going to incorporate the strange wreck into his plans. To Bangau, an Ibani sea-Dayak, or *orang laut*, whose ancestors had been formidable pirates, the old ship emanated foreboding.

'Spirits, sir?' A visceral sensation was uncoiling in McGuigan's belly; Kirton was a Catholic after all.

'Well human remains actually, Sar'n't,' Kirton said, his voice resuming its natural brisk tone, 'and before anyone else goes aboard you and I are going to have to go and dispose of them. Not even Her Majesty's Royal Marines can be expected to make skeletons their bed-fellows.'

'They're just bones then, sir.'

'Yes, just bones . . .'

'Well we can deal with them while the men are preparing breakfast.'

'Quite so, Sar'n't.' It would be a neat juxtaposition, bones then breakfast.

'Will that be all for tonight, sir?'

'Yes, I think so.'

'I'll post the pickets and catch some shut-eye. Good night, sir.'

'Good night, Sar'n't.'

Lieutenant Charles Kirton lay for some time on the fetid forest floor staring through the drips of water that fell from the canopy high above. After dark it had rained heavily again and he was pretty wet, but it was not physical discomfort that prevented him from sleeping, or the nocturnal noise of the mangrove swamp; it was the effect of those fifteen minutes spent aboard the strange old wreck. And it was only partially the human remains that had so disturbed him: ghosts came in other guises, though the skeletons were real enough seen in that crepuscular gloom.

He could not escape the conviction that had gripped him that not only would the old sailing vessel prove the answer to the mission's quest, but that there was a disturbingly personal element to his finding her, a supernatural connection that his rational mind found it difficult to throw-off.

'Well, Charles,' the C.O. had said at his briefing back in Tawau as they pored over an almost featureless Dutch map—featureless in terms of features but covered in the conventional signs for 'jungle,' 'swamp,' and bearing the legend *niet onderzocht,* or *unsurveyed* in English. 'I can't tell you exactly where in all this bloody jungley stuff this bloody river is, but it's there somewhere. From what intelligence is telling us is appearing further along the border with our friend's here . . .' the C.O.'s right fore-finger traced the wriggling line of the uncertain national demarcation westwards, away from the coast which the Malaysians and their British allies dominated, 'the Indos are moving men and *matériel* up to the border with Brunei and Sarawak at too fast a rate, and the equipment is too heavy, for most of it to be airlifted. There has to be a water route through here somewhere,' and the senior officer's finger retraced its path to circle an area perhaps thirty miles south-west of where they then were in Tawau. 'From this *kampong* here,' he tapped the little black rectangles representing an Indonesian village, 'to which there is a half metalled road, and then into *perahus* or whatever they use hereabouts and upstream.' The C.O.'s finger shot back to the border through the 'unsurveyed' jungle. 'There *has* to be a water route, d'you see?'

'I do sir.'

'Now to the secret aspect of all this,' the C.O. went on. 'Intelligence indicates the Indos are preparing for a major offensive connected with some date significant to President Sukarno's regime—I don't know what it is, but I do know that there are several options and that the first is inside a month, his birthday on the 6th of June, the anniversary of D-Day! So, we want you to locate the river and find somewhere we can mount at least a 7.62 to interdict this traffic and generally bugger-up their line of communications. All classic stuff really; just the job for you and your new boys . . . So there you have it: Find somewhere suitable, bit of hard ground, or make a platform of tree-trunks, you know the kind of thing, then send back word by way of the Dayak Ranger and a couple of men and we'll move ammo and supplies up to you, by air preferably, over all this jungley stuff.'

Kirton had not really listened to the little pep-talk with which his boss concluded the mission briefing, though he gave something of the sort to his men a bit later as he passed on a redacted version of the C.O.'s briefing to his men. Their travails as they fought their way through first the rain forest and then this abominable swamp had been a minor epic. He had only the sketchiest notion of distance, though a slightly better understanding of direction. Willing and helpful though he had proved, his jungle-craft being indispensible, this was not territory with which Bangau was familiar. And how did you become familiar with 'all this jungle stuff' that covered the land with a profuse monotony? He recalled his days as a boy-scout and the certainties of laying and blazing a trail, of following compass bearings and crossing streams on rafts made of matches and match-boxes! They seemed to have been sent on a fool's mission, for even if they found the river no-where seemed to offer the slightest prospect of what they were looking for: hard ground. And how far *ulu* did one go before drawing too much attention from the Indonesians' forward base? And then, that very evening, without really trying, he had found the place. Well no, that was not quite true, for it had found them and they had merely stumbled across it.

And it most assuredly *was* full of spirits.

His mind drifted, running over that strange encounter with the old ship. Now that really was weird. Like Sergeant McGuigan he too had wondered if that long, over-hanging counter stern would take the mounting of a heavy machine gun. He had stamped hard on the deck, even with some difficulty opened a small wooden hatch that led into what was either a lazarette or a store, but the gathering gloom told him nothing other than she *seemed* sound enough. He had begun his sailing in old boats, one of which had been a little teak-planked Victorian cutter, and he knew teak from oak at the very least. And this old hooker looked to be teak-built and solid as a rock.

He had lain down on the deck and peered over the stern. There was no taffrail, only a low toe-rail and he could see right under her long overhanging counter, down to the upper edge of her rudder. The swiftly fading daylight, reflected on the river's surface, threw the carved decorations under the peeled paint into relief. There was some gingerbread work which looked as though it had once been decorated with gold leaf—*gold* leaf? And he could read her port of registry in its mirrored carved letters: LONDON. But it appeared that a short piece of dangling plank—a rotten soft-wood presumably—had been screwed over the top. There was nothing much left of it so he could read nothing but the single suggestion of the letter 'J'. Or had it been an 'S'?

'Singapore, probably,' he had murmured to himself.

And just above was her name. And here came his first shock; anyone—anyone in the whole fucking world except Lieutenant Charles Henry Kirton, RM—would have had trouble reading it upside down, let alone of pronouncing it or of knowing its significance, for that applied only to himself. But Kirton knew almost before he had picked out all of the mirror-imaged letters and it made him shiver, almost as much as the sudden anxiety to get back to camp before total, tropical darkness and a downpour of monsoon *hujan* enveloped him and the Dayak Ranger.

'Bloody hell!' he had muttered, rising to his feet.

As he had turned forward he had found himself facing a companionway which led below. Consumed by a powerful curiosity, yet concerned about the failing light, he had dithered before scrambling hurriedly below. What he found there had sent him back on deck, badly shaken and eager to pick up Bangau and return to camp and the company of his men.

'Plenty spirits, Bangau,' Kirton said abruptly, his mouth dry, setting off the way they had come just as night fell.

They had made it by the skin of their teeth, guided by the low sound of voices and the hiss of the small stove heating the dehydrated pot-mess, their nervous state causing them to move carelessly, involuntarily snapping that dead wood. After the meal and his conversation with McGuigan, Kirton had prepared himself for sleep. It had begun to rain and he had heard the muttered curses of the marines around him, already vociferating their loathing of the so-called 'icky-gribblies' that took their prostrate bodies as highways to their own suppers. He had silently offered up his evening prayers, commending his badly disturbed soul to God, undemonstratively crossing himself and composing himself for sleep.

But—unusually for Kirton—it did not come easily, despite the exertions of the day.

He lay there, staring up at a sky now completely clouded over with heavy rain-bearing cloud and thought of what he had found: that upside down, back-to-front name he had seen but an hour or so earlier and the human remains. He felt certain, viscerally positive, that he knew the identity of one of them. It was a weird conviction that left him musing on the strangeness of it all, of the nature of so-called coincidence and on the circularity of all things.

But there was also the distasteful task he had to undertake the following morning.

Almost his final act that day was the subconscious breathing of the name of the ancient Greek goddess that appeared on the old vessel's elegant counter:

'*Tethys* . . .'

PART TWO

Chapter One

Singapore

Captain McClure was a hot and irritated man as, standing on her starboard bridge-wing, he conned the auxiliary steam-vessel *River Tay* of 1,860 gross registered tons through the anchorage off Singapore. The Lion City lay sweltering in the heat although, judging by the clouds banking up over the Riau Archipelago to the southward, and the islands surrounding Pulo Bukum ahead, there would be heavy and drenching rain before long. It was windless in the anchorage but he knew this was only temporary; such lulls in the monsoon did not last and the energy in those clouds was palpable.

He steadied the Chinese quartermaster at the helm onto a new course to bring the *River Tay* closer to the Esplanade and nodded to the junior apprentice who, having bent the requisite signal flags onto the halliards, was waiting for the order.

'Hoist away, there.'

'Aye, aye, sir,' the lad said, smartly, running aloft the signal for the *River Tay*'s agent. The boy belayed the halliards and stood back for a moment to see that the signal flags flew free alongside that for pratique and the ship's 'numbers,' then turned to the master.

'Signal hoisted, sir,' he reported formally.

'Very well,' responded McClure, not taking his eyes off the anchored ship under the stern of which the *River Tay* now slid through the perfectly calm blue waters. It was one of the new Holt steamers, the first of which had come into service the year before, 1866. *Achilles*, he read on her counter stern.

'Port easy. . . stop engine,' McClure ordered.

'Port easy,' repeated the quartermaster.

'Stop engine,' responded the senior apprentice, bending to the engine-room voice-pipe and waiting for the answer which he called out to McClure across the bridge-wing of the *River Tay* in the still hot afternoon air.

'Steady . . . steady as she goes . . .'

'Steady on west by north, sir.'

McClure lifted his telescope, held it against a dodger stanchion, and levelled it at the distant signal station on Mount Faber. He was too far away to make much of the flags that hung limply from the yard-arm, so he shifted his attention to the cluster of boats milling around Collyer Quay and Johnston's Pier. He was impatient now; this call at Singapore was entirely unnecessary, or would have been had not Henry Kirton, his second mate, broken his leg so badly that he required urgent medical attention. The *River Tay* ought to have been heading for the Sunda Strait on her long passage across the Indian Ocean to round the Cape of Good Hope on her way to London.

'Signal station's acknowledged, sir,' reported the senior apprentice, lowering the long glass.

'Thank you,' McClure said. He was a smart lad, McClure thought, with damned good eye-sight. He would get a step in rank as uncertificated third mate for the run home, profiting from Kirton's misfortune.

'I think that's port health coming off now sir, and possibly the agent's boat close behind,' the senior apprentice added ingratiatingly. McClure raised his own glass again. A small sailing vessel slid across his field of vision before he saw the large pulling boat that he recognised as the port health officer's gig; not far astern another boat was heading their way and flying the house-flag of the *River Tay*'s owners: the Scottish River Line's Singapore agent, Mr Cha Lee Foo, a quiet dignified Chinese merchant who was reputed to be worth a fortune, an *orang kaya* if ever there was one and with whom McClure had been doing ship's business for twenty years, ever since he had been chief mate of the barque *River Carron*.

McClure looked over the side; the ship was barely moving now. He cast a glance round. He wouldn't be anchored long if he had his way, unless Cha could get him some coal in short order.

'Half astern,' he called over his shoulder and heard the reassuring response from down below, then observed the roil of white water under the counter that he was watching for as he leaned over the bridge-wing. He let it work its way up the ship's side until almost directly beneath him.

'Stop engine!'

'Stop engine, sir.'

'Give her three shackles and let go, Mister!' he shouted forward to where the waiting chief mate and the carpenter stood-by the windlass on the foc's'le. There was a pause, then a roar as the starboard anchor dropped out of the hawse-pipe and the cable flew over the windlass in a cloud of pungently rusty red dust, thundering on the gypsy whelps. The carpenter rang one bell as the first shackle—fifteen fathoms—shot over the side, closely followed by the second, with its two bells and then the third.

A few moments later McClure felt the gentle tug as the anchor gripped the sea-bed and the *River Tay* brought-up to her cable. Half a moment later the mate straightened up from staring down into the blue waters of the road, crossing his forearms to signify all was secure and bellowing: 'Brought up, three in the water, sir.'

McClure waved acknowledgement, then turned to the wheelhouse door.

'That'll do the helm. Finished with the engine, but pass the word for steam again in a couple of hours' time . . .'

Having heard his order acknowledged he turned back to the open roadstead with a sigh. Now there was the bloody business of the paper-work with port health and the discharging of Mr Kirton. He looked over the side.

'Lower the gangway!' he shouted and heard 'Aye, aye, sir,' from the main deck below. Then, delaying the moment of going down to his cabin for a little longer, he turned his attention again to the approaching boats, wishing young Kirton had taken more care, but he was a clumsy young man, efficient enough at his job, but no smart shaver like the two apprentices he had had on the bridge that afternoon. Both were ex-

Conway boys, keen and sharp as Chippy's copper tacks, whereas Kirton was something of a dreamer, a product of a less prestigious training establishment. He had already been in trouble twice in the voyage, once when he had tripped and fallen down a companionway, spraining his ankle in the process, and on a second occasion when he had over-stayed his shore leave by half an hour in Yokohama. McClure was not a man disposed to appreciate such conduct from a senior officer.

The captain had lost sight of both boats now and it was some moments before he located them again as they came into view from under the long counter of the little sailing vessel anchored between the *River Tay* and the Esplanade. For a moment he allowed his eye to linger on the brigantine; she was an anachronism: very sweet on the eye, if one liked that sort of thing, with a greenish hull and a long counter that befitted a yacht—perhaps that was what she was. He supposed Mr Kirton might like her; he had expressed a certain penchant for sailing vessels, but then McClure realised the heat and his irritation was making him judge his second mate unfairly. The young man had been doing his utmost for the ship when he had injured himself.

Bowling along under sail and steam, the *River Tay* had been caught in a vicious squall in the South China Sea. Just relieved by the chief mate, Kirton had pointed out the dark cloud and the white line on the horizon to his relief, saying:

'We'd better get some canvas off her . . .' and had gone on deck to cast off halliards as the mate blew his whistle for all hands and informed Captain McClure of the approaching squall. As the hands began clewing-up the sails the squall hit them and the ship heeled right over to leeward, whereupon there was a noise like a gunshot followed by a thunderous shaking of the whole vessel as the large fore-topsail blew out of its bolt-ropes. Kirton had been first into the rigging and raced aloft like a monkey, working his way out along the bucking yard. He reached the windward topsail yard-arm just as the sheet block shackle shook loose, its seizing failing; the pin flew into Kirton's face, the bow struck him hard on the breast, but the flaying dashed him flying from the foot-rope.

McClure had arrived on the bridge to see the second mate fall. He might have bounced on the lower shrouds and been flung overboard—in which case he would have drowned before a boat could have got to him; or he might have hit the deck, in which case his death would have been almost certain and quicker than drowning. Instead he entangled his leg in the lower-mast rigging which arrested his descent with a bone-shattering wrench. Captain McClure swore that he had heard the snap of Kirton's femur above the howl of the wind. There he hung for a few minutes, twisting and jerking in his agony until the squall was past and a panic party extricated the poor fellow from the mess he had got himself into.

Well, there was not much anyone could do for him after that except staunch his bleeding face, dose him with laudanum from McClure's medicine chest, and get him to Singapore as quickly as possible. Now McClure watched the port health boat round up alongside the gangway and gave a casual wave to the smiling face of Mr Cha, as the agent's *sampan* awaited permission to come alongside astern of the official gig.

Half an hour later, having cleared port health and secured a bed for Kirton at the British Military Hospital, McClure waved Mr Cha into a chair in his cabin.

'Whisky?' he asked, already pouring the Chinaman's favourite tipple.

'Velly good Captain,' said Cha appreciatively. 'I not expected to see you homeward-bound this voyage. I understand you have sick man for Militaly Hospital.' Cha spoke excellent English, only descending occasionally into the pidgin that was the *lingua franca* of the Straits Settlements, though like so many Chinese he had trouble pronouncing the letter 'r.'

'Yes. I shall have to pay him off and leave him in your hands. He's my second mate, Mr Henry Kirton.' McClure handed a chit with Kirton's name spelled out in capitals. 'Try and get him a berth so that he works his passage home when he is fit again.'

'You no want company to pay for passage home,' Cha said grinning, his shrewd eyes twinkling under their heavy folds as he regarded McClure over the rim of his glass.

'No, I don't. And if you cannot find him a berth, send him home as a Distressed British Seaman.'

'Velly good, Captain. How long you stay?'

'No longer than I have to, why?'

'I have some small parcels of cargo and some personal effects which I could get aboard you before tonight if you will take them. You have space?'

'Let's get Mr Kirton into your boat first, Mr Cha, then I'll get the chief mate to join us and we'll see what we can do to oblige you . . . Oh, and by the way, if we're going to take on cargo, how soon could you lay on a lighter of good coal?'

'Velly quick, Captain. We talk cargo over second glass of your number-one whisky. Just now I tell my boat-man to order you coal.' The old man put down his glass and left the cabin. McClure could hear him shouting down to his *sampan* in Cantonese.

'Cunning old bastard,' McClure chuckled to himself. Sending his boat off meant that Cha would stay on board until it returned, by which time he would have emptied the captain's whisky bottle. Kirton would suffer for the delay but the laudanum would help with that.

Hal Kirton was only vaguely aware of what was happening to him as he was carried down the narrow gangway and aboard Mr Cha's boat. There he was laid in the stern-sheets and a red face bent over him. Kirton could smell whisky and dimly realised it was the *River Tay*'s master who attended him.

'I'm very sorry to lose your services, Mr Kirton,' McClure said with a formality that Kirton took to be sincere. 'Mr Cha will see you into the right hands and you must get better as soon as you can.'

Kirton managed a wan smile. The effect of his last dose of laudanum, administered to him on the master's orders by the steward, was already taking hold and he relapsed into a state of semi-consciousness. As the *sampan* pulled away from the steamer's side he caught a glimpse of Captain McClure at the top of the gangway, then the trucks of the fore- and mainmasts of the ship before he closed his eyes.

It was some time before he opened them again. He lay in a bed, tucked under a spotlessly white sheet with a *punkah* flapping lazily overhead. He looked about him, realising he was in a hospital ward, a light, airy room with windows opening onto vegetation. There were about twenty other beds, most of them occupied. Suddenly the light went out of the day and after a few moments the heavens opened and the temperature plummeted. The noise of rain battering the roof seemed disproportionately loud and it came with a return of the pain which made him gasp. A few minutes later he passed out.

The next thing he knew a short stocky man in a white coat stood at the foot of his bed along with an orderly and a nurse. They were talking over a few notes and all three looked up at him as he groaned.

'Well, well, young man, you've certainly badly injured yourself,' the man in the white coat remarked. Partially drugged as he still was, Kirton noticed the strange contortions of the doctor's clipped moustache as he formed the words: 'It'll be some time before we have you back on your feet, I'm afraid. You've a compound fracture of the femur, to say nothing of other complications including three cracked ribs and a contusion on the side of your head the size of an ostrich's egg. D'you understand what I'm saying?'

Kirton nodded obediently as the doctor went on: 'You're what I think you sailors say is well lashed-up while your bones set, and you're damned lucky not to have fractured your pelvis, but you've torn a lot of ligaments and I'm afraid you are going to have a bad limp for the rest of your life.'

With that Parthian shot they shuffled off to the next bed where he heard the doctor ask: 'Well, Sergeant Morris, and how are we this evening?'

Kirton tried to process the extent of his disability and its permanence and it took him back to those few seconds of terror as he flew backwards off the fore-topsail yard thinking that in another he would strike the deck and his life would be over.

Over the next few days he realised that the 'lashing-up' had eased his pain a good deal and they had begun to wean him off the laudanum. He knew by then that he was in the British Military Hospital and was a lucky man to have been landed in Singapore. He knew too that he was on the mend when he began to think of what would happen to him when he got out having discovered the bundle of papers left in the locker by his bed. A letter in Captain McClure's distinctive hand-writing informed him that the *River Tay*'s owner's agent would look after him and find him a homeward berth, that Mr Cha also held his balance of wages outstanding, less, of course, those sums he had drawn against the ship for a few runs ashore and his mess-bill on board. Mr Cha also had his sea-chest, his sextant, his set of nautical tables, and his two elderly 12-bore shotguns. McClure's letter finished with a flourish, recommending Mr Henry Kirton for his sobriety, efficiency, and reliability as a ship's officer to any prospective employer, should such a testimonial be required.

But the sawbones had said he would have a limp; the horror of the implication struck him. A limp would be a permanent disability; it could render him unfit for sea-service, in which case God alone knew what he was going to do with the rest of his life.

After ten days he wrote a note to Mr Cha, requesting him that if the pressure of business allowed it, would he be kind enough to attend the hospital and discuss his, Hal Kirton's, homeward passage?

He received a courteous reply written in perfect copper-plate script, the nub of which was that Mr Cha had already tried twice to see him but had been told by the medical orderly in charge of the ward that 'no damned Chinese monkey' was allowed into a British military hospital.

Kirton attempted to remonstrate with the duty orderly who merely responded that 'it was against regulations and that he—Kirton—was bloody lucky to have been given a bed there.' He was, after all, only a merchant seaman and 'not worth half the buttons on a hussar's breeches,' so the best thing for him to do was to 'lie quiet and get bloody better.'

After a while Kirton managed to raise the subject of his discharge with the senior nurse who only usually put in an appearance with the doctor, whom he now knew as Surgeon Major Jeffries, the assistant chief medical officer of the establishment. Nurse Trimm was scarcely more helpful, though she did evince some sympathy.

'We'll send a note to your Chinese friend,' she said, as though talking to a servant, 'when you are ready to be discharged and he can come and get you in his rickshaw.'

And with that he had to be content. Nor were his fellow inmates much help to him. Kirton was a species of alien: neither fish nor fowl. They had no way of setting him in the pecking order of the military life, despite the fact that he said—several times—that he was, or had been, the second officer of a smart, barque-rigged auxiliary cargo steamer and was, to boot, the holder of a First Mate's Certificate of Competency.

Even on the day of his discharge, when Mr Cha duly arrived with his clothes, his blue uniform jacket with its brass buttons, his white duck trousers and small-crowned peaked hat with its gold badge failed to impress, and it was with a great sense of relief that he limped out of the hospital ward on his crutch noting that 'the damned Chinese monkey' was allowed to pay his fee before joining his charge in a smart trap.

'You stay in nice hotel for a few days, Mr Kirton, get more better, then I find a job for you.'

Aware that the nice hotel along with the hospital fees would be drawn from the wages Cha held for him he replied: 'Thank you Mr Cha, but I think I must get the first ship home, and as a Distressed British Seaman if necessary.' Such a plan would speed him on his way at no cost to himself and, haunted by the uncertainty of his future, he must eke out his money.

As if reading his mind, the little Chinaman beside him said, 'You go home England side maybe not get job on ship because your leg no good, eh?'

Kirton nodded dejectedly. 'Maybe. Yes.'

'You mallied?'

'What?' Kirton was taken aback, both by the Chinaman's directness and the fact that Cha also considered his career might be at an end. It was one thing to harbour private fears and apprehensions but to have them articulated by a third party practically confirmed their likelihood. There were hundreds of young fit men eager to get to sea and the shipping companies took their pick of them. He might find a berth on some old hooker, but that was not what Hal Kirton wanted in life: He felt a wave of panic rise in his gorge like vomit.

'You mallied?' Cha repeated his question.

Kirton shook his head. 'Er, no, no, I am not married.'

'Maybe you stay Singapore-side and I find you job here. Make plenty money . . .'

Kirton scoffed, replying in the *lingua franca* of the coast, 'I make plenty money mean you make plenty money but I savee you want me to do something li'le bit bad.'

'No, no, Mr Kirton,' Mr Cha said firmly, beating his robed breast and clearly offended, 'I straight business man, honest as day long. I have idea for you; by'm'by I tell you . . .' Cha paused, as if considering something; 'maybe we talk tomollow.'

They did not talk tomorrow, or the day after that, or indeed for a week, by which time Kirton was thoroughly fed-up. In a desperate effort to improve his fitness and improve the strength of his wounded leg he took to the habit of walking along the waterfront every forenoon before returning to his rather mean hotel where he would lie down for an hour every afternoon during the heat of the day, his leg throbbing painfully. If and when the rains came he would get up and, when the deluge had passed, sally out in search of a meal from one of the Chinese stalls on the Esplanade.

He noticed the pretty brigantine lying off Collyer Quay on the very first morning of his daily exercise. That forenoon he had gone in search of a Malacca cane to help him walk, eschewing the use of the crutch he had been reluctantly supplied with by Nurse Trimm and ended up by purchasing a fine sword-stick from the emporium of a Sikh merchant in Change Alley. Captain McClure would have been surprised to learn that the 'clumsy' Kirton had been an adept at single-stick aboard the school-ship *Canopus*. Not that Kirton felt the necessity of having a weapon for self-defence, but the sword-stick was the only cane that the Sikh had in stock that was of the right length to aid him in his perambulations. He was more preoccupied with handling his new acquisition as an aid to his weak leg to take much notice of anything else, but on the third morning the brigantine again caught his eye and on the fourth morning he popped his pocket-glass into his trousers and stopped to give her the once-over.

She was very pretty, about one hundred feet long with a sharp rake to her two masts, a long jib-boom, and a lovely bow and elegant, attenuated elliptical counter. Her hull was dark green with what looked like two gold ribbands which caught the sun. She had a broom hoisted to her mast-head indicating that she was for sale. He did not think the broom had been there the previous day and on the following morning it was gone so that he wondered if his eyes had been playing tricks; after all, he murmured to himself, 'you have had a blow on the bonce that might account for a hallucination or two, to say nothing of a large quantity of laudanum thereafter.'

Then the following day, whilst staring at the brigantine through his pocket telescope, he felt a tugging at his sleeve. Swinging round he found an emaciated rickshaw 'boy' of indeterminate age at his side. Instinctively checking if the contents of his pockets had been tampered with, he brushed the wretch aside, but the man would not go.

'You b'long Mister Kirton, eh? Mr Cha send me fetchee you, chop-chop.' The fellow backed away beckoning Kirton to follow him and climb in his rickshaw. 'Mr Cha pay for lickshaw,' he said smiling. 'You no trouble me, *Tuan*.'

Kirton regarded the man for a moment, recalled his recent purchase, and climbed into the rickshaw. As he sat behind the bony body of the trotting Chinaman, Kirton's mind drifted to the little brigantine. He had precious little else to think about other than his forthcoming interview with Mr Cha but the acquisition of the sword-stick, the appearance of the brigantine, and the memory of his days in the old *Canopus* off Ney-land at the head of Milford Haven gave him a painful reminder of his circumstances.

Each evening aboard the training ship the boys were allowed an hour of free time before colours, their evening meal, evening parade, prayers, and pipe-down when they were allowed to 'skylark.' This customarily meant some form of mock fighting in a 'bundle,' or at their most civilised a game of British Bulldog.

One evening, as they charged from one side of the old gun-deck to the other in a riotous game of British Bulldog one of their instructors had appeared on deck and roared 'Stand-fast!' at which the cadet-captain had blown his whistle and they had all come rigidly to attention. Such an interruption to their tomfoolery was unusual. The last time it had occurred, one of the cadets, Benning he recalled, had been called out and whisked away before they were allowed to resume their licensed riot. Only later, when he did not appear at dinner did they learn that poor Benning's mother had died. On this occasion, however, the intervention was for all of them.

'Some of you,' the instructor boomed portentously, 'will work out your sights in the best appointed chart-rooms of the finest mail steamers afloat . . . others on an upturned cask on the deck of a South Seas schooner . . . and the time to choose is *now*!'

This had set them all talking about the future over that evening's meal and Hal Kirton clearly remembered being torn between the two images, each of which possessed an allure of its own. In the end—and being a young man of caution having only an unmarried older sister left alive—he had made his choice. If the *River Tay* had not been a first-class mail steamer she was a crack vessel, belonging to a first-rate steam navigation company—the Scottish River Line—and he had been immensely proud of being her second officer.

Now, however, with his career prospects in grave doubt, even the brigantine—which had clearly seen better days, and had reminded him of that South Seas schooner whose attraction had vied with a steamship all those years earlier—suddenly seemed utterly beyond his reach.

Mr Cha had commercial premises close to the waterfront just behind the godowns of the European merchants and forwarding agents. Its exterior bore the legend that its business was that of 'Shipping, Forwarding and Commission Agent,' and beneath this a proud addition proclaiming that the House of the Green Dragon was the Sole Agent for the Scottish River Line of Glasgow as well as a couple of Scandinavian shipping firms. Inside an imposing counting-house a score of Chinese clerks, or *cranis*, laboured; from this large room a staircase led to the roof where a constant lookout was kept during daylight hours for the signals of ships for which Mr Cha acted as Singapore agent. At the rear of this office was a substantial godown policed by half-a-dozen tall Sikhs, each man armed with a P53 Lee Enfield rifle and wearing blue tunics and green turbans.

Kirton was met at the doorway by the senior tally clerk, who introduced himself as Lee and who conducted Kirton up a flight of stairs to Cha's private quarters. In a large room almost the size of the counting-house below and smelling heavily of incense and something else, Cha sat at a low table smoking a small opium pipe. As Kirton was ushered in, the old *towkay* laid the pipe aside and clapped his hands, whereupon a young woman in a long blue robe brought in tea. After dishes of the beverage had been set before Cha and his guest, the old Chinaman asked, 'How you feel now Mr Kirton?'

'Fine, thank you, Mr Cha. Ready to go home as soon as possible.'

'What doctor say about your leg, eh?'

'You mean my limp?' Cha nodded. 'That I will have a gammy leg for the rest of my life.' Kirton tried to keep the bitterness out of his voice.

'Gammy mean no good, eh?' Cha enquired and Kirton nodded. 'Maybe end all your happiness, eh?'

'If you mean my career at sea, that is a distinct possibility . . .'

'Distinct possibility,' Cha repeated, as though testing the phrase with which he was not entirely familiar. 'How you like to stay here one, two year, make money, be captain?'

Kirton frowned. What was the old chap talking about? He thought that he had put that idea firmly out of the old Chinaman's head days ago; he certainly did not wish to become an agent's runner with a phoney title. As for becoming a ship-master, well that was out of the question. 'Mr Cha, I don't think you understand, I am not qualified to sail as master, having only a first mate's—*Da Foo*'s—certificate of competency.'

'*Da Foo* velly good; *Da Foo* good enough to be captain of small vessel under other flag, not Blitish . . .' Cha paused to let the possibility sink in. 'My fliend Captain McClure say you good seaman, but he wanchee you found berth quickly. I have small sailing ship, I just buy it. I think you like. I know you look at it everly day. She under allest by Admilalty Marshal, now I buy her . . .'

'The brigantine? The brigantine anchored off Collyer Quay?' Kirton suddenly felt his heart hammer in his breast at the sudden flood of possibilities that presented themselves to his imagination.

Cha nodded. 'She velly good li'lle ship. I have survey done. You can take it back to your hotel and lead it, but more better to go aboard tomollow, have a look-see for yourself.'

Kirton's brain was racing. 'But what flag?' he asked.

Cha shrugged. 'Maybe Siamese flag; maybe flag of Sultan of Tidore, or Sultan of Sulu, I need to decide . . .'

'And what trade will you engage her in?'

'Oh, usual inter-island tlade, copra, coconut, gutta-percha—good freight rates for gutta-percha jus' now—maybe some rattans, plenty t'ings to fill small ship like this. Sometimes take passenger and personal effects. But Captain,' Cha said smiling subtly, 'you neglect your tea . . .'

'That is most discourteous of me, Mr Cha, please forgive me.'

Kirton felt his mood shift alarmingly. Old Cha had a reputation throughout the Laird fleet; the Scots directors in Glasgow were the only British owners to employ as agent a company run by a Singaporean Chinaman. No-one was quite sure how the two businesses had come together some thirty years earlier when the old East India Company had finally lost its monopoly of the China trade, but the scramble by enterprising ship-owners eager to fill the vacuum had led to what was known as the Scottish River Line quickly hitching its wagon to the House of the Green Dragon.

The old man waved aside the apology. 'It is good for young man to be excited by *distinct possibility*,' Cha said savouring the phrase and nodding sagely. 'Now, before you make up your mind, you go aboard ship tomollow, make survey for yourself, and come back here in evening. About six o'clock. We discuss business then.'

CHAPTER TWO

The Brigantine

THE FOLLOWING MORNING, DESPITE THE DULL AND PERMANENT ACHE in his leg, Kirton woke with an unusual feeling of optimism and it took him a moment or two to fathom its origin. An hour earlier than had become his custom he was on Collyer Quay and hailing a *sampan* only to be intercepted by Cha's boat-man.

'No, no, sir. Boat all make leady for you. Mr Cha make special order.'

Kirton stared intently at the brigantine as they approached her. Distance had certainly lent enchantment to the eye for she looked shabby and down-at-heel as the *sampan* approached her. As they drew closer he could see that in her rigging there were a number of what seamen called 'Irish pennants,' loose ropes' ends from which the whippings had worked off, or the result of rot and the parting of the strands, yarns, and fibres. These were particularly obvious in the ratlines and along the foot-ropes on her foremast yards where the servings had frayed adrift. And while she retained what did indeed look like two gold ribbands, her green paintwork was patchy and peeling, though the copper visible above her waterline looked in good condition. She was light, of course, devoid of any cargo, though she would have contained some minimal ballast.

Taking his eyes off her he stared at the boat-man and made a circular gesture with his right hand.

'You take me right round, please.' The boat-man nodded, used to taking ships' officers round their vessels to check trim and read their draughts.

They circled the vessel not five yards off her and Kirton reviewed her with a keen eye, sensible that she might be his first and only command, a vessel in which he might make a quick pile which would save him from destitution if he was lucky. She certainly had more than mere pretensions to good looks, for the sweep of her sheer was lovely, though he thought the rake of her masts excessive, marking her as a real old-timer. From where he now sat bobbing alongside her, her two masts soared into the sky for around one hundred feet, he guessed, roughly the same as her length, if one excluded her bowsprit and jib-boom. The foremast crossed three yards, a fore course, a topsail yard, and a topgallant, which, he judged, meant that she had a deep topsail. He thought of his recent adventure trying to disarm such a sail and viewed this one with suspicion. He would have to have a crew to match such an ungainly beast. On the other hand, being a brigantine her mainmast was more simply rigged, with a spanker boom and gaff, and a tall topmast that undoubtedly bore a large triangular gaff-topsail, though no sails were bent on the yards nor nestled along the other spars. The yards were not exactly cock-billed, but they were not squared and appeared to have braces of some light or local rope, not much more substantial than the flag halliards on the *River Tay*, and they were devoid of blocks.

They passed round the bow and Kirton was astonished at the length of the sharply steeved jib-boom: almost a third of the vessel's length, he thought, though later he learned this was not quite so. Her quite lovely clipper bow bore no figurehead, only some elegant scroll work and her name, though the weather had rendered this illegible despite its being carved into the woodwork of her sheer strake. Passing down the port side they reached the stern, a long overhanging counter. He could see more lettering there, in better condition than that forward, along with some gingerbread-work, but so long was her overhang that it was virtually invisible from a boat a few yards off since it faced almost directly into the water. Returning to the starboard waist where a tattered pilot ladder hung down her topsides, Kirton grabbed the man-ropes and tried the wooden rungs before trusting his body-weight to it; he had no desire to end up in hospital again.

Climbing cautiously, aware of the new handicap of his gammy leg, he swung it over the low rail and got himself aboard somewhat inelegantly. An elderly Malay in a dungaree suit and the cotton hat worn by Muslims who had made the *haj* seemed to be waiting for him and made a gesture much like a salute.

'Belong *Casab*, *Tuan*, *Casab* Ibrahim to your service . . .' Kirton smiled at the old man and, on impulse, held out his hand. The old fellow regarded the outstretched open palm of the *orang puteh* with a moment's suspicion before wiping his own on his cotton dungaree shirt and tentatively taking the younger man's with a sort of bow. 'Mr Cha tell me you come today, you want me show . . .'

Kirton shook his head at the old ship-keeper. 'No, thank you Ibrahim. I look-see myself. Maybe take long time.'

Kirton limped forward, embarrassed by his handicap, hauling himself up onto the low forecastle and limping forward to the knightheads. A capstan served the two anchors, one of which was, of course, on the seabed, though a lighter spare, or kedge, was lashed down on the deck. The ship's bell in its brass belfry consisting of the conventional two stylised dolphins bore a legible name: *Tethys*.

'Who or what in the name of Hades is Tethys?' he asked himself before noting the date, that of her building: 1836. He pulled out his pocket knife and began to stick it into the timbers of the catheads, the deck, and, under the break of the forecastle, the deck beams. Her timbers were as hard as iron. Just abaft the break of the forecastle a windlass was bolted down, driven, he realised by a shaft from the capstan on the forecastle deck above. Abaft this the foremast rose from its cluster of fife-rails. Most of the running rigging had been stripped off and, he presumed, sent below, along with its blocks, which argued that the vessel had not been abandoned but left with some care.

Opening the nearest door of a deck-house set between the foremast and the hatch he discovered a small carpenter's workshop in which all the tools remained in their lodgements and included a range of sail-maker's gear. There was also a door to a companionway which led directly below. Having no artificial light he descended into this space only far enough to learn that it was the crew's accommodation, eerily lit by a number of bull's eye glasses in the main deck above. There were bunk spaces for twenty-four men, a large crew for such a small vessel by European standards, he thought, a suspicion forming in his mind as to the origins of this curious *Tethys*. 'Bloody odd name,' he murmured to himself. Turning, he scrambled awkwardly back on deck, quietly cursing his leg.

The third door—actually a double set of donkey doors, the top half of one of which was open—revealed a well-appointed galley. A lit fire in the black stove kept a kettle of water hot between its iron fiddles. Presumably Ibrahim liked his *chai*.

Passing the hatch on which the old man sat and worked, neatly serving a wire strop which had been removed from a newly oiled brace block that lay beside him, Kirton dragged himself onto the long and low poop. At the forward end the sharply raking mainmast towered into the blue sky. To his astonishment at the hances there were two quadrants of iron laid into the deck.

'What belong these, *Casab*?' He called down to Ibrahim, pointing at the iron inserts. The old man looked up, his face breaking into a smile. 'For guns, *Tuan*. Two brass cannon all safe down below.' Ibrahim patted the hatch tarpaulin upon which he sat at his self-appointed task.

Kirton concealed his surprise; the existence of two brass cannon was more evidence to add to what he was thinking. The long poop had no deck-house as such and no skylight, but a low coach-roof lined with ports and a companionway at its after end, indicating a break in the line of the main deck with a lowered second deck below. A row of bull's eyes extending right aft presumably let light into the spaces underneath this. He walked aft until he stood at the elliptical curve of the counter, some several feet abaft the steering position with its wheel, steering-box, and binnacle.

'If I'm right,' he thought to himself, regarding the long poop and its unprotected counter, 'and this *Tethys* was built for what I think she was, this must have been a liability in a typhoon. Still,' he mused on, 'she is still afloat, so I suppose that says something . . . and perhaps I am unduly suspicious . . .'

Having poked his pocket knife around a small hatch which presumably led down to a sail locker or a lazarette for their powder and shot, he moved forward again, coming to the companionway doors at the end of the raised—or was it a sunken—coach-roof. It was solidly decked, he noted, and in teak too, though that in itself was not unusual; the *River Tay*, built on the River Clyde, had teak decking.

If anything on deck had surprised him by its unusual nature what he found below simply astonished him. The companionway descended onto a flat about five feet below the level of the deck above. He passed a neat chart-room, its clock, barometer, and brass-edged chart-table as spick and span as if she was in commission. Beneath a rack still containing pencils and dividers a set of parallel rules lay on the table, and along the bulkhead were a number of pasted notices and quick reference tables: speed and distance; seconds of arc converted into the decimals of minutes; distances off by vertical sextant angle. To port was a small bookshelf containing an out-of-date nautical almanac, a volume of Imray, Norie & Wilson's nautical tables, and a thick leather-bound note-book which, Kirton discovered on opening it, contained pilotage and cabotage notes for locations all over the South China Seas and beyond, along with some drawings of significant navigational marks. There was also a copy of the latest edition of James Horsburgh's *The India Directory*. Opening the drawers underneath he found folios of charts covering most of the Indian Ocean and the Western Pacific from Japan as far south as Torres Strait. The chart-room brass gleamed and would, Kirton noted wryly, have kindled a reflected gleam of satisfaction in the eye of even Captain Douglas McClure. The only thing that hinted at neglect was the fact that the gimballed chronometer in its mahogany box lay unwound and stopped. He was tempted to get it going, but decided that such an act would smack of presumption, for the more he found the more he could hardly believe his eyes.

Along with a growing sense of unease about the origins of *Tethys* was the notion of accepting the command of her that Mr Cha had offered him. The expression 'fallen on his feet' occurred to him, loaded as it was with irony, given his physical condition.

He moved from the chart-room into the officers' capacious saloon off which were lower alleyways leading to the master's and officers' cabins. All was beautifully appointed, the woodwork was well varnished, the table—though dusty—bore a deep polish once he dragged his figure across it. Lower alleyways leading aft contained the steward's store rooms.

He gave the officers' cabins a perfunctory look. There seemed to be a lot of them—six in all—and each was better appointed than its neighbour, arguing a rigid hierarchy. The master's cabin was, if not sumptuous, worthy of a ship far larger than a small brigantine. Polished panelling lined the bulkheads; it was thoughtfully furnished with a double-bunk mounted above four large drawers. The washing-place facilities were of the latest enamel-ware, the privy a neat bucket in a teak box; all-in-all it practically begged for a new and appreciative occupant.

It was clear that no expense had been spared in the construction or fitting-out of this fine little ship, and he was now possessed with a consuming curiosity to know her history. He opened the master's desk hoping to find log-books, her certificate of registry, and perhaps a letter book containing correspondence, but all here was as bare as Mother Hubbard's cupboard and he realised that if Mr Cha had indeed purchased the vessel, all her papers would now be in his custody. Nevertheless, he thought, Ibrahim might be able to enlighten him, if only a little.

Back on deck he found that the old Malay had lifted the corner of the hatch tarpaulin and removed one of the hatch-boards. 'See down below, *Tuan?*'

'Maybe later, Ibrahim . . .' The old man's face fell visibly and Kirton peered down into the stygian gloom. He did not fancy poking around in the hold with his bad leg. It already ached intolerably from the unaccustomed exertions of the last hour and a half. He should, of course, have gone round sticking his knife into the lowest timbers in the ship and discovered how much water lay in her bilge, but instead he slapped his right thigh.

'I have bad leg, Ibrahim,' he said. 'Not good to climb too many ladders on same day but tell me, you ship-keeper, what down below? Hold space all empty, except for guns? Not very interesting . . .'

The truth was that subconsciously he did not want to find anything wrong with the *Tethys* and Cha had already offered the surveyor's report for him to read. Besides, he reasoned to himself, Cha was too shrewd a businessman to invest in a wreck.

But Ibrahim had his own agenda; the suggestion that the hold was empty annoyed him.

'Hold no empty, *Tuan!*' he exclaimed. 'All running gear, blocks, sails and guns struck down below before crew leave her. Me only man left . . .'

'You were part of her crew before she was out up for sale?' he asked, Ibrahim having explained the untidy appearance of the brigantine's spars.

Ibrahim nodded. 'Sure *Tuan*. I *Casab*, look after ship; turn-in first-class work . . .' He indicated the meticulous serving he had just finished which lay on the hatch tarpaulin beside him. 'Make sure all running gear in tip-top condition.' He gestured towards the poop, 'also look after all accommodations. Upper rigging is big problem,' and here he waved his right arm aloft, 'too much work for one man but brigantine very good little ship. I serve for twenty years man and boy.'

'Where was she built?'

'Long time ago, Moulmein, all Burma teak, first captain plenty money.'

'He was the owner as well?'

'Part-owner with Parsee house in Bombay, Muckerjee Brothers, plenty money,' and then Ibrahim let drop the fact that had been troubling Kirton since the suspicion first arose in his mind.

'Very fast, *Tuan*; maybe fastest in opium trade.'

So there it was, whatever 'Tethys' signified, she was, or had been, after the abolition of the slave trade, that most reprehensible of all British merchantmen, an opium-clipper.

'You can smell in the hold, *Tuan* . . .' Ibrahim waved his hand at the uncovered portion of the hatch-square and Kirton learned over again. Now he could smell the full and undisguisable odour of the drug, similar to that being masked by incense in old Cha's private quarters. It was, he knew well, an astonishing fact that some cargoes left their odour behind long after discharge. Perhaps, he thought inconsequentially, 'Tethys' had something to do with the white poppy itself; a native name, for it was something of a lisping tongue-twister for an Englishman.

'How long since she carried opium?' he asked his informant.

'Oh long time,' Ibrahim said, waving his hand aloft. 'Long time ago had studding sail booms, now all irons take away, so not so fast, but still fine li'le *perahu, Tuan*.'

Or big *perahu*, Kirton thought, asking, 'How did she come up for sale?'

'After she sell out of opium trade she bought by Singapore men, put into island trade. Then captain die. Chief mate made captain. He drink too much, we lose money on cargo, then new captain caught doing bad things; owners in Singapore find-out he cheating them, carrying own cargo, not keep his books prop'ly . . . Company lose face and become bankrupt. One day last year come Singapore side; Admiralty Marshal come aboard arrest ship, put up for sale . . .' Ibrahim stopped for a moment then, cocking his head on one side asked, 'I know Mr Cha buy ship. You new captain or chief mate?'

Kirton stared at the old man and expelled his breath. 'Mr Cha has offered me the job of master, yes.'

'You take job, *Tuan*,' Ibrahim said firmly. 'Stay honest, not drink too much, and make money. You English gentleman, more better than last captain; he no good . . .' Ibrahim hawked loudly and, with considerable emphasis, spat clean over the ship's rail. Then, before Kirton could say anything, he added: 'Ship teak, all teak, last forever. Ibrahim see that all running gear in good order. Standing rigging not so good; need proper overhaul; need money; you find a good mate and, *Tuan*, you keep Ibrahim as *casab*. Mr Cha will not let you choose crew, he will want all Chinamen, but perhaps you speak good words for *casab* as important person, number one after officers. Ibrahim know *Tethys* like some men know wife; I no wife, no home, just *Tethys*. Served good English captains since a boy. I good Muslim, no drink, no gamble. Chinaman all gamble. And drink. *Samsu* plenty strong.'

Kirton's mind was whirling. Could this old man undertake the job? Ibrahim's strange *patois*, his mixture of pidgin and colloquial English, amused Kirton, but he would undoubtedly be an asset if he had kept the brigantine's gear in such good condition all on his own and on his own initiative.

'Are you capable of going aloft, Ibrahim?'

'Me not that old, *Tuan*. You want me to show you?'

Kirton smiled. 'No, I take your word. But I cannot go aloft. Last time I go top-side I catch bad injury,' he slapped his right thigh again.

'Bad luck, *Tuan*, but good luck you come aboard *Tethys* today, good luck Mr Cha your friend. He good man for an unfaithful Chinaman.

Sometimes Allah's will works behind clouds and then the sun shines. All men connected like links in anchor chain but have bad link and chain parts; now you find good mate and maybe second mate. Old ship be like new and you be proud captain for young man.'

Kirton reeled at the old fellow's philosophical turn. Never mind his pride in command of so lovely a craft, where in Heaven's name was he going to find a chief mate? He knew no-one in Singapore . . . Suddenly the responsibility of what was on offer swept aside the romantic notions the near perfect condition of the brigantine—inboard at least—had been inflaming his imagination with. Was this something he really wanted to undertake?

But short of going home to do God knew what, a lame man with little future, what else could he do but accept Cha's offer; or at least, give it a chance?

Give it a chance . . . a *cha-nce* . . . He found himself chuckling at the silly semi-pun. He could always change the vessel's name and, whatever flag Mr Cha decided his vessel would sail under, he, Hal Kirton, would be her 'Master under God.'

'Maybe I see you tomorrow, Ibrahim,' he said abruptly. He needed to think, and he could not do that aboard the *Tethys*. He went to the ship's rail and called Cha's patiently waiting boat alongside, scrambling down into it. As the *sampan* drew away from the brigantine's side, Ibrahim waved from the rail before turning away to resume his serving of the brace block strops.

Chapter Three

The *Towkay*

At six o'clock that evening Kirton returned to Cha's place. He was admitted by the chief *crani* Lee, who was just then closing-up for the day. Kirton found Cha in his quarters waiting for him, smoking his opium pipe. He clapped his hands and the serving girl appeared.

'You like opium, Captain? It help your leg.'

Kirton shook his head. 'Thank you no, Mr Cha.' Nurse Trimm had given him a severe warning not to succumb to any such temptation after he had been weaned off laudanum. Cha laid down his own pipe with a sigh.

'You see ship?' Cha asked indicating he should sit.

'I see ship, Mr Cha. She is a very fine little vessel but there is some work to be done before she could be taken to sea . . .'

Kirton sat as Cha waved him to silence before he could outline a specification of the most obvious tasks. 'We discuss details concerning ship by'm'by. Tonight we discuss you, and how you work for me. Bring tea,' he ordered the girl, before settling to the evening's business.

'To begin I pay you small salally and cover your hotel bill and expenses. After first voyage we agllee proper salally and allowances. I look after you Captain, if you look after my intellests. You pick officers; I pick crew; twenty-four men, all Chinese . . .'

Kirton set aside the problem of finding officers for the time being. It was perfectly understandable that Cha would pick a Chinese crew—

drawn no doubt from those whom he wished to place under obligation to him—but he felt a powerful loyalty to the old man who had kept the *Tethys* in relatively good condition. He was also wary of having a crew consisting of a single nationality, well-knowing that they could quietly combine against and mutiny against him; a couple of European mates, if he could find anyone suitable, would be no defence against twenty Chinese with murder in their hearts. Bearing in mind the *Tethys* was a brigantine, he did a quick calculation as Cha continued:

'. . . Plus you have own tiger.' The prospect of having his own steward, or 'tiger,' was seductive, though Kirton guessed the man would be Cha's on-board spy—all-of-a-piece with his own 'low salary' during a first probationary voyage. 'You agllee?'

'No, Mr Cha. Ship no need of twenty-four men. Say sixteen Chinese sailors, one bosun, one carpenter, one cook, and one officers' steward. I keep same *casab* who is looking after ship now as sail-maker; he is a very good man and knows the ship. That makes twenty-two including my tiger. Then you allow me to have four Sikh *jagas* like you have as guards. They work as quartermasters and carry arms . . .'

Cha did not react to this counter-proposition; instead he asked: 'Who you have as officers? Two or three mates?'

The prospects of finding one seemed remote, so Kirton answered as far as optimism carried him. 'Two . . . at least to begin with.'

Cha considered matters for a moment, then asked, 'You not trust all Chinese crew, Captain?'

'It is better to mix nationalities, sir,' Kirton responded with a rather stiff formality.

'You consider Chinese man a monkey?'

'Not in the way you were treated at the hospital, Mr Cha; that was disgraceful. Of course, I, like any seaman who has to go aloft, needs to be agile like a monkey. I was,' he indicated his leg, 'not good as a monkey myself, and look what happened to me!'

Cha smiled. 'Good. I would not like to hear you call me "Chinese Monkey" behind my back . . .'

'Mr Cha,' Kirton said, looking directly into the old man's deep-set eyes behind their Mongolian fold of skin, 'I am not in the habit of insulting someone who is my benefactor.'

'Not all Blitish gentlemen regard Chinese like-so, Captain Kirton.'

'Maybe not, Mr Cha, but I am an ordinary Englishman that must earn his living by his own wits and skills. Please believe me when I say this, you have saved me from a life of beggary and I agree to command your brigantine. My only demand is that you consider my requirements as regards crew.'

Cha had obviously been doing his own calculations; he had—as Kirton had pointed out—Sikhs in his own employ and finding four sufficiently obligated to him by ties connected with these men would not be hard, brothers and sons, for example. Besides, he had his own plans for Kirton's mates.

'Then it is only the mates that must be found, Captain? How do you propose to do this?'

'Well,' Kirton responded without much conviction, 'I thought that I might board one or two ships in the port and offer a berth to anyone willing to accept.'

'That does not sound velly satisfactory . . . no lecommendations . . . no testimonials . . .' Cha paused and scratched his round head. 'You eat on Esplanade tonight? Maybe I find you a chief mate.'

It was on Kirton's lips to ask how, but he swallowed his words before he could utter them. Instead he turned the conversation to the business of making the brigantine seaworthy again, requesting a budget to have her hauled out on the slip so that any damaged copper might he replaced and her under-water body checked over, something the surveyor could not possibly have done while she lay afloat.

It was nearly eight o'clock when Kirton left Cha and limped seawards to the Esplanade and his, by-now, usual table.

He was half-way through his meal of egg *foo yung* when he was aware of company. He had brushed away several youngsters, mostly Chinese boys intent on beating him at noughts-and-crosses to mulct him of some cents for their own subsistence, and the hovering presence irritated him. In truth he was lost in thoughts concerning the brigantine, making a list of things to be attended-to which he was jotting down on a scrap of paper, kicking aside the problem of how and where to find officers until the morrow.

He waved the shadowy figure away with a peremptory gesture that fell just short of provoking an oath from him. But the figure stood his ground.

'Captain Kirton,' a voice said, compelling Kirton to look up. Everybody was deuced keen to call him 'Captain' these days, so-much-so that he thought the world had embarked upon a campaign to seduce him into falling in with all Cha's plans willy-nilly. It was all decidedly odd and he wondered if he had, as yet, entirely thrown off the effects of the drugs he had been taking at the hospital.

A tall, lanky European stood at the table. He was young, younger than Kirton, and wore the cotton singlet and cheap cotton trousers and sandals of a Chinese *crani*. Kirton had the vague feeling that he had seen the young fellow before, but could not place him.

'What d'you want?' he asked curtly, seeing signs that the stranger was begging.

'A berth aboard the *Tethys*, sir.'

'What?' Kirton exclaimed.

'A berth, sir, aboard the *Tethys*,' the younger man repeated.

'In what capacity?' Kirton asked.

'Mate; second mate; even third mate . . .'

'And what are your qualifications for any such berth?' Kirton enquired as the young stranger manoeuvred himself opposite Kirton and stood behind the empty chair facing him.

'Three and a half years of my time worked out, sir. Then I got stranded here in Singapore . . .'

'So you're an apprentice who broke his indentures . . . yes, yes, sit down, sit down . . .' he said testily. The young fellow had hardly taken his seat before the Chinese waiter who managed Kirton's table appeared and Kirton asked, in a slightly exasperated tone of voice, 'Are you hungry? Would you like a drink?'

'May I have the *foo yung*, sir, and a beer?'

Before Kirton had given his consent the waiter had vanished to take the order to the stall that served as kitchen to the dozen tables that marked the territory of his concession.

'Thank you very much, sir.'

'What's your name?'

'Christopher Rodham, sir. I'm usually called Kit by my friends.'

'Are you indeed. Now tell me more about yourself. What are you doing here, beach-combing. And I want the truth.'

'I was serving under Captain Richard Richards, in the *Seawitch*, and we were waiting for the annual crop of tea, engaged in the usual local trade up to Japan and back to Foochow in time to load for home. I had a run ashore in Yokohama and missed the ship . . .'

Kirton pricked up his ears at this; he had almost committed the same offence in the same port and could guess the cause, but he said nothing.

'Captain Richards was a driver, sir and would not wait. He was anxious to be the first to start loading in the Min River and left word with the agent that I was to follow. How was up to me . . .'

Rodham's beer had arrived and he took a draught, provoking Kirton to wonder if he was a drunkard or merely wanted relief from his somewhat humiliating confession.

'How long were you adrift?'

'About three hours, sir,' Rodham said after wiping his mouth.

'Go on.'

'I managed to get a passage to Shanghai then to Foochow but when I got there I learned that the *Seawitch* had sailed for home, so I came here and I have been here ever since . . .'

'How long ago was that?'

'About eight months, sir.'

'Why didn't you get a passage home? What kept you here? Why didn't you return home as a Distressed British Seaman if you couldn't find a berth?'

The fried rice arrived and Rodham refused the proffered knife and fork, taking up chopsticks which he handled like a native Chinaman.

'I decided not to go home, sir, I got a job . . .' He was tucking into the rice dish, his youthful features lit by the paraffin lamp that hung over the table. Kirton studied him for a few moments. The lad was clean-shaven, though his beard was showing at the end of the day and his dark hair was long enough to flop over one eye. Captain McClure would have had something to say about that! Then a suspicion quickened in Kirton's mind and he knew where he had seen the young man before.

'With the House of the Green Dragon. . . as a *crani*, I suppose?' he ventured.

'Yes, sir,' Rodham admitted. 'Not a proper job for a white man, I admit but . . .'

Kirton smiled, 'But not a bad one for someone who's taken up with a local woman, eh?'

Rodham stopped masticating, swallowed, and stared at Kirton. 'How did you know that, sir?'

'I didn't, I guessed. You were adrift in Yokohama because you had got involved with a woman; you did the same thing again here in Singapore, only this time it was more serious. Now I suppose you have fallen out with your concubine and want a way out, a rehabilitation, so-to-speak . . .'

'No, not at all, sir,' Rodham said with an almost offended air, 'unless by rehabilitation you mean a change of employment . . .'

'A move to something more suitable to a European . . .'

'I'm not ashamed of my wife, sir,' Rodham said with a sudden ferocity, 'but . . .'

'Your wife? Good Lord, you're married then.'

'Yes, sir. I'm married to . . .'

But Kirton forestalled any further remarks, asking, with a narrowing of his eyes, 'Did old Cha send you to find me here this evening?'

Rodham smiled and nodded. 'It suits us both.'

'What d'you mean by that? Does "both" mean you and I, or you and Cha?'

'Perhaps both "boths," sir,' Rodham said mischievously.

'I think you had better explain yourself, Mr, er, Rod . . .'

'Rodham, sir, with an H.'

'Well go on Mr Rodham with an H, tell me why this proposed arrangement suits you and Cha.'

'I am married to his daughter, sir. Between ourselves, he has no sons and is beset by many relatives who would fleece him of his wealth given half a chance. He offered me a job as tally-clerk with a view to my rising in the firm and, I hope—as he hopes—learning sufficient to make me a partner. But I need experience in the trade and he wants a greater part of the trade than acting for others, *ergo*, he buys the brigantine . . .'

'So this, this venture is all for you,' Kirton remarked, disappointed that Cha was not the *deus ex machina* who had come to his own aid.

'Not entirely sir; he is thinking chiefly of his daughter and our sons.'

'You have children too,' enquired a bemused Kirton.

'Well, not yet, Captain Kirton, but one is on the way and a son is expected.'

Realising he had made a bit of a fool of himself, Kirton coughed and said, 'So you add your name to Mr Cha's as the, er, directors of the House of the Green Dragon, is that the idea?'

'Well, the idea is that we become Rodham & Son, and take our place among the other major agencies. The old man is getting on, you know . . .'

'But why come back to sea as chief mate?'

'To learn the trade and, if you do not take me as such, I will be appointed *comprador*, since I assume you know little more of the matter than I do.'

'Hmmm, that may be true; so if I don't take you as mate . . .'

'I should be disappointed, sir.'

'And who would serve as *comprador*, assuming that we require one?'

'I would, saving you the trouble . . .'

'But,' Kirton broke in only to be interrupted by Rodham.

'We'd ship an old *shroff*. He'd be my mentor and act as interpreter; that way we'd all maintain our "face."' Rodham paused, then added, 'it would make life very pleasant for you, sir, almost like having your own yacht!'

The younger man's enthusiasm and conviction was so patently sincere that it made Kirton laugh. 'Well, you seem to have got it all worked out . . .'

'For both the "boths," sir,' Rodham added with a wide smile, adding, 'It's a pretty lucrative trade, you know.'

Kirton grunted and sat back, considering the younger man as he finished tucking in to his *foo yung*. Howsoever such an arrangement played out, he himself was still too young not to view the proposition of such a future as alluring as it was exciting. Even if the adventure did not last more than six months at the end of which he was compelled to relinquish his chosen avocation, he could return home in the satisfaction that he had achieved his school-boy ambition to command a merchantman.

Rodham, feeling the eyes of the other man on him, laid down his chopsticks and sat back, wiping his mouth. The two regarded each other for a moment or two before Kirton grunted. 'It's all very pat, isn't it?' He shook his head. 'And what makes you think you would be able to fulfil the position of chief mate?'

'I know my stuff, sir . . .'

'Do you? Yet you missed your ship's departure from Yokohama. I take it the lady was worth it.'

Rodham grinned and finished his beer. 'I'd prefer not to discuss the lady's accomplishments if you don't mind, sir.'

Kirton grunted again. He knew he was on shaky ground here, having himself infuriated Captain McClure from a similar cause, though the unapproved extension of his shore-leave had only been half an hour and occasioned not by any tardiness on his part, but a failure to fight his way through a press of traffic—well, that was what he told McClure for fear the older man would think the worst of him.

'You've been to Yoko' yourself, sir?' Rodham asked cheerfully.

'I'm not the one answering the questions, Mr Rodham,' Kirton said, pricking the younger man's bubble before going on to ask, 'what d'you think Mr Cha would say if I refused your importuning?'

Rodham shrugged. 'I'd happily sail as second mate . . . but my guess is you'd find me on board as *comprador*.'

'That's not a guess, is it? From what you told me just now I am here precisely to facilitate your gaining experience in the trade whether as chief mate, *comprador*, or both . . .'

'Another "both," sir,' Rodham said with a note of facetiousness that struck a nerve in Kirton. There was a touch of precocity in this youth that he, Kirton, at twenty-two, found irksome, despite the otherwise likeable enthusiasm. A fourth-year apprentice might make a decent third mate, he thought, but chief mate might be a stretch too far. On the other hand, where in Hell was he going to acquire a competent mate? And the lad had been in sail in a tea-clipper under a master with a formidable reputation. He himself had never occupied any position higher than that of second mate and whilst he understood the rudiments of ship's business and the stowage of cargoes, and although he had served his own apprenticeship in sail, his own deficiencies would be easily exposed. An experienced mate would soon discover that his commander was possibly less qualified than himself, whilst Rodham would present no such problem. Besides, with his disability Kirton would need an active second-in-command, one not so experienced that he was unwilling to go aloft should conditions warrant it, or stand on the dignity of his rank in case he lost 'face' in front of a largely Chinese crew.

'Captain Richards was a driver, sir. I know how to handle a watch, sir, and a ship under sail.' The lad seemed to be following Kirton's train of thought.

'What about the Rule of the Road?'

'No problem there sir. I was swotting for my second mate's ticket in the *Seawitch*.'

'Hmmm. If I appointed you chief mate and asked you how we ought to fill the other two vacant officers' berths, what would you say?'

'I'd say not to bother with a third mate, sir. We'll be in the interisland and local trade and I could work watch-and-watch with a competent second mate. There's a *nakoda* from Calcutta looking for work whom I happen to have run across the other day; he was asking if I knew anything about the *Tethys*. I think that he would accept a berth as second mate. I heard you wanted armed *jagas*, bring the senior of these aft to occupy the third mate's berth and the ship's other afterguard berths can be used for the bosun, the saloon steward, and the *shroff* . . .'

'You certainly have got it all worked out, Master Rodham,' Kirton remarked drily.

'I've thought of little else during the last week, sir, since old man Cha mentioned his plans to me. Isn't that what the chief mate's job entails?'

It was a radical solution to the manning of the brigantine, Kirton thought, musing on the notion. 'You think a hugger-mugger bunch like this living cheek-by-jowl under the poop will work?' he asked.

'I've spent some time here in Singapore now and I know that if you employ a single race you may have trouble, but a mixture prevents cliques and combinations.'

'How old are you, lad?' Kirton asked, extremely conscious of his own youth.

'Nineteen, sir.'

'And how old is your Indian *nakoda* that you just happened to run into the other day?'

Rodham screwed up his face in thought. 'About thirty, I'd say.'

Kirton grunted again. 'And how d'you think he'd feel working under a mate of your youth—or a master of mine, come to that,' he added frankly.

Rodham shrugged. 'He can take it or leave it. You and I are *orang puteh*, sir, white men. Besides plenty of the old opium clippers and the country-*wallahs* were commanded by young British masters with older Indian and Malays in their crews.'

'And what d'you think of the old *casab*, Ibrahim. If you've been aboard you know him.'

'I'd say he would make a useful hand, sir. I don't think we should make him the *tindal* though, Mr Cha will want the sailors all to be Chinese, so a Number One Chinaman will have to be bosun, but old Ibrahim has kept that vessel in as good a condition as any one man could have done . . .'

'You've had your eye on her for some time then?'

'Absolutely, sir. From the moment I heard about the scandal of her arrest. In fact it was me who drew my father-in-law's attention to her, only to find, of course, that he knew all about her anyway. The green hull clinched the matter, I think.'

Kirton laughed. 'I was hoping it was the survey . . .'

'That too . . .'

'And what languages d'you speak, besides English?'

'Cantonese—which all Cha's *cranis* speak—though not very well, and some Malay . . .'

Both men had long since finished their meals and their beers and the intensity of their conversation had deterred the waiter from pressing them further. Now Kirton called for the bill and as he paid it he said: 'Very well. I'll give you a trial period as chief mate as long as my own as master. When do you think you can report for duty?'

'Tomorrow morning, sir,' Rodham said firmly. 'And thank you, sir.'

'Now you had better go home to your wife and tell her what you have let yourself in for.'

'Thank you, sir.' Rodham stood up and offered his hand. Kirton shook it warmly.

'I hope we get on, Mr Rodham and that I do not live to regret this moment.'

The younger man grinned in the lamplight. 'I am sure that you won't sir. I'll see you tomorrow.'

Kit Rodham was on board by the time Kirton reached the *Tethys* at nine o'clock the following morning. He was going about the upper deck with a note-book and pencil when Kirton asked for assistance to hoist his own gear on board.

'I shall be living on board from now on,' he announced, 'but I'll be spending the first few days ashore making arrangements with our owner . . .'

And with these words was initiated six weeks of furious activity in which the brigantine was transformed from a rather neglected little vessel to a smart, if old-fashioned, craft, and Hal Kirton and Kit Rodham began their fateful partnership.

CHAPTER FOUR

Master Under God

FOR EIGHT DAYS THE *TETHYS* LAY ON THE SLIP WHILE NOT FAR AWAY
coolies toiled on the digging of a large graving-dock. The work aboard
the brigantine was no less intense than the expansion of Keppel Harbour as Cha provided a gang of Chinese, most of whom were to become
permanent members of her crew. After her copper had been cleaned and
restored to a serviceable condition, the loose paint on her topsides was
scraped off and the vessel was primed and painted, keeping her green liv-
ery which, by happy coincidence had indeed greatly pleased old man Cha
who saw it as a most propitious omen. On deck the teak deck-houses
were rubbed with coconut husks and lovingly coated with copal varnish
so that they gleamed under the tropical sun. Aloft, the standing rigging
was overhauled, replaced where necessary, seized, tarred, and rattled down
to the dead-eyes. Almost single-handedly effected by Kit Rodham, the
running gear was hove out of the hold and, directed by Ibrahim, sent up
to grace the masts and spars.

Rain frequently interrupted the work of the score of labouring Chinese; during the deluges, these men were hustled down into the hold
where they cleaned the bilges and spread a mixture of oil and tar on the
teak timbers. The smell gradually overcame the slight odour of opium
which many of the Chinese drew in with enthusiasm. The task was
enlivened by the periodic hunt for rats chased out of their cover by these
activities, so that the *Tethys* was rat-free by default.

The two patented brass breech-loading guns were lifted on deck
and measured for new traversing carriages. These, made by a short, lean

Chinese *tomelo*, along with their iron wheels were then mounted at the hances, the forward ends of the poop, port and starboard, to command fields of fire on both sides.

'Enough to deter any *orang laut*,' Rodham declared knowingly, referring to the old sea-pirates, or 'men of the sea,' such as the Bugis, after whom a *kampong* in the Lion City was named, situated along the very creek on which the slipway was situated.

Hampered by his gammy leg Kirton was happy to leave the physical supervision of much of this work to Rodham and his petty officers. Ibrahim worked tirelessly and the bosun, a middle-aged Chinaman named Tan, proved a tower of strength once he had joined the vessel. He, like all the Chinese, was bound to Mr Cha by some unspoken tie of familial or commercial connection. As for himself, Kirton pored over charts, consulted James Horsburgh's *East India Navigator*, and sought from every possible source he knew of details of the inter-island and local, or 'country,' trade upon which he was about to embark. *Comprador* or not, he was determined to master as much detail as he could, to prevent the exposure of any deficiencies occasioned by his youth and inexperience.

In this he was greatly assisted by the second mate, the Indian *nakoda* who, like the bosun, late arriving on board for 'personal reasons,' nevertheless proved a veritable mine of information, supplied some charts of his own, and sent ashore for more where the ship's inventory fell short.

When this officer had reported aboard Kirton had asked him his name, only and somewhat mystifyingly, to be told that it was Vic Jones. Though the man was of obviously Indian colour Kirton held his peace, sensible to the nature of 'Vic's' hurt pride in having to accept a rank far lower than he had previously held. That the man swallowed his conceit was to his credit, but Kirton had no desire to further humiliate him and showed every symptom of his gratitude at 'Vic's' assistance as they traced over the likely tracks the *Tethys* would cover in the weeks to come.

Only old Cha was absent from the noisy vessel; he left everything to those he had engaged to undertake a task that lay beneath his dignity and which they knew better than he, wishing to avoid any solecism that might seem a loss of face. His remoteness was mollified by Kirton's own reports to him as to progress and the expenditure he was undergoing, a quotidian process that strengthened the bond between the two men since Kirton was punctilious in calling his ship's owner 'sir.'

Mr Rodham, for such as mate he was known by convention, was allowed to sleep at home, not being required to come aboard until they signed the Articles and came together as a proper, organised ship's company. One evening as he knocked off and, having cleaned himself, Rodham came to report the day's work to Kirton only to find that the captain had a task for him.

'Mr Rodham, being a domicile of Singapore, before you rejoin tomorrow morning, please do me the service of hunting out an establishment of public education and discovering who, or what, is, or was, Tethys.'

The following forenoon, later than usual, Rodham appeared and informed his commander that Tethys had been queen-consort to Okeanos, the first Greek God of the Oceans. She was, therefore, mother of seas and rivers, the couple 'preceding Poseidon and Amphitrite, in this role,' he had added didactically.

Kirton nodded his thanks. 'Well, now we know; a goddess of the ocean and mother to seas and rivers; it seems a trifle pretentious.'

Despite the monsoon rains, by dint of activity and some cash inducements by way of *cumshaw*, eight days after being hauled out, the *Tethys* was run back into her natural element. The last task had been the recovery of her ranged and overhauled anchor cables and their restoration into her tarred-out cable lockers, freshly marked in their fifteen fathom 'shots' or 'shackles' of chain cable. Only some of her fore-and aft canvas had as yet been bent-on for the purpose, but she made her own way out from the wooden piles to the anchorage where the rest of her suit of sails was sent up and bent on. By the tenth day her gleaming fore yards bore their complement of course, topsail and topgallant, her jib-boom its fore-topmast staysail and jibs, her main topmast and topgallant stay their staysails, and the mainmast its spanker and gaff-topsail.

Two days later the *Tethys* lay ready for sea and began taking on a modest general cargo of necessaries, some consigned and some loaded 'on spec.' That evening Kirton dined with Mr Cha, who explained the arrangements he had set up for the appointment of the *shroff*, the desire he had for Kit Rodham to act as both chief mate and 'makee-learn' *com-*

prador, to all of which Kirton had long since reconciled himself. They wound up their business with Cha explaining the registration of the brigantine as a vessel wearing the ensign of Jamal ul-Azam, the Sultan of Sulu.

'The Dutch will not touch you, Captain, especially as you are Blitish master and have guns, but most of your trade I 'spect to be within the sultan's kingdom.'

Passing a bewildering number of documents, some covered in Chinese characters, two in Spanish and four or five in a script with which Kirton was not familiar, Cha told him that although beneficially owned in Singapore, the *Tethys*'s port of registry was henceforth 'Jolo' and that he should have the carpenter prepare a board suitably carved with that name and screwed over the old opium clipper's original port of registry: London. The document in the unfamiliar script was, Cha explained, a copy of the vessel's Certificate of Registry; it was in the *lingua franca* of the Suluese. The version in English, signed by both Cha in his capacity as vice-consul of the Sultan of Sulu, already bore his own name and Cha asked him to sign the Suluese version to avoid trouble with the Spanish. The *Tethys*, Cha explained, had a nominal majority share-owner in Jolo, the old *towkay*'s nephew, Ban Guan. Here the two Chinamen owned a godown.

This set of ship's papers he finally handed over to Kirton in a beautiful folio of green leather marked ostentatiously with the title: *Brigantine Tethys, The Green Dragon Shipping Company, Jolo & Singapore, 1867*. Last, but by no means least, Cha passed to him three scrolls. All bore heavy red seals and an elaborate 'chop' or stamp of authorisation.

'These,' explained Cha, a twinkle lighting his dark and deep-set eyes, 'are your certificates of competency. They are all in English.'

Kirton frowned as he saw after his own name the inscription in an elaborate copper-plate script the word 'Master.' 'How. . . ?' he began, but Cha waved him to silence.

'Cha is vice-consul in Singapore for Sultan of Sulu, Captain Kirton,' the old man said formally, referring to himself in the third person. 'Now, you go, sail when you are ready and I will see you when you come back Singapore-side by'm'by.'

Kirton rose awkwardly, finding it difficult with his bad leg. He gave Cha a short bow, as had become his custom on departure, and the old man clapped for the girl to clear away the dishes before reaching for his opium pipe.

Five days later the *Tethys* lay at anchor in a shallow bay on the coast of one of the Anambas Islands, a Dutch outpost in the South China Sea. She had arrived that afternoon and her boat had been pulled ashore to advertise a stock of paraffin available for sale, along with lamps and lanterns, steel cutlery, and other domestic articles. Kit Rodham had come back with a promise of brisk trading on the following morning and, after dinner, Kirton and Rodham were sitting in deck-chairs on the *Tethys*'s long poop, smoking the cigars that they habitually enjoyed in the evenings and which served the dual purpose of providing pleasure and keeping the mosquitoes at bay. After the short twilight of the tropics, the long beguiling evenings with the sky bright with stars were a cool and welcome relief of the heat of the day. Much of the monsoon had lost its effect in the China Sea and it had taken them some days to work their way north-east of their departure point off the Horsburgh lighthouse.

After their Herculean labours in Singapore the passage east had been a joy, almost a yachting trip, as Rodham had predicted, but for the fact that the *Tethys*'s crew needed the time to settle down. Kirton blew smoke at the heavens and viewed his companion who was staring at the whorls of thick blue smoke that rose from his cigar, making idle gestures to weave fantastic figures in the still air.

In the late twilight the younger man's dark good looks gave him a 'native' appearance, in real contrast to Kirton's own features, fair and burned by sun under a shock of blond hair. Even in the prevailing light, or lack of it, Rodham's shaven jowls showed a beard where Kirton's was a plain pale oval. Kirton had to admit that, given his own physical shape, the presence of so active and willing a young man had proved a God-send. His leg was set now, and the join had not been well made. Privately he raged against the poor attention he had received in the British Military Hospital in Singapore, but then he was not a soldier, though had he been a naval officer he was certain he would have received better treatment than he had had. He had never felt more like a piece of imperial flotsam than the moment when the full impact of his future had finally struck him. Still, he was man enough to admit the turn events had taken had been more than fortunate.

'This is, I suppose,' ventured Kirton, 'the nearest thing to heaven a man can find.'

'I can think of another, sir,' Rodham responded with a chuckle.

Kirton did not react; though wanting two years to his majority, Rodham clearly had both an appetite for and enjoyed success with women. Kirton had not met Rodham's 'wife,' but had convinced himself that the young woman was little more than a concubine except that he could not see Cha allowing such a liaison under his nose without some form of formal union. The old man's plans, revealed by Rodham and confirmed by Cha himself, indicated that Rodham was indeed being groomed for at least a nominal partnership in the House of the Green Dragon.

'You have not been married long,' he remarked, implying he knew that the joys of the marriage bed wore off.

'I didn't know you were married, sir,' Rodham said, drawing himself upright in the deck-chair and stubbing his cigar out in the ash-tray alongside it.

'I'm not,' replied Kirton, 'and not likely to be with a leg like a strained shackle pin . . .'

'Come, sir,' consoled the younger man, 'many a comely Chinese girl would happily serve you as a wife; you are a wealthy man, an *orang kaya* . . .'

'Hardly,' chuckled Kirton despite himself. 'Anyway,' he hauled himself awkwardly to his feet, walked to the ship's rail and, with a deft flick of his fingers, shot his cigar stub overboard before turning and saying, 'I never found a discussion about women enhanced any such evening. They are best enjoyed for what they are . . .' He paused, looked about him, at the loom of the island covered by its abundant rain forest, and then up at the over-arching constellations as he stretched contentedly. 'Will you join me in a night-cap?'

'With pleasure, sir, but I think we should . . . ah, here he is.' It was Rodham's turn to haul himself up from his recumbent position as 'Vic' came on deck. The older man had kept quietly to himself since they had left Singapore, and as he emerged from the companionway he seemed suddenly awkward.

'Come join us,' said Kirton, 'Kit, there is another deck-chair somewhere.'

Rodham went aft, opened a locker alongside the steering gear, and drew out a third chair, setting it up. The second mate sat, drawing a silver cigar case from the pocket of his nankeen trousers, and removing one offered both his colleagues another smoke.

'Thanks but I have just finished one,' said Kirton.

'Me too,' added Rodham, though somewhat reluctantly.

'Now what may I get you to drink?' Kirton asked.

'Thank you but no, sir. I do not normally drink spirituous liquors,' he said in his slightly awkward English.

Kirton reached for a small hand-bell set on top of the adjacent coach-roof and on the appearance of his tiger, Ah Chuan, called for two whisky sodas.

A slightly uneasy silence descended on them for a few moments, broken by the second mate—who had paused in the preparation of his cigar to say: 'I hope that I am not intruding.'

'Not at all,' said Kirton. 'I was just about to send word for you to join us if you had not turned-in as this is the first chance we have had to get together properly since we sailed from Tanjong Pagar.' Then, ever conscious and slightly embarrassed by the other man's experience, he added, 'I should not like to think you felt excluded, though our conversation has been no more than idle chatter.'

'No, no, sir, that was kind of you, I am not troubled by such matters; if you and Mr Rodham have matters to discuss, they are not the business of myself.'

'My God, "Vic," what is it that you are smoking?' Rodham asked, as the second mate conjured a large cigar into life and the aroma from its glowing end coiled about their heads.

Removing the cigar from his mouth and regarding the lit end, the second mate answered, 'It's Sumatran tobacco, wrapped in Deli leaf. As good, if not better than anything you'll get in Manila. Would you care for one?'

'Yes, by God, I would, though I would not want to deplete your stock,' Rodham said, changing his mind.

'I have sufficient,' 'Vic' said in his quiet voice. Rodham took the proffered cigar from the case and lit it from his own match.

'Captain, sir?' Sorely tempted, for he enjoyed smoking, Kirton demurred. 'That is most kind of you but I think not. I try not to indulge too much in such things.'

The whiskies arrived and Kirton went on, addressing the second mate, 'I hope that you are content with your present berth,' he said, and without waiting for a response, added, 'This is a night for yarning and it is too early for turning-in, tell us what sort of vessel you commanded in the country-trade?'

'A fine, heavily-sparred full-rigged ship,' 'Vic' responded, 'running from the Hugli to Hong Kong but, unfortunately the owners—a Parsi house in Bombay—was bankrupted in the crash of '65 and I lost everything . . . I tell you gentlemen, a seaman's life is at the mercy of a fickle fate though such are the ways to enlightenment.'

'I don't think I should have found such a thing enlightening,' Rodham remarked drily.

'The individual can do nothing in such circumstances . . . the tea freight rate had dropped to £3 per ton . . .'

'Didn't one of Jardine, Matheson's steamers clean-up by beating the mail packet to every port and buying-up with paper money all the gold and specie the master could afford?' Rodham asked.

'Indeed, it was a ruthless year . . .'

'It was cleverly done, though,' remarked Rodham.

'Without a doubt,' agreed the quondam *nakoda*, 'but it left very many, many others eating humble-pie and finding it not much to their liking.'

Silence fell upon the three men, then Kirton announced that he was going to turn-in, leaving the others on deck. After the master had gone below Rodham said:

'Vic, I couldn't help seeing that on the Articles you signed-on as V. Jones . . .'

'This troubles you?'

'No, not at all, but I am somewhat curious by nature, and probably should hold my tongue. However, I have enjoyed a good dinner and a pleasant glass and a smoke of your truly excellent cigar. We are likely to be ship-mates for some time, so forgive me if my question is impertinent.'

'I am sailing in a Suluese vessel under a master who does not have a proper master's certificate and am junior to a boy who broke his indentures to sleep with a woman he had lost his head or his heart to. Perhaps I wish to keep my proper self to myself . . .'

'Oh, come on, that's a bit harsh, is it not?'

'Mmmm, not from my perspective.'

Rodham's protest was in defence of himself, but a moment later he had digested the import of what Vic had said about Captain Kirton and he asked: 'Are you saying the Old Man has not got a proper Certificate of Competence?'

'Not as issued by the British Board of Trade. Like you he hides under the artifice of a Suluese ticket.'

'Well I'll be damned!' For a moment Rodham remained silent, digesting this intelligence. Then he sighed and said, 'I suppose we all have our secrets.'

The second mate chuckled. 'Not too many at your age, I am hoping,' he said.

'I have been a bad lad,' Rodham confessed.

'Women or wine?' the other asked.

'Women,' Rodham paused. 'But that is over now. I am married and have a good future . . .'

'You have a very good future married to Mr Cha's daughter. I am supposing you are to become a partner in the business one day.'

'I think that is in the old devil's mind,' Rodham answered disingenuously.

The second mate laughed again, but this time with a touch of bitterness, pitching his cigar-butt over the rail into the sea. 'Of course it is in his mind; he has no sons, only a daughter and a number of useless relatives. It is necessary that he have a successor and what better than a young white man to elevate his trading house with a British name and a white man on the Board of Directors . . .'

'I'm sorry if that . . .'

'Not at all, but it makes sense.'

'Yes, I suppose it does,' a chastened Rodham admitted.

'As for my name, which you are so *curious* about, my name is Vikram, or Vik for short. Vik with a *k*, that is.'

'And you do not mind my calling you that?'

'Not in the least; as long as you remember that I am not pretending it is an English name like Victor, which I rather think you at least might have thought to be the case.' The second mate paused for a moment then added, 'I would be obliged if you would remember that, young fellow.'

'Of course,' said Rodham, leaning across and, in his impulsively boyish manner, extending his right hand, 'and you must call me Kit, Kit with a *k* being short for Christopher.'

'So you are named after your God,' the older man laughed quietly, rolling his head from side to side. 'No wonder that you are senior to me.'

They both lolled in their deck-chairs and stared into the velvet softness of the night in companionable silence. Then Jones said:

'You are what I calculate to be a forward young man Kit, but I concede this is an evening for exchanging confidences and there is the matter of my surname after which you so impertinently enquired . . .'

'I did not mean to pry . . .'

'It is no matter. If we are to work together it is as well to be clear about such things. My real name is not Jones alone, but Vir-Jones . . .'

'Isn't that unusual?' ventured Rodham, blundering into territory an older and wiser man would have avoided.

'Not so very unusual in parts of India where the British have long been resident. My grandsire was a man from Wales who had come out to work for the old East India Company. Though my father was born illegitimate, the old man recognised him on condition he retained the name; thus I *am* Jones by birth. While I might run the risk of insults in Calcutta, an officer identified on the ship's papers as "V. Jones" is less likely to raise the eyebrows of those pigs, the Dutch.' Jones paused, then, reminded of past unpleasantness, went on: 'I would not wish to hear you remark on the mixture in my blood.' Then, thinking of Rodham's own marital entanglement and how it levelled matters between them, added: 'You will understand, being married to Mr Cha's daughter.'

Rodham chuckled contentedly, the whisky having warmed his belly. 'And very happily too, Vik. And since this is indeed an evening for confidences, I was myself born illegitimate, orphaned and put in an institution from which I was sent to sea ...'

'And that is why you do not mind settling in Singapore?'

'Exactly.'

'Well, my young friend,' Jones said rolling his head and regarding his empty glass, 'I think that is as far as discretion should take us this evening, I am all for turning-in.'

'Eight bells, sir.' They were interrupted by the duty *jurmudi*, or quartermaster, reporting the end of the watch to Rodham.

The young mate nodded. 'Then make it so,' he said. Leaving the Chinese quartermaster to ring the ship's after bell, Rodham yawned, then said, 'I'll check the cable, there's little to see by way of bearings in this darkness and then she's all yours, Vik.'

'I'll see to it, my dear fellow. You need your beauty-sleep more than do I, but please, call me Vee-Jay, it is what my friends do.'

'Vee-Jay,' repeated Rodham, as if testing the contraction. 'Very well ... so good night ...'

Kirton came on deck again later that night. He was unable to sleep and decided to stand the remainder of the middle-watch himself, resolving to ensure that he trained the *jurmudis* to manage an anchor-watch in the future. Both the mates would be busy on the following morning, so he explained his intentions to the second mate, dismissed him and began to pace the long poop.

With all the scuttles open, he had heard much of the conversation between his two officers. The night had been too still and silent for him to even pretend to ignore it, and it had disturbed him to the extent of preventing sleep. But there were other, vaguer thoughts and deeper longings that the evening had stirred-up.

It had been the first evening of relaxation since he had joined the *Tethys*, and in some way it annoyed him that in the end it had been soured by the knowledge that both his officers knew of his lack of a British master's certificate. Not that the passage across the South China Sea to the lovely archipelago off which they presently lay at anchor could possibly have revealed any deficiencies in his ability. He and Jones had managed their sights perfectly and, although his own physical incapacity prevented him from agile movements, he had got sail off the brigantine quickly enough when they had experienced a sudden and violent squall and brought her in to a difficult enough anchorage under sail with a quiet skill that would have astonished Captain McClure.

As for the matter of a British certificate, well, there was nothing to be done about the matter for the time being and he hoped it did not trouble his junior officers over-much, but one could never be too sure of such things on a ship, especially so small a vessel as the *Tethys*.

Walking the deck that night Kirton recalled that distant afternoon aboard the old wooden-wall *Canopus* and the interrupted game of British Bulldog. Well, it seemed he was destined not to command a first-class mail liner—or even a crack cargo-ship of the Scottish River Line—but a South-Seas schooner after all, or at least an East Indian brigantine with a disreputable history. His tenure of command would be short, he thought with more than a hint of bitterness, terminated when old man Cha had no further use for him, or when his bloody leg gave out. As for that mangled appendage, it gave him a good deal of pain and, though he found it impossible to reconcile himself to the fact that this was to be a permanent legacy of his attempt to end up a gentleman captain with passengers dining at his table and several hundred horse-power at his command, he stared out over the taffrail into the velvet darkness of the tropical night and drew into his nostrils the smell of the shore with a sudden and overwhelmingly deep contentment. If Henry Kirton had learned one thing in his short career at sea it was to—what he called to himself—*log the moment*.

If one failed to do this, a life of toil and hardship found no relief and he knew that his sense of embitterment would, in the end, triumph over his youthful love of his avocation. He would turn to drink, or opium, both of them tempting analgesics not only for a wounded soul, but a humiliating disability. He drew himself upright from the ship's rail and turned away to pace irregularly up and down, smelling the scent of the island, borne offshore by the breeze.

Chapter Five

Shaking-Down

From the Anambas they ran north-east, through the Balabac Strait, and swung south into Telok Marudu, anchoring in turn off the *kampongs* that lined the shore of this large inlet. To the south of them, rising from the dense green of the rain forest reared the mighty peak of Kinabalu, its summit shrouded in orographic cloud, but its mystical majesty dominating the whole of this north-east coast of Borneo.

At each place Rodham, accompanied by the *shroff*, a reserved Chinaman of indeterminate age named Ching who kept to himself, went off in the ship's boat with the usual supply of domestic wares for sale or barter. In return they picked up small parcels of island produce which were hoisted aboard the *Tethys* by her crew and stowed in her hold. From the last of these villages they stood out into the Sulu Sea to the isolated island of Cagayan Sulu, before doubling back to the main island, anchoring off the brown cliffs of Berhala, and sending the boat in to Sandakan.

Everywhere they found a brisk if modest trade; whatever internal factions divided the Sultan of Sulu's subjects, the sight of the purple and white ensign at the brigantine's peak was welcomed; anything was better than the Dutch tricolour. Moreover, to capture a warm trade Cha had instructed Rodham and Ching not to drive too hard a bargain, but to begin to build a loyal clientele.

From Sandakan Kirton laid a course for Jolo, their port of registry where they found a warm welcome. The immediate waterfront of the township consisted of a small village on stilts and cargo-work was consequently slow. Nevertheless, Cha had sent word ahead whilst the *Tethys* still lay on the slip in Singapore, and his nephew there had a substantial quantity of produce ready for them such that there was little for Rodham to do but see it stowed safely. On weighing for their passage to Tawau, Ching suggested they salute the sultan's flag ashore with a few discharges of their breech-loaders, a task embraced with gusto by Rodham and the Sikh *jagas*.

As the smoke streamed to leeward and Vee-Jay ordered the setting of the fore course, the *Tethys*, already leaning to the breeze under her jib, fore-topmast staysail, fore-topsail, and spanker, drove along at a cracking pace, exchanging the emerald green of shoal waters for the dark blue of the deeper Sulu Sea, the wake curling astern in a roil of marbled movement, the bow wave thrusting out from under the flare of her lovely bow, the spray glistering like the parcel of pearls that Kirton had taken charge of and secured in the ship's safe.

'Give her the t'gallant and main staysail, Mr Jones,' Kirton called out to the men coiling down halliards in the waist before walking aft and taking the helm. He sent the *jurmudi* aloft to cast loose the main topsail, stopped down in the cross-trees, and when the quartermaster returned to the deck, Kirton ordered him to 'hoist away!'

It was hard work for one man to run the large triangular sail up its jackstay to the main truck, and Rodham, just then coming aft from seeing the starboard anchor secured at the cat-head, jumped to the Chinaman's assistance; up went the sail just as the fore-topgallant, having been swiftly mast-headed, was sheeted home.

Standing at the wheel, Kirton felt the brigantine heel further, and dig herself into the grain of her course, throwing off a larger set of pearls from the lee bow as she increased her speed. Watching the length of his ship, with his crew coiling down the halliards and sheets, working together as a team gave him an immense sense of a satisfaction he had not known since he had first taken command of a cutter in Milford Haven manned by his fellow cadets, to reach down the length of the ria to Dale Roads before being obliged to hand over to another lad for a similarly exhilarating reach back to the grim black and white hull of the old *Canopus*.

Nothing, not even the quickest passage of the full-rigged ship *Cormorant* in which he had served his four-year apprenticeship, still less the setting of sail in an auxiliary steamer like the *River Tay*, had ever given him so much pleasure. In the first there had been too much hazing, or bullying by the mate, the assigning of a score of menial tasks on a daily basis; and in the latter no real pleasure in employing canvas when a steam-kettle down below continually reminded you that you were in some ill-conceived mule of a vessel that might be pointing the way to the future, but indicated that the years to come would lose much of the pure joy which provided a sailorman with the sops of his chosen way of life—or so thought Hal Kirton.

No, this was sublime; flying-fish sailing with no Cape Horn to fear before one returned home, no doubling of the Cape of Storms, which was the better name for Good Hope to any sailing ship man. Not even a typhoon could catch them here, for the Chinese called Borneo the 'land below the wind,' of a latitude incapable of generating such a vicious storm, though only a little further north the Philippines were vulnerable. Provided he and his mates kept the *Tethys* from striking a coral reef or an isolated rock and navigated these island-studded seas with the caution and respect that could trap the unwary or the cocky, the prospect of commanding the old but lovely little vessel filled Kirton with unutterable joy.

It was almost with regret that he handed the wheel over to the *jurmudi* and fell again to hobbling up and down the deck. Flying fish could be seen now, leaping ahead of them, panicked into flight by the shadows of their sails and the onrush of the brigantine. A pair of dolphins came leaping in from the starboard side to ride the pressure wave the *Tethys* was pushing ahead of her, to the childish delight of several of her crew who chattered excitedly at the prospect of catching one and eating it. They made good *chow-chow*, Kirton knew, but these creatures avoided the lure hurriedly lowered and, after twenty minutes, peeled away and disappeared.

Bowling along on a north-westerly course, by the wind, to clear the land, they passed island after island until nightfall, and when they were out in the Sulu Sea, they tacked and shortened down. Kirton had no desire to run aground in the darkness and their next port of call, Tawau, required a daylight transit of the Sibutu Passage into the Celebes Sea.

Although they had not exhausted the coastal settlements under the sultan's jurisdiction, the hold of the *Tethys* was filling rapidly and

Kirton was keen to sail further south, beyond Tawau, into the waters of the Dutch East Indies, to try their luck somewhere on the coast of Kalimantan.

'It's certainly worth a try, sir,' agreed Rodham, relishing his role as *comprador*. 'We can be in and out before the Dutch know anything about us, even supposing they are going to bother about a small, inter-island Suluese vessel.'

They were sitting at the saloon table as *Tethys* ghosted along, her lookouts doubled and instructed to keep a sharp eye out for the extensive reef that lay off Bum-Bum in the approaches to Tawau. If they had not spotted any breakers by nightfall, Kirton intended to haul round to the south and heave-to for the night, but just now, at their midday meal, there was a chance they might pass the reef before sunset.

They sat at the saloon table at the far end of which the silent Ching ate his rice. 'What d'you think of *Da Foo*'s idea of trying for trade further south, Mister Ching?' Kirton asked.

'Velly good,' said the *shroff*, barely interrupting his meal.

'The question is where exactly?' Kirton said.

'You tly mouth of Sesayap Liver, Captain. Anchor . . . send boat . . .'

'I'll get the chart . . .' volunteered Rodham cheerfully.

At the end of a three-month voyage they returned to Singapore with a hold full of rattans, coconuts, copra, hemp, and gutta-percha, the latter much then in demand for electrical insulation. Their arrival, of no particular interest to anyone other than the waterfront idlers, established for the crew of the *Tethys* what was to be a regular routine, though the periods of their absences varied according to their luck with cargoes. Thanks to Kirton's good nature and his lack of alternative accommodation, he released his two mates from duty for a week of their ten-day turn-round, happy to live aboard the *Tethys*. Besides the eager Rodham, Kirton had discovered that Vik had a wife and three small children and by this act of liberality he greatly increased his popularity. For the crew he devised a system of long and short leaves, with a similar result; given a ten-day stay in their home port, one watch would take a week's leave, the other three days, reversing this on their next homecoming.

After the five capacious holds and 'tween decks of the *River Tay*, supervision of the discharge and cleaning of the *Tethys*'s single 'tween deck and hold was far from an onerous duty, even given his crippled state. Every evening, after the duty *jaga* had taken over the anchor watch for which he and a *kurmudi* had soon been trained, Kirton would take a boat ashore. Sometimes he dined with Cha, but more commonly he was free of obligations to the owner and went and dined with his own kind, occasionally meeting a former ship-mate either on the Esplanade or in one of the colonial establishments.

In this way the *Tethys* became a regular sight in the waters east of Singapore, and Captain Kirton's smart brigantine established a reputation for fast passages, so that now-and-again, she would embark a passenger or two, for which the *jagas* were obliged to sling hammocks in the 'tween decks or on deck just under the break of the low poop. The fact that her ship's company consisted of several races and religions made her cook an adept at producing a multiple menu, thus attracting Muslim and Chinese merchants who had dealings with the Sultanate of Sulu.

The success of the *Tethys*'s voyages began to pay dividends to Kirton himself, as Cha put him on a generous salary as he had promised and matters ran along smoothly in this way for over a year. But the fates, the gods, providence, or what-you-will abhor the status quo as much as nature does a vacuum. In truth, there is no such thing as the status quo; subtle changes are constantly being wrought by the actions of humans as much as by exterior forces wheresoever they originate. Since a ship is but a world in microcosm, in the case of the *Tethys* it was the senior members of her afterguard who wrought this change over a period of time.

Captain Kirton was not a religious man; he had long ago abandoned the guidance and supposed certainties of the Church of Rome, in which he had been brought-up, and those of the Church of England whose doctrine was at such odds with the quotidian conduct of his superiors in their tyranny aboard the *Canopus* where he was obliged to pay his respects to the Established Church. But like so many sailors he was deeply spiritual; in the ignorant this could manifest itself in a deeply-rooted superstition.

But men of Kirton's enlightened stamp, who brushed with the numinous as much as the scientific every time they took their sextants out of their boxes, often possessed an awareness of some form of natural laws which, like the attraction of the poles upon their compasses, affected the affairs of men.

Thus, in his somewhat aloof station, a station rendered thus by both his semi-isolation as commander of the brigantine and his personal life lived almost entirely on board, he saw with greater clarity than his shipmates the changes that they were slowly undergoing.

He himself, he acknowledged, was growing tired of an existence the challenges of which he had mastered. Not that this was evidence of the slightest dissatisfaction in his professional position; on the contrary, he had quickly grown into it, assuming a quiet authority which, by virtue of a compound of his intellect, his bearing, his abilities, and all those nuances that go to make up a man's character, had produced a fine ship-master who was as near revered by his crew as was possible.

But this had come with consequences. Those closer to him than the hands found him less of a subject for adoration. Though he never lost his temper with his officers, his bad leg could make him tetchy. But if by strength of will he avoided open ruptures with his mates, he was slow to praise them when they did well, and when they earned a reproof, as all subordinates are subject to at some time or another, Kirton's silences were taken badly, especially so by Vikram Vir-Jones. Kirton had grown steadily away from that early heavy reliance on his second mate which the older attributed to the wrong causes.

The second mate's age, his past experience, and, most of all, his race, made him susceptible and highly sensitive to this unintended spurning by Kirton. The captain himself was unaware of the effect his confidence was having on his junior mate, always treating him with the respect his rank, abilities, and age were due. Indeed, Kirton paid little heed to the colour of a man's skin and acknowledged he owed Vee-Jay a great deal in establishing the success of the *Tethys*; but he was unfortunately oblivious of those occasional irritabilities caused by the pain in his leg and the constant reminder of the limitations the growing deformity of the twisted limb imposed upon him, both of which produced occasions when, if matters did not fall out quite right, produced in him a sense that the quondam *nakoda* had somehow failed him.

Vikram Jones was a loyal man, grateful to have found employment in such a generally congenial vessel as the *Tethys*, but his own sensitivities were not always helped by the third player in this intimate, slow-burning little drama, Kit Rodham, whose influence on affairs grew almost by the month, or by the constant ambitions of his own wife, whose life had suffered as a result of her husband's loss of prestige in the banking crash of '65. She, alas, could not perceive—as her husband could—that he had at least a comfortable and steady berth in a little vessel that had made a name for herself among the many archipelagos east of Singapore. Jones was, therefore unpleasantly caught in a trap of his own making and in his discontent he sought a revival of his own career, an objective blocked by both the younger white men aboard the *Tethys*.

It was, therefore, the young man in the middle whose ever extending influence began to force matters apart. The boyish enthusiasm and energy with which Kit Rodham had begun his career as chief mate and *comprador* aboard the *Tethys* soon combined with his natural intelligence. While old Ching continued to manage the ship's monetary affairs and, under Cha's strict instructions, oversaw Rodham's dealings, it was not long before the young man could stand on his own two feet where his job of bartering in trade-goods and acquiring a decent homeward lading for the brigantine was concerned. As for his task as chief mate, this was rendered easy by both of his colleagues, who from a standing start of both assisting Rodham had gradually subsumed much of the mate's duties. None of them minded this; it was a convenience and worked well, provided Rodham stood his sea-watches, all of which amounted to an easy-going regime which suited them all—up to a point.

As for the crew, the Chinese seamen were excellent fellows, who in their own manner, kept to themselves and as long as their *tindal*, the bosun Tan, enjoyed the prestige and respect from the officers that his rank entitled him to, were fine ship-mates. The small group of Sikh *jagas*, whose daily chores consisted chiefly of keeping watch on the poop as assistants to the officer-of-the-watch and maintaining the ship's small arsenal of rifles, shotguns, and the two breech-loaders, were also semi-autonomous, though they messed with old Ibrahim, the diligent *casab* whose occasional arguments with Tan over the fabric of the *Tethys* caused a good deal of amusement to the rest of the ship's company.

Although they involved a fair amount of exceedingly bad language, largely consisting of racial slurs from each party, these rows were generally good-natured. Pidgin was the language common to all of them, pidgin laced with a good deal of Malay, for most Singaporeans born and bred in that mixed-race city spoke a smattering of Malay, including the Chinese, and Vikram Jones and Kit Rodham both spoke it quite passably.

However, one morning, when the *Tethys* lay becalmed in her homeward approach to the Balabac Strait, Tan—as was customary—came aft at sunrise to discuss the day's work with the chief mate. Rodham habitually consulted Kirton over much of this, the captain having developed decided views on the appearance of the brigantine when she arrived at Singapore, besides taking a keen interest in the general maintenance of the fabric of her hull and her gear aloft.

Rodham, distracted by the haze of the early morning preventing him obtaining accurate bearings as they drifted about, was anxious about the vessel's position. During Jones's middle watch the *Tethys* had been hit by a strong and sudden squall, the rain had come down in sheets, and she had driven south-west at her best speed. Now she lay motionless, but the question of quite where she was gnawed at Rodham's guts. Captain Kirton would be on deck shortly and he did not wish to be found wanting.

At this point Tan came onto the poop, gave Rodham his usual morning salutation when they were at sea, and began discussing the work that the hands should be getting on with. Rodham waved him away.

'Too busy just now, *Tindal*,' he said sharply, 'plenty problems with navigation . . . ' As Tan turned away, Rodham recalled such a curt dismissal was discourteous, and would play ill with Kirton, who insisted on a proper code of conduct aboard the vessel.

In a spontaneous and therefore ill-considered attempt not to show the Chinese petty-officer disrespect in front of the duty *jaga* and—more importantly the *jurmudi* at the wheel—Rodham called the *tindal* back and in a temporising tone of voice said:

'Talk to *Casab*, he want some work done topside . . . ,' before resuming his anxious scanning of the obscured horizon.

Tan had turned, but hearing the mate's words he stiffened. 'I no take orders from *Casab*,' he snapped, before going forward and turning the hands to on several tasks of his own devising. It was a small enough matter, but the bosun burned from what he considered loss of face in front of witnesses, all of which soured matters for some time thereafter and led to a permanent breach—at least upon Tan's part—between the mate and his right-hand man where the ship was concerned.

The truth was, the double task of being the *Tethys*'s executive officer and her business manager was not entirely a sensible one, especially in the hands of one so inexperienced as Rodham. He was no longer an eager lad, but a father, with growing ambitions of his own, ambitions that the hot-house atmosphere of Singapore in the latter part of the 1860s offered in the form of almost unlimited opportunities.

CHAPTER SIX

An Uncertain Future

IN MAY OF 1868 A NEW-COMER NAMED MANSFIELD FROM TEIGNMOUTH in Devon had arrived in Singapore to establish a new agency on behalf of Alfred Holt's Ocean Steam Ship Company of Liverpool. Holt's blue-funnelled steamers with their revolutionary steam engines were eating into the China trade dominated by Skinner's 'Castles,' MacGregor Gow's 'Glens,' and Laird's Scottish 'Rivers.' The House of the Green Dragon took this muscling-in by another European company badly, and although it increased the amount of tonnage available for the carriage of inter-island commodities to the West, old man Cha saw it as a slight to his own ambitions. The *towkay* was increasingly eager to get Rodham ashore, but he was as yet too young to hold a directorship under the colonial regulations. Rodham himself, showing an aptitude for the matter of commerce, and a greed for the rewards it would bring him, grew impatient. By now a first-class *comprador*, he had become a second-class chief mate, so-much-so, that Kirton was, upon occasion—and even though his duties were of the lightest imaginable in that capacity—obliged to quietly upbraid him. Such humiliations were as offensive to Rodham as his own tetchiness had been to Tan and had, in their own way, contributed to the latter. Not knowing where they were as they approached the Balabac Strait that morning might have earned Rodham yet another rebuke from a man he otherwise regarded with both fondness and respect.

Of course, neither Vikram Jones nor Kit Rodham could appreciate the degree to which Kirton's injuries excoriated him. The physical pain, which to some extent came and went according to the monsoon and the humidity, was bad enough; but the moral effect began to bite deep. To be sure he was happy enough in his command; the little brigantine answered all the secret desires nurtured by a romantic sailor like Kirton, employed in so delightful a trade as she was. Indeed, the burdens of command could scarcely have been lighter and, providing his leg held out, the years ahead offered the prospect of more happiness than he had dared hope for in the miserable days following his discharge from the care of Major Jeffries and Nurse Trimm. But a man had other needs and the constant uxorious chatter of his mates, with their wives and families, reminded him of his enforced celibacy.

As first it had seemed a small thing; he had, after all, had a good run ashore in Yokohama and women were cheap enough in Singapore if a man wanted to buy his pleasures, but he began to yearn for something more permanent. The deep contentment of his two mates began to eat into Kirton's inner self. Most white men took a Chinese, Tamil, or Malay mistress, according to their preferences, employing her as a cook-cum-house-keeper and referring to her, at the club among their male friends, as the 'walking dictionary,' since they tended to learn the local language from such women. It was all pretty louche and considered harmless. Kirton was no angel, having been eight years at sea since leaving the *Canopus*. And even when in the training ship the senior boys had found ways and means to enjoy the favours of a small number of willing girls in nearby Neyland. This had caused the occasional rupture with the local lads and declarations of unofficial hostilities had resulted in bloody noses, all of which had to be concealed from the training-ship's officers.

But Kirton had reached that age when he thought increasingly of a permanent establishment like Rodham's. That young man's future was cut-and-dried in a way that Kirton's could never be, what with his twisted leg and his limp. Vikram Jones had once confided in him that he thought that had he, Kirton, turned-up footloose in Singapore before Rodham, the shrewd old Chinaman would have settled the inheritance of his business on him, so desperate was Mr Cha to elevate his trading house into the first class, with note-paper and documentation that was not so obviously Chinese in constitution as the House of the Green Dragon. Kirton had dismissed this as pot-stirring on the part of the Indian officer, but the thought surfaced from time-to-time and its impracticability always rested on his twisted frame. Most of the time he could suppress such thoughts, busy man that he was, for he was not fool enough to take his good fortune for granted, but there were moments, long languorous moments, when he longed for female company.

There were but a few white women in Singapore; those that were not married to the senior members of merchant-houses, agencies, or banks, or wedded to garrison officers, were either tough single women like Nurse Trimm, or the young daughters of the aforesaid married couples. Such girls were soon shipped back home for their schooling, and in any case few of any of them would have regarded the limping skipper of the little brigantine *Tethys*, who worked for a Chinaman, a 'catch' of any kind. According to their myopic view of life even Cha's rumoured wealth carried little weight; not only was the man a 'Chink,' but he was in a *low* form of trade, despite his connections with the Scottish River Line of Glasgow and the Copenhagen Steam-ship Co. And he smoked *opium*!

Unless one was blithely unaware of such subtleties, one simply 'kept' one's walking dictionary until the time came to go home. Miscegenating young men like Rodham who took local wives were, of course, utterly beyond the Pale, a disgrace to the name of Englishman, and not made welcome in the social circle of the Europeans.

But Kirton could not go home. There was no point to it; he had no-one except his sister to go home to and she had written to announce she was engaged to be married. He could, of course, sit for his full British master's certificate, but his leg would prevent him from obtaining 'respectable' employment, so he had little else to look forward to but a life aboard *Tethys*, or her successor, in the employ of what would, everyone supposed, shortly become Rodham & Son.

The facts had been rubbed-in by an encounter on Collyer Quay one day. He had come ashore in the ship's boat, smartly pulled by four Chinese seamen and with a 'guard' of two *jagas* to signify his rank and importance—a stipulation of old Cha's, who never went anywhere without an escort and the clanging of gongs to announce his progress. As Kirton had limped up the steps and walked along towards the Esplanade a voice had hailed him.

'Kirton! Henry Kirton! Is that you?'

He had turned to find Captain McClure following him, having himself just landed from his own ship.

'Captain McClure, good to see you,' Kirton had ventured in a sudden access of pride, eager not to show subservience to a fellow master, but holding out his hand as one equal to another.

'I heard that you had settled down here and taken command of that odd little brigantine under Old Man Cha's colours,' McClure said somewhat patronisingly.

Kirton gave a short laugh. 'The colours are the Sultan of Sulu's, to be precise, Captain McClure.'

'And you're doing pretty well, I understand from what Cha tells me. He seems to think I dropped you in his lap deliberately when it was your leg . . .' McClure, aware of his tactlessness, let the sentence go unfinished.

'Yes, it was my leg,' Kirton said, irritated by McClure's smooth manner.

'How is it, my boy?' asked the older man, in a feeble attempt to make amends.

'Crooked,' Kirton answered sharply. 'They didn't make much of a job of it in the hospital, not unless they thought that I'd enlist as a cavalry trooper out of desperation.'

'Well, it's good to see you; Cha's gain is the River Line's loss.' He paused, then added, 'I guess you are going my way? To the House of the Green Dragon?'

Kirton grunted in the affirmative, then changed the subject. 'I saw the *River Spey*. I take it she's yours?'

'Yes, maiden voyage. Fine vessel and I have James Lawlor as second officer . . .'

'Lawlor?'

'Senior apprentice when you were with me; fine chap. Old Conway, of course. You are a Canopian, if I recall.'

'Yes, I am.'

'I think this new idea of young apprentices serving their time in steam rather than in sail will catch-on. The Laird ships have pioneered it and it took a deal of arguing to get the Board of Trade to agree to it, but

I have no doubt in my mind that it is the proper approach. The *River Spey* carries no sails to speak of bar a few fore-and-aft rags, as you probably noticed.'

'And I carry no engine in the *Tethys*,' Kirton riposted with a wry smile.

'I suppose you buzz-nack round the islands. It must be rather a pleasant occupation for a man like you ...'

'You mean a cripple?' Kirton bridled.

'Not exactly, my dear chap,' McClure said soothingly in a vain attempt to limit the damage to Kirton's self-esteem, but only adding to it as he blundered on. 'But, of course you'd not be able to find a berth in any of the River Line these days. The Board of Trade are slowly tightening their grip on the mercantile marine. Still, the little ... what's she called? *Tethys*? She'll see you out, I'm sure. Make something of a *Nabob* of you even though she is only a country-*wallah* ...'

By this time they had reached the House of the Green Dragon, but instead of going in with McClure, Kirton took his leave of his former commander.

'I've one or two things to attend to, Cap'n McClure. Good day to you.' He touched the peak of his hat and turned on his heel.

McClure stared after him, noting the pronounced limp and Kirton's reliance on his heavy stick, then turned to the green painted door of Cha's counting-house and tapped on it with the head of his own Malacca cane.

Kirton had been lying, of course. He had himself been on his way to see Mr Cha, but McClure's patronising condescension had upset him more than he could admit to himself. He was certain that at any moment the man would quiz him about his lack of a 'proper' master's certificate and he was damned if he would put himself through that humiliation.

He took himself off for a long and painful walk, returning to the *Tethys* late that night.

The old *casab* Ibrahim was on deck smoking and gave him a salute.

'Good evening, Ibrahim,' Kirton said, suddenly feeling his loneliness intensely.

'*Jaga* say you stay ashore, *Tuan*. Maybe love woman. Now you come back to ship; maybe you love *Tethys* better than woman.'

Kirton covered the need to respond by lighting a cigar. It was not his practice to relax in front of members of the crew but his relationship with Ibrahim went back to his first hours aboard the *Tethys* and there were those shared moments that their subsequent change in status could not quite erode.

'The *Tuan* has not been drinking,' Ibrahim boldly ventured, sharing the same sentiments as Kirton.

Kirton grinned and took his place beside Ibrahim, leaning on the rail and gazing at the lights moving hither and yon along the Esplanade, taking his cigar from his mouth and blowing a long curl of smoke into the windless velvetiness of the tropical night. 'No, the *Tuan* has not been drinking. Did you expect me to be drunk?'

'The white man likes to drink . . .' Ibrahim said with an uncomprehending shrug.

'This white man likes to drink, but not too much. Too much bad; bad things happen . . .'

'Like when Malay man run *amok* . . .'

'Yes, maybe,' Kirton responded shortly, knowing the *casab* was Malay. He drew on his cigar again and looked up at the stars. 'You not run *amok*, Ibrahim, from staying too long ship-side?'

Ibrahim gave a short laugh. 'No, *Tuan*. *Amok* always get shot. Not proper way to go to Paradise.'

'No . . .' Kirton responded as a silence fell between them.

Then Ibrahim asked with disarming candour: 'If no drink and no have woman, what *Tuan* do to come ship-side this late?'

'I walk, Ibrahim, long, long walk, out past the Bugis *kampong* and then I think of the ship and, as you said, maybe *Tethys* my wife . . .'

'That *bagus* for old man like Ibrahim, no good for young man like the *Tuan*. Maybe you catchee nice young woman. Plenty Chinese girls' family sell you. You keep in cabin . . .'

Kirton laughed bitterly. The conversation had taken a dangerously self-revelatory turn. 'My tiger would not like that.'

'Ach, tiger heathen infidel Chinaman. No worry about that man.' Ibrahim dismissed the Chinese steward Ah Chuan.

'Ah, but I do, Ibrahim,' Kirton said in a self-revelatory moment. 'I worry about all of you aboard the ship.'

'What you think about on your long walk?'

'What d'you think about while smoking on deck?'

'Paradise, *Tuan*, Paradise; and sometimes what Ibrahim do tomorrow to look after ship.'

'Well, I think of ship too.' Kirton paused and then asked, 'Are you happy Ibrahim?'

Kirton instantly regretted the question for he felt the old man next to him almost physically shrink; the chat between an old and a young man shifted a gear as the Malay confessed: 'Ibrahim not happy since all family lost.'

'Oh, all your family were killed? I'm so sorry . . .' Kirton attempted an apology, aware of the clumsy way McClure had trampled all over his own feelings earlier that evening.

'Allah willed it, but hard for me. I lose two wives and four childer. Bugis raided my *kampong*, take all away. I was fisherman then.' He paused, as if to master his feelings. 'After, I come to sea. One year later I join *Tethys*, just after she no longer carry opium to China. Never go home to *kampong*; home here.' He slapped the rail upon which both men leaned.

They smoked in silence until Kirton had finished his cigar and, as he straightened up to pitch the stub overboard, he yawned and said, 'We must sleep, Ibrahim.'

'Yes, *Tuan*. I check anchor light then see if *jaga* on anchor-watch is awake before I turn-in.'

Kirton glanced up at the poop where the tall figure of one of the Sikhs could be seen leaning against the main shrouds.

'Good night,' Kirton said, walking aft to the poop ladder, leaning heavily on his stick for his long walk had tired his bad leg.

'Good ni', *Tuan*,' the old man responded.

Just as Kirton reached the poop Ibrahim called after him. '*Tuan!*' Kirton turned. '*Tuan, Allah panjankan umor dan mengawalkan Tethys*,' the old man called after him: 'May Allah prolong your life and protect *Tethys*.'

'Thank you, Ibrahim. May Allah bless you too,' he responded, almost involuntarily, a sudden odd sensation passing through him. But he was too tired to give it any thought; his leg hurt abominably and he had yet to negotiate the companionway ladder, which would take all his concentration and a good deal of his strength.

When he had reached the companionway doors he heard Ibrahim call after him again. 'Captain Kirton!' Slightly exasperated after his exertions, Kirton raised his head.

Ibrahim's wrinkled old face, barely perceptible in the starlight, just rose over the break of the poop as he stood at the after end of the main deck.

'What is it?'

'You keep ship safe, *Tuan*, long time after Ibrahim . . .' The sentence was left unfinished and Kirton did not know if it was a question or an instruction, but he sensed again, something insecure about the old fellow.

'Yes, yes, or course, Ibrahim. Always . . .' He began to lift his gammy leg over the companionway sill.

'You promise, *Tuan*?'

'I promise, Ibrahim.'

'On your honour as an English gentleman?'

'On my honour as an English gentleman.'

At that the *casab*'s face disappeared and his figure retreated into the night.

As he slid between the sheets Kirton's last thought was that it was odd that the old man's anxiety for the *Tethys* matched his own ambitions for the brigantine. Thanks to his employer's generosity, the success of his voyages, and his frugal way of life, Kirton had an idea. He had intended to lay the matter before Cha that day, but the encounter with McClure had dissuaded him, though the long walk that had resulted from it had coalesced his thoughts. He had forgotten about the odd sensation Ibrahim's words had stirred up inside him and went to sleep, a half-smile on his face.

The following morning Kirton was awoken to the sound of shouts of alarm. He leapt out of his bunk when he heard one of the Malay-speaking Sikh *jagas* call out: '*Sudah mati! Casab sudah mati!*'

77

Kirton's Malay did not extend to the understanding of this phrase, but he knew instantly that it involved Ibrahim—that much was obvious—and his intuition told him even before the Sikh knocked on his door, that the old man was dead.

And so it proved. Ibrahim lay in his bunk, a shrivelled corpse bereft of all the vivacity that had kept him going about his duties so sedulously in the years that he had served Kirton aboard the *Tethys*. Kirton felt a hard lump in his throat, turning away to order Tan to wrap him up and take him on deck. Had Ibrahim died at sea matters would have been simple, but now it would be necessary to inform the port authorities and the local imam, so that what remained of the poor old man could be buried before sun-down. Back on deck shortly before eight bells ushered in the forenoon watch, Kirton ordered the *Tethys*'s Suluese ensign worn at half-mast for the day.

By the time the two mates arrived on board, Kirton had called for a boat and, leaving them to see the corpse was taken ashore, Kirton went ashore himself. After dealing with all the business attending a death in port and securing a doctor to certify this had been due to natural causes of old age and cardiac arrest, he made his way to Cha's premises.

It was not essential to inform Cha of the death, but he felt as a last mark of respect to the man who had done more than any other to maintain the brigantine, that Cha should know. Moreover, Kirton had the matter of yesterday's deferred business to discuss with the *towkay* and was, in a sense glad that Rodham had his hands full delivering Ibrahim's body to his co-religionists.

To his intense annoyance, however, he found Captain McClure ensconced in Cha's private quarters, all too obviously at ease. There was also another master present, the commander of a Danish steamer, and the three men were so comfortably situated that Kirton felt like an intruder. But Cha waved him to a seat and clapped his hands so that the serving girl brought in a tea-bowl, and poured the thin aromatic green liquid into it from her pot.

'We were just saying, Captain Kirton,' McClure announced airily, 'that the freight rates on China tea are pinching the clippers. Swire is getting Holt's blue funnels £12 per ton and Captain Mortensen here has been offered 10 for a cargo to Copenhagen.'

'Really?' responded Kirton, pretending interest.

'Blue funnel ships top dollar,' added Cha, and Kirton sensed his annoyance that the new house of Mansfield had scooped up the agency for these new-fangled ships with their reputedly superior engines to those of the Scottish River Line or any other British shipping company, let alone the Scandinavians.

'Ver' economical ships dose blue funnellers,' put in Mortensen with a shake of his head.

The conversation rambled for another half an hour before the Dane rose and took his leave. 'Hoping for *samsu*,' opined McClure under his breath in what was supposed to be a cosy aside to Kirton and a knock at the Scandinavian. Kirton gave McClure a thin smile, not enough to suggest complicity in the man's casual disdain, merely to acknowledge that he had heard his former commander. Then, mercifully, Cha thanked McClure for coming to see him, explaining that he had important business to discuss with Kirton; the implication that this was private produced a somewhat put-out expression on McClure's face, but he rose, shook hands, and departed cordially enough, wishing both Cha and Kirton a good morning.

'You no come to see me yesterday, Captain,' Cha began. 'Captain McClure said he walked here with you . . .'

'Yes, that's correct, Mr Cha, but I had much on my mind that could not be discussed in front of Captain McClure.'

'No ploblem,' Cha waved the matter aside. 'Now you tell me what make tlouble for you.'

'First I have sad news,' Kirton began, telling the old Chinaman about the *casab*, Ibrahim. Cha approved all that Kirton had done, after which Kirton coughed and launched into the speech he had tried to rehearse on his long walk the previous evening.

'You will remember, sir,' he said respectfully, 'our early conversation about my prospects as master of the *Tethys* . . .' Cha inclined his head. 'Well, I hope that I have given satisfaction in that regard and I am wondering if you would consider my buying into the ownership of the vessel.

You have been most generous in your employment of my services, but I am in need of some reassurance that if and when my leg prevents me from going to sea I am not cast upon the beach. If I owned some shares in the *Tethys* . . .'

'How long, Captain, do you think the *Tethys* can continue trading as she does now? Four, five years? Soon steamship come into coastal trade; al'eady I hear the Honourable House of Mansfield talking about a new steamship company all same Swire in China to feed blue funnel ships here. *Tethys* too small to compete then—you waste your money. Better you help House of Gleen Dragon, maybe old Cha set up steamship company, eh? Anyway, you buy half of the ship, then you pay half of the lunning expenses. That not good business. More better I pay all lunning costs.'

Kirton considered Cha's arguments and his proposition; it all made good sense, of course.

'And you become first captain of the company, you have steamship expelience,' Cha continued.

'That is a most interesting proposition, Mr Cha,' Kirton replied, 'but I should still like to buy into the *Tethys* for the remainder of her time in your service. I have become very fond of the ship . . .'

Cha shook his head and wagged his right fore-finger at Kirton. 'That is not sensible, Captain; sometimes I do not understand you Englishmen. You walk into country, take over as Number One, then become like stupid coolie boy over a rich girl who give you two cents more than her fare along with a big smile.'

Kirton could not but laugh at the other's analogy. 'Well, sir,' he said, 'the *Tethys* has become my wife, some would say.'

'Yes, too many say "why Captain Kirton no take nice Chinese girl? He very lich."'

'Do they indeed?' responded Kirton wryly. 'Well it is Captain Kirton's own business. Come, sir, what do you say to a half, thirty two shares? What have you got to lose?'

'People will say I cannot afford the ship, that I sell-out to Englishman, that I lose control of my company . . .'

'That you lose face?' Kirton asked abruptly, at which Cha inclined his head slightly, without articulating an acknowledgement of the fact.

'But no-one need know and besides, do you not intend leaving your business to your son-in-law?'

The presumption roused Cha. 'Not all, Captain Kirton, he will inhelit part, part will go to my chief *crani*, Lee. He is a distant cousin and a good man. Mister Lodham still ver' young to take my place when I join ancestors.'

Feeling thwarted in what he thought would have appealed to the old Chinaman, Kirton rose to leave. Then he remembered his promise to Ibrahim of the night before. It seemed a foolish thing to keep when commercial imperatives drove matters of business, but he felt he could not abandon the old ship so quickly. Subsiding into his low chair again he made another proposition.

'Sir, may I ask that if and when you decide to dispose of the *Tethys* and go into steam, you will give me the first option on her purchase. I will offer you a good price.'

Cha looked at the younger man and said, 'More better you catch a good wife, Captain, but if you still want ship when time comes, yes, you can make me an offer. And if I die I leave half-share in *Tethys* to you, not the company, with option to buy out other half-share on condition you retain company as agents.'

Kirton smiled. 'I wish you long life, sir, but I cannot argue with your kindness; thank you.' Kirton paused and then said, 'Mr Cha, there is just one other thing, the matter of my qualifications . . .'

CHAPTER SEVEN

The Burning *Kampong*

ON THEIR RETURN TO SINGAPORE AFTER THE VOYAGE FOLLOWING THIS agreement between Cha and Kirton, the latter informed his two mates that he would be interrupting the regularity of their domestic bliss to the extent of requiring a week's leave, free of the ship. He did not explain why, merely told them to make arrangements between themselves and handed the ship over to Rodham. After this he took a small portmanteau ashore and booked himself into a back-street hotel run by a Chinese family. For the next few days Kirton sat for his British Master's Certificate of Competency at the offices of the Board of Trade. He had been nervous at the beginning of the process of proving his sea-time, the clerks giving him a rough time, regarding the ornate declaration of his otherwise entirely satisfactory sea-service provided by Mr Cha, but his orals ended with a long conversation with the examiner in which the prospects of the future trade of Singapore and the geography of the eastern part of the Malay archipelago—of which the examiner was ignorant—entirely eclipsed concerns with the Rules for the Prevention of Collisions at Sea.

As Kirton rose with the all important chit signed by the examiner, the two men shook hands like old friends.

'You are perhaps the most interesting candidate I have examined for a long time, Mr Kirton,' the examiner said. 'I am newly out here and this morning has been a revelation.'

'That's most kind of you,' Kirton said, rising to go.

By a terrific effort Kirton had walked to and from the examination rooms without his stick and by bandaging a short bamboo splint to his leg had almost eliminated his limp, or so he thought. But as he walked towards the door, the examiner asked, 'D'you have a limp?'

'A very bad sprain, sir,' he lied with a smooth eloquence of which he was afterwards partly ashamed. Thank heavens the examiner was a new man, not yet party to the tittle-tattle about a certain Captain Kirton of the brigantine *Tethys*. It was therefore with some relief that two days after his orals he surrendered his chit and received the properly drawn-up document declaring his new status. That evening he checked out of the hotel, ordered a rickshaw and hired a boat from Collyer Quay, returning to his cabin aboard the *Tethys*.

As he sat on the edge of his bunk massaging his leg, badly bruised and abraded by the expedient of the bamboo splint, he nursed a secret smile, envisioning McClure's astonishment if he had only known that he was, at last, his former commander's equal.

The *Tethys* lay at anchor on the western shore of Marudu Bay. The sun had yet to show itself and was hidden behind banks of cloud to the east. Mist hung over the low valleys seaming the undulating rain forest that faded and rose in the distance through innumerable foothills drained by hidden watercourses until breaking out into the magnificent peak of Gunung Kinabalu, the greatest mountain in south-east Asia.

Leaning on the teak box that contained the *Tethys*'s steering gear, still in his night attire of cotton *sarong*, Kirton enjoyed his first cigar of the day, watching the mists slowly burn off as the sun rose and threw its sudden warmth across the bay, turning it from a dull slate grey to a sparkling blue. He had long finished his smoke by the time his tiger brought him his morning coffee, and still he did not go below, such was the quiet beauty of the morning. Kirton had come to love these first two hours of daylight with the beguiling scent of the land brought offshore by the *terral*; later the sun would often crush him with its heat and only the wind of a sea-passage could restore the perfection of his day, or the ship herself would demand his full attention, but those hours of quiet limbo were a pure joy.

They had anchored late the previous evening, after dark, with only the looming summit of the great mountain against the afterglow of sunset to use as a mark, creeping in towards the land under a fading breeze, the leadsman in the chains calling out the soundings. As a consequence they found themselves about a mile further offshore than was customary when seeking a cargo off the *kampong* they called No. 5. There were six villages along the shore of Telok Marudu with which they habitually traded and Kirton had allocated them numbers as he was unsure of the names, two of which sounded very similar. No. 5 was usually productive and to signal a desire for trade, the headman would order a Suluese flag, or at least his own interpretation of the sultan's colours, hoisted on a conspicuous *nipah* palm near the beach.

As the mist lifted and Kirton began to feel the heat of the sun he went forward to the companionway doors. Just inside it the ship's long glass nestled in a rack, but before he reached the entry Rodham emerged with the large telescope in his hand.

Kirton backed off and let Rodham scan the shore. He had not been able to make out anything hoisted in the tree with the naked eye, and the windless morning did not help. But he could see the smoke of cooking fires already rising above the distant huts.

'That's odd,' said Rodham, lowering the glass and turning to Kirton with a puzzled expression on his face.

'What's the matter?' Kirton asked.

'I know we're further offshore than usual, but you'd expect the trading flag to have been run up by now.'

'There's not much wind yet,' said Kirton.

'No, but I'm sure that I'd be able to see it sir, even hanging slack.'

'Well we'll move further in as soon as the wind stirs.' Kirton looked about him. 'About an hour should do it, after a shave and some breakfast.' And with that he betook himself below, calling his tiger for hot water. In his cabin Kirton hummed contentedly to himself as he shaved and then washed himself, pulling on the clean shirt and white duck trousers laid out for him by Ah Chuan. Slipping his soft leather shoes on he went into the saloon and had just tucked-in his napkin when he heard Rodham's voice call:

'Sir!' It had more than a hint of anxiety in it and, with a sigh, Kirton waved aside the kedgeree the saloon steward set down before him and went on deck.

'What is it, Mr Rodham?' Kirton asked with just a hint of irritation at being thwarted of his breakfast.

'There's still no flag, but the smoke looks rather more than just cooking fires and I can see some big *perahus* drawn up on the beach. Something's not right.'

'Let me have a look-see.' Kirton took the proffered glass, steadied it against a backstay, and refocused it. The strip of beach and the estuary of the river upon which '*Kampong* No. 5' depended swam into focus. Drawn up on the beach were the usual small out-rigger boats that the inhabitants used for fishing, but alongside them three larger craft lay. Kirton could see one or two figures hanging round them; they seemed to be looking in their direction. Then something else caught Kirton's eye and he shifted the telescope to bring it fully into his field of vision: an orange flicker of fire.

'By God, you're right, Kit! The bloody *kampong*'s on fire; those *perahus*, I'll lay money on them being Bugis raiders.'

Kirton's brain whirled then settled on a plan. 'Right,' he said decisively, 'Get the derrick up and hoist out the boat! I'll call out the *jagas* and take an armed party ashore . . .'

'Surely you should stay on board, sir . . .' Rodham began, but Kirton cut him short.

'If anything happens to me, Kit, it doesn't matter. But you and Vee-Jay are married men. Do you heave short and the minute the wind serves stand inshore. You'll have to man the guns yourself if I take all the Sikhs, but I shouldn't think that will trouble you unduly will it.'

'No, or course not.' Rodham could not suppress a boyish grin at the prospect.

'A couple of rounds will doubtless drive them off if I haven't done the business myself. But don't over-do it, for God's sake.'

A few minutes later Kirton was cursing his gammy leg as he clambered over the ship's rail and lowered himself down into the waiting boat. Four Chinese sailors were at the oars, the armed *jagas*, one forward and the remainder after, were already fingering their ammunition belts. Tall to a man, with their green turbans and simple white tunics and trousers, their short swords—worn by every Sikh male—in their belts, their brown feet in sandals, they were imposing enough, grinning to each other relishing an encounter in which they could use their arms. All had been soldiers and bred to the profession of arms and they listened attentively as Kirton, siting at the tiller, called them to order.

'Bugis pirates are setting fire to *kampong*, maybe burn everything they cannot take away. We must drive them off and help people. Ship come close in as soon as wind blows and use big guns. Best we do not kill them but make them run away . . .'

'You not want to shoot holes in their boats, *Tuan?*' the senior Sikh, Pritam Singh, asked.

Kirton shook his head. He did not want more trouble than was absolutely necessary. 'No, we must make them get out of the village . . .' Kirton's voice trailed off for as they approached the beach a number of figures could be seen running down to the large *perahus* drawn up on the strand. Some carried loot, others had women over their shoulders, but it was what lay behind them that captured Kirton's attention; they had a clearer view of the village longhouse now and it was ablaze from end-to-end, a mass of crackling orange flame which roared upwards into the clear morning air which it disfigured with a black pall of smoke.

'My God!' he breathed, appalled at the wanton destruction. He was not in the habit of landing at these outlying trading posts, leaving all that to Rodham and his *shroff,* but he had formed the opinion that the various tribes that inhabited the coast of Borneo were, in general, a peace-loving people and the Rungus, who lived in this remote corner of the great island, had always seemed a most attractive race when they had come out in their dug-out canoes, some to traffic for small items of goods in which the *Tethys*'s Chinese crew speculated, or simply to stare up at the brigantine out of a delightfully naïve curiosity.

These thoughts were quickly driven from his mind as a bullet whizzed over the boat and the *jagas* stirred with impatience.

'Return fire, *Tuan?*' the one in the bow asked.

'Yes,' Kirton said shortly, and as the boat drove in towards the sand some one hundred yards to the south of the Bugis' *perahus*, an exchange of fire began. Kirton's heart was in his mouth and his mouth was dry. He had never been under fire before, though he had witnessed the enforcement of public order by rifle-fire in several ports during his time at sea, mostly in China, but once in San Francisco and a couple of times in Valparaiso. He lugged out his own weapon, a heavy old Colt revolver that Cha had long ago presented him with telling him it had been found on the *Tethys* when he had acquired the old brigantine.

He had only fired it a couple of times at sharks, just for the fun of it, and once at a gibbon that had got aboard and defaced the *Tethys*'s deck with his ordure. Now he looked down the long barrel and drew a bead on a man who levelled a gun at them from behind the protection of the nearest *perahu*.

Kirton saw the puff of smoke from the gun's muzzle and something whizzed past his head and, almost in reaction, the Colt barked in his hand. It kicked like a mule and the shot missed. Looking at his enemy he saw the man reloading with what appeared to be a ram-rod and in the next second he squeezed the trigger of the big revolver a second time. He saw the man's head turn, caught a glimpse of the brown face just before it disappeared.

A moment later the boat grounded on the sand and Kirton was scrambling out in the wake of the Sikhs. Pritam Singh directed three of them to head for the village and beckoned the remainder to follow him as he loped towards the *perahus*, firing from the hip as he went. The P53 Enfields barked as one or two of the *jagas* dropped onto one knee and took a careful aim. Kirton, hampered by his leg, stumbled after them and when he reached the first *perahu* he found two of the Bugis in its shelter crouching in fear, staring down the barrel of one of the Sikh's rifles. Beyond them lay the man Kirton had shot; the bullet had blown his jaw away and he lay writhing in agony. Pritam Singh, came up to him with a wry smile on his handsomely bearded face.

'Not shoot to kill, *Tuan*,' he remarked with irony. Taking out his short sword he despatched the wretched Bugis, before bending over the corpse and picking up the man's gun. Pritam Singh looked at it with contempt.

'Muzzle-loading musket,' he said shortly, tossing it aside, before removing the dead man's *kris* and longer *parang* from his belt and shoving them in his own.

They found another Bugis pirate hiding in the shadow of the last *perahu* guarding four or five terrified women and a handful of children. Having secured their prisoners, Kirton and his party turned their attention to the *kampong* from which came shouts and shots. Four men dashed out of cover, as if making for the *perahus* but seeing the line of Sikhs coming up from the strand, they doubled back and disappeared in the smoke and the rain forest that came up to the end of the longhouse.

Following the *jagas*, Kirton saw the pathetic sight of the purple and white flag laying at the foot of a large palm tree, ready for hoisting, and a pile of baskets woven from *atap* leaves and containing some of the trade goods, recognising the sea-snails of which the Chinese were particularly fond, along with bundles of rattan and some bales of copra surrounded by a cloud of black copra bugs. But such observations were *en passant*; his main attention was what lay ahead where the Rungus' longhouse, now almost entirely burnt, was collapsing in upon itself in showers of sparks, leaving stark vertical timbers, some black and smouldering, some still burning like torches. Dead bodies lay everywhere, a score or so—old men, women, and children chiefly—slaughtered by the Bugis raiders whose attempt to carry off heaven knows how many month's produce and domestic animals had been interrupted by the arrival of Kirton and his Sikhs. Pigs ran about squealing, many severely burned and in terrible pain, but by the time Kirton had limped up to the carnage and wreckage of the longhouse the 'enemy' had either fled into the rain forest, or lay dead among their own victims. Three were prisoners of the separate party of Sikhs who had made directly for the village; they squatted on the ground, their eyes large with fear as they regarded the gigantic men in their green turbans and the *orang puteh* who seemed to saunter up to see the work his minions had accomplished. Possessed of a deep hatred of the Dutch colonial masters of Sulawesi from whence they hailed and whose ruthless habits they knew well, they presumed they were about to be killed and were astonished when the white man ordered the surviving raiders trussed and bound, and thrown into one of their own boats.

Arming the waiting women with the captive's own *parangs*, Kirton left them to stand guard over their attackers, enjoining them—as far as he could stretch his rudimentary Malay and make these women understand him—not to kill them, however much they wished to. Kirton and his men then turned their attention to a search of the *kampong* without finding anyone else. Kirton ordered his party to withdraw to the beach; just as the wind began to rustle in the fronds of the *nipah* palms, glancing seawards Kirton saw the fore-topsail of the *Tethys* being mast-headed and watched for a moment as his ship hauled round and stood inshore. Twenty-minutes later, as she swung to re-anchor, Rodham backed the fore-topsail and Kirton saw the splash of the anchor. Then the port breech-loader barked in a terrific crack that echoed away into the distance. The gun was unshotted and Kirton called for the trading flag to be quickly hoisted to deter Rodham from any further heroics.

Kirton paused for a moment, fascinated by the sight of his vessel, realising how rarely one had the opportunity to see one's own ship as others did. But he found himself trembling from the exertions of the last half an hour and the reaction shook him. Then Pritam Singh approached and saluted, requesting orders.

Drawn back to the present, Kirton was non-plussed. He found he had eight prisoners who, whatever their felonies, had committed a capital offence under the colonial law of Singapore, and must be brought to some kind of justice. As he stood scratching his head some figures emerged from the rain forest and Singh's men immediately drew their bolts back with a series of threatening clicks. But these were the handful of survivors from the longhouse who had been woken from their dreams by the hollering of the attackers as they put flame to their dwelling, and had fled in sheer terror. They were mostly young men who had run off into the interior, and they came now to see what damage had been done, reassured by the crack of the *Tethys's* ordnance which they knew was beyond the power of the *orang laut*—the men of the sea—to command.

Kirton turned his attention back to his prisoners whom he had left in the charge of the women; it was then that he noticed the most prominent of these. She seemed taller than her fellows, wrapped in the simple *sarong* in which she had been sleeping. She held the long *parang* she had been given and her eyes were full of fire as she stood guard over the Bugis raiders as they cowered in the bottom of the *perahu* in which they had been tumbled after being bound with strips of mangrove by two of the Sikhs.

Kirton directed one of the *jagas* to take over the duty of watching the prisoners, but the young woman would not budge and in her protests drew attention to herself. Kirton noticed her fine features, the high cheekbones, the dark, almond eyes which flickered only once in his direction and—he was sure—took in his maimed leg at a glance. Feeling awkward and clumsy he turned away, calling Pritam Singh to get the prisoners taken off to the *Tethys* under guard in the ship's boat.

As these arrangements were being made, more villagers emerged from the forest, including the headman, and the forenoon was spent in sorting matters out. The language barrier proved almost insuperable under such unusual circumstances until Kirton got a message off to the ship and had Rodham and the *shroff* Ching landed. The Chinese *chin-chew* was able to act as interpreter and it was agreed that Kirton would land as many domestic articles as would assist the villagers to rebuild the longhouse, thereby depleting the *Tethys* of every axe and saw, nail and hammer in his 'tween deck. He would give them credit beyond the value of what he could carry off in the way of prepared cargo they had waiting for him. This beneficial act would either curtail his voyage, or require him to purchase the remainder of his lading at other ports with *sycee* silver from his imprest.

He had already decided to alter his plans after calling at the other *kampongs* in Telok Marudu to check on their well-being as much as take any opportunity to trade. After this he would sail for Jolo in order to hand his prisoners over to the sultan's justice. He had no wish to become involved with the authorities in Singapore, and the fact that the *Tethys* was a Suluese vessel and wore the sultan's colours made this the most logical course of action, for the raid was upon the sultan's territory.

It was late afternoon before Kirton returned to the *Tethys* with Rodham and Ching. They left with three large pigs, recently dead from their wounds, by way of thanks from the village headman, an old Rungus who acted with great dignity in the aftermath of the catastrophe that had overtaken his little fiefdom.

The Bugis raid was not, Kirton learned, an isolated incident, but it bit hard into the economic life of the otherwise seemingly happy existence of these 'natives,' as Kirton noted in his journal much later that evening. As he was pulled out from the shore in the ship's boat and the stench of burnt pig, death, and smouldering wood was cleared from his lungs by the land breeze that would carry the *Tethys* some miles offshore before she had to anchor again, Kirton reflected on the events of the day. Had he acted properly? Would there be repercussions? If so, how would he handle them? Should they have destroyed the Bugis *perahus* and not left them to the villagers? Was he guilty of murder in killing the man who had turned out to be the Bugis' leader?

Suddenly he felt very, very lonely.

'What do we do with these bastards?' Jones asked as soon as Kirton regained the brigantine. The second mate was clearly nervous at having such a dangerous gang on board, notwithstanding the fact that Tan had them in chains, shackled to ring-bolts on the main deck.

'Feed 'em, I suppose,' Kirton replied wearily. 'They can sleep where they are ...'

'And what about her?' the other man persisted.

'Who?'

'That woman ...' Vee-Jay pointed. In the shadow of the forward deck-house the tall young woman, still holding the *parang*, squatted, her eyes fixed on the prisoners. 'She frightens me,' he added, only half in jest. 'By the gleam in her eyes she may run *amok* with that bloody *parang*. She hasn't taken them off the prisoners since she came aboard with them, and she refuses to go ashore. In a moment it will be too late,' he added as the ship's boat was hoisted in and the sailors stumped round the capstan singing the monotonous chant they used instead of a shanty.

'Feed her then,' Kirton said, staring at the woman. Then he turned aside, much in need of a wash, some food, and a cigar.

Chapter Eight

The Pearl

Fluky winds delayed their passage to Jolo, and the ship was kept in a constant state of anxiety over the presence of, not so much the shackled prisoners, as the woman who watched over them. She refused to move, except to use the crew latrines forward and to eat, and even then her gaze continued fixed upon the shackled Bugis.

It began to dawn on Kirton that perhaps she would be the biggest problem he had confronting him in the next couple of days. However, much to Kirton's relief, when the *Tethys* anchored off Jolo and he paid his respects to the sultan's *shawbunder*, the head customs collector greatly eased his mind. Datu Mohammad bin Yusuf, a sleek rotund individual, informed him after a certain amount of silver *cumshaw* had passed from Kirton to the Suluese official, that His Highness the Sultan would be delighted to dispense justice to men who had the temerity to raid his territory. Moreover, at the same time, His Highness would, the *shawbunder* felt certain, make a formal complaint to the Dutch vice-consul for forwarding to Batavia.

The *shawbunder* also interviewed the young woman, discovering that she had stood guard over the Bugis so vigilantly because one of them had killed her parents and younger brother before attempting her own rape and abduction. Once it was explained to her that all the pirates would be executed she seemed to relax and the *shawbunder* requested that Kirton take her back to her *kampong* on his homeward run to Singapore, a request to which Kirton agreed with a readiness that surprised himself. Nevertheless he asked:

'Does she have a name?'

Datu Mohammad waved the question aside. 'She is a no-body,' he remarked dismissively before going over the side of the brigantine.

While all this was going on, Rodham and Ching were compensating for the losses of the voyage by taking on extra lading for Singapore from Jolo. It would, Rodham, informed Kirton, take a few days to garner what they had been promised by Ban Guan on very good terms. This additional good news only left a much relieved Kirton with one problem: what to do with the girl?

It offended his instincts to leave her to sleep on deck any longer and he was reluctant to upset the sensibilities of any of his officers, petty or otherwise, by turfing them out of their own cabins, however temporarily. Such matters as status being extremely important to the delicate balance of hierarchy aboard the *Tethys*, he thought it best to make the sacrifice himself, his own position being unassailable. He was not only '*Tuan*' to his men but—and especially to the Chinese—he was '*Ch'uan Ju*,' the lord of the ship.

Ah Chuan, his tiger, disapproved, of course, but Kirton's temporary removal to the chart-room which was provided with a narrow settee for the master to lie down fully-clothed in time of danger when his presence on deck might be instantly required, provided him with a rudimentary bed-place. Having lived for four years in a sailing vessel's half-deck, a few days in the chart-room troubled Kirton not at all.

Feeding the young woman was a somewhat different matter. Now that old Ibrahim had gone there were no other Malays on the ship and, in any case, the Rungus were a primitive people and the poor lass would be seen as an inferior by his Chinese sailors. Jones and Ching the *shroff* suggested she was simply fed on deck, fearing, Kirton suspected, that if he followed his instinct and sat her at the saloon table, they would take offence while the girl herself would be intimidated and completely overwhelmed by the strangeness of it all. In the end he had her eat in the chart-room, where she cowered on one end of the settee until left alone to address her meal.

Kirton had no way of knowing the effect of all this on his guest, though he was not insensible to the young woman's simple beauty and graceful movements. In her grief she did not smile, said hardly a word, and simply did as she was bid by Ching acting as interpreter. She refused to relinquish possession of the *parang*, a fact that seemed to worry everyone except Kirton who, when asked by Rodham why he showed no concern, could find no logical reason for his lack of anxiety. They were all terrified that in her distress she would run *amok*, a contention that Kirton refuted with some vigour. Seeing the lack of reassurance in Rodham's eyes, he added with a false callousness, 'She keeps that thing wrapped up in a cloth, but should she decide to do so, we will have to shoot her, Kit,' it being common practice in Singapore to gun down an *amok*, as Ibrahim had pointed out, such a disturbed individual having passed beyond the realms of human reason. 'Anyway,' he had added, 'I have never heard of a female *amok*, have you?'

'No sir,' responded a slightly crestfallen Rodham.

However, in the following days, Kirton and his Colt were never far from each other and he took to using his stick on deck; its concealed blade was longer than his guest's *parang*. While he had to admit to himself he had not even considered that the young woman might run *amok*, somewhat disingenuously assuming she would be grateful for the intervention of Kirton and his ship's company, he found her scrutiny of himself deeply unsettling, for he was ever conscious of his crippled leg and increasingly thought of himself—in her eyes—a woeful, even a contemptible figure.

True he had made some attempts to converse with her, using the honorific form '*Puan*' to convey respect, but he failed to elicit any meaningful response, let alone her name.

But for the young Rungus woman, contemplation of the strange *orang puteh* was such a source of fascination that her grief grew manageable, especially so after she had learned that the pirates delivered into the hands of the sultan's law officers had been beheaded.

The *Tethys* lay for a week off Jolo and took aboard sufficient lading to enable her to return to Singapore with credit. Further credit of a rather different kind was accrued when, on clearing outwards for the British colony, the *shawbunder* presented Kirton with a large and very lovely pearl.

Ching translated, informing Kirton that: 'It is a mark of the esteem of His Highness Sultan Jamal ul-Azam and is a gift from him to you, Captain Kirton. His Highness considers your conduct in his service merits such a gift and calls down the blessings of God upon your head, infidel though you may be.'

Kirton bowed to a smiling Datu Mohammad bin Yusuf as the beautiful thing was handed to him on a square of dark silk. 'Please convey my sincere thanks to His Highness,' Kirton replied, enquiring of Ching whether protocol required him to do anything further.

'No, *Tuan*; the sultan is discharging his debt to you for your action at *kampong* No. 5.'

Kirton nodded, then smiled at the *shawbunder*, adding, 'Please also inform His Highness that he may rely upon Captain Kirton to uphold order wherever he trades in his ship among His Highness's dominions.'

Afterwards he had no idea why he had appended this pompous declaration, only that the receipt of such a stunning personal gift seemed to warrant something more than a bland expression of gratitude. Always attuned to the sensibilities of those with whom he interacted, Kirton was assiduous in cultivating others, particularly when his livelihood and that of the *Tethys* depended largely upon their goodwill. In this way the little brigantine carried his reputation as obviously as if his name was writ large upon her green top-sides. If few people actually set eyes upon Captain Kirton the man, his ship was as conspicuous as a heavy rain cloud obscuring the sun before a deluge of *hujan*.

It was late on a Tuesday afternoon by the time the hatch was covered and secured, the boat hoisted in on its chocks, and the hands sent to the capstan. Kirton had been taking 'a lie-off the land' on the chart-room settee when Jones woke him from his snooze with a rustling of the charts and the information that 'Mr Rodham had the fore-topsail and topgallant mast-headed and loose in their gear, with the men stamping round the capstan.'

Running his hand over his face, Kirton swung his feet to the deck and shoved them into his leather pumps.

'Where's our passenger?'

'On the poop, sir,' Jones informed him with a certain amount of distaste. 'I have the courses laid off for Telok Marudu,' the second mate added as if only too willing to speed the woman on her way and off the ship.

'Very well,' said Kirton formally, making for the companionway.

'Oh, and sir . . .'

Kirton turned: 'Yes? What is it?'

'There's a Spanish man-o'-war lying off the outer islands . . . bit unusual . . .'

'Indeed,' grunted Kirton, grabbing the long glass as he passed up the companionway.

Twenty minutes later, having dipped her purple and white ensign and fired one of the guns to salute the sultan's standard ashore, the *Tethys* gathered headway and leaned to a spanking breeze and stood out of Jolo Road under all plain sail. The sun was already low, setting in what Kirton judged would be a blaze of glory, and he wanted to get clear of the land before the sea-breeze died and he was obliged to wait for the *terral*.

Once well under way, the sheets secured and the hands coiling down the halliards, Kirton cast about the seaward horizon which was dotted with islands; it took him no time at all, however, to locate the foreign man-of-war, an auxiliary steam corvette, he judged, her white hull coming into full view as the *Tethys* cleared the shore. She lay stopped, right ahead of them, hove-to under a backed main topsail and with a cloud of smoke rising from her buff funnel.

Kirton walked aft and stood beside the *jurmudi* on the wheel.

'Ease her a point,' he said and the quartermaster put the helm over a spoke or two. 'Braces, Mr Rodham,' he called out to the chief mate as he came aft from securing the catted anchors. 'We've a stranger to dodge round,' Kirton added by way of explanation, pointing with the long glass as the weather luffs of the square sails shivered to the small alteration of course.

'Aye sir.' That done Rodham came aft and stood beside Kirton where they were joined by Jones.

'Spaniard,' said Rodham shortly, identifying the huge red and gold colours that flew at her mizen peak. 'That's bloody unusual.'

'That's what I said, Kit,' Jones remarked. 'What's she doing here?'

'Territorially ambitious would be my guess,' said Kirton, raising the glass and studying the strange sight. 'Going to grab the Sulus before the Dutch, perhaps?'

'That would have implications for us,' said Jones.

'Yes, by God it would!' exclaimed Rodham. 'It'd shut down the whole trade if either power got hold of Sulu by heaven!'

They were fast approaching the Spaniard, heading to pass under her stern, and they were already close enough to see figures on her bridge and on her deck.

''Take a look-see at her, Kit,' said Kirton, handing over the telescope and walking aft to stand by the helm as they closed with the man-of-war.

'Sir! I think . . . !' Rodham shouted, but he was cut short as a column of water rose up on their lee bow and a puff of smoke drifted lazily away from the Spanish corvette. A second or two later the concussion of the discharged gun rumbled over the water towards them.

'They want us to heave-to,' Jones said anxiously.

'Damned if I am going to do that!' snapped Kirton suddenly resolute. 'Lay our position on the chart Mr Jones and be quick about it, stand by to tack, Mr Rodham, let's ensure we are in Suluese waters . . .'

Rodham called out the order to tack to the hands, most of whom, having finished their coiling down were lingering out of curiosity at the presence of the strange vessel. Seeing the men at their stations, Kirton walked aft, stood beside the wheel and ordered the helm put over. The brigantine came upright, passed through the wind with a clatter of blocks, a whirring of sheaves, and a thunder of sail before leaning over to the new tack which would take her inshore again.

Kirton looked aloft, the Suluese ensign snapped out like a board; should he dip it as a mark of respect to a man-of-war? Strictly speaking flag etiquette required him to do so, but a sudden truculence welled up inside him as Jones reported them still well inside Suluese territorial waters.

'Thank you. Vik?' Kirton asked with a disarming lack of formality, 'You're absolutely certain?'

'Absolutely, sir. There are islands all round us . . .'

A second shot plunged into the sea off their starboard side and Kirton snapped: 'Bugger this! Cast off the main flag halliards, Vik, I won't be a second . . .'

Dashing below to his cabin he flung the door open. The young Rungus woman was naked to the waist and washing herself. With a word of apology Kirton flung open a drawer and drew out a bundle of red bunting and fled. On deck he handed the toggled end of the flag's fly to Jones and bent on the eye to the end of the halliard the second mate passed to him. A moment later the British red ensign was run up to the main truck.

As Kirton handed over his bight of the flag halliard to Jones for belaying Pritam Singh was beside him saluting. 'Do you require me to fire one of our guns, *Tuan*?' he asked eagerly, a wide anticipatory grin below his splendid whiskers.

'For God's sake no!' Kirton snapped, adding 'at least, not now,' as he watched the reaction of the Spanish man-of-war. Then seeing the downcast expression on the Sikh's handsome features, he explained, 'We must not make trouble.'

'Yes *Tuan*,' Pritam Singh responded disconsolately.

A third shot plunged into their wake but they were now rapidly drawing away from the corvette, disappearing into the scarlet splendour of the sunset. Kirton stood at the stern watching whether the Spaniard would give chase, but whatever her orders, they lay off Jolo and did not include chasing impudent brigantines. He lit a cigar and ordered the red ensign lowered. Only when he was carefully rolling-up the flag, just as he had been taught long ago on the *Canopus*, and was on his way to stow it below did he think of the young woman in his cabin.

CHAPTER NINE

The Rungus Woman

THEY MADE SEVERAL STOPS ON PASSAGE BACK TO TELAK MARUDU AND *kampong* No. 5, Rodham and Ching being eager to capitalise on their otherwise erratic voyage; thus it was that the *Tethys* bore a quantity of deck cargo as she finally crept into the anchorage off the Rungus village one afternoon a fortnight later.

Kirton had no way of knowing what effect this delay had on the young woman, but when she realised that they lay off her home and Ching told her to prepare to leave the vessel she made it very clear that she would not comply. Her eyes filled with the fury she had formerly reserved for the Bugis pirate who had murdered her family, and she writhed away from the one attempt Tan made to force her to the ship's rail beneath which the ship's boat bobbed expectantly. Eventually Kirton, who was in the chart-room signing the ship's log-book, was made aware of the commotion in the waist.

Hoisting himself up on the coach-roof he stared down at the little drama taking place below him. 'What the devil is the matter?' he called and Ching turned and explained.

'Missee no wantchee leave ship, *Tuan*. She say ship now her home ...'

'*What*?' exploded Kirton. 'Tell her that is impossible.' He turned to return aft when a torrent of Rungus dialect erupted from the waist. He turned round to see the young woman in a fury of expostulation, jabbering nineteen-to-the-dozen, the circle of seamen growing by the minute at the entertainment. Most of the Chinese seamen could scarcely conceal their amusement and Kirton sensed they were probably making bets on whether their English master would throw in the towel and adopt the woman as his concubine as any sensible fellow would, faced with such a beauty. Indeed, he heard the expression '*nyai*' used just as the woman's tirade came to an exhausted end.

Kirton had to admit to himself that the idea had crossed his mind, but the looks of contempt she had thrown at his leg had built a wall of indifference between them. Now, quite suddenly, as she stared about her awaiting the response to her rant, he realised that she was not only beautiful, but the visceral attraction of her was more than strong, it was irresistible. And regarding the assembled men, he could see a hunger in their eyes too, a hunger he knew only too well and it boded ill.

'Bring her aft,' he ordered curtly, stumping away to stand at the end of the steering-box where he lit a cigar. *What in God's name was he to do with the wench?* he asked himself as his heart thumped in his chest with an unexpected nervousness as he stared over the ship's side. A small *perahu* was putting out from the beach. Maybe whoever was in her could resolve the situation, but such thoughts of a *deus ex machina* were blown away by a cough and the voice of Pritam Singh: '*Tuan?*'

Kirton turned to see the woman standing between Pritam Singh and another *jaga*. All three were ramrod straight and the chief *jaga* had his hand to his turban in salute. The sight of the proud Rungus woman hit him like a kick in the solar plexus. Behind the little group stood a rather weary-looking Ching.

Kirton met the woman's eyes and for a moment they stared at each other, an experience Kirton found so disarming that he was for a moment tongue-tied before he coughed and, turning to Ching, said, 'Ask why she refuses to leave the ship, if you please Ching.'

'She alleady tell us, *Tuan*. All her family dead and if we make her stay shore-side *kampong* No. 5 she must mally a man she not like and she say she will run *amok* and kill him so that she die herself . . .'

Such was the tension he was under that Kirton almost burst out laughing at this little native drama, except that in some way the woman hooked his gaze and he was compelled to regard her: She was serious; *deadly* serious in fact. Quite suddenly, and with that impulsiveness that lay at the heart of his character, Kirton did not want to put her ashore.

He turned to see how close the little *perahu* had drawn and, in doing so, drew the attention of the woman to the approaching craft. Immediately she began talking again, this time dropping to her knees and plucking at Kirton's trousers so that he turned and, embarrassed, said, 'Get up! Make her get up!'

Before Ching could translate the two Sikhs had hauled her to her feet and held her wriggling body between them.

'She say man who she hate is in *sampan, Tuan*. You must choose. Maybe you go ashore and buy her, take her to Singapore and sell her to brothel . . . Live cargo,' the Chinese *shroff* added with a sly smile.

Kirton revolted at the notion, though Ching was only being the ever pragmatic *chin-chew* for which he was paid. Whether or not the woman guessed something of what was being discussed, she threw fearful glances at the *perahu* and suddenly broke free from the *jagas*, ran to the rail and shouted what appeared to be a stream of invective at the young Rungus who stopped paddling and began shouting back.

'For God's sake,' Kirton mumbled, his patience wearing thin. This was all an appalling farce. 'Stop it!' he roared, regaining the woman's attention. 'Listen to me,' he commanded and without looking at Ching but holding the gaze of the woman he said, 'If I pay headman money and take you to Singapore, is that what you want?'

The minute he heard Ching say 'Singapore,' the woman shook her head violently and spoke again. This time her sentences were short and measured. Ching translated.

'She want to stay ship; she say you not buy her, her father dead, no-one own her, she free, she make herself useful, help cook, clean, do woman's work. No woman on board . . .'

'That will cause no end of trouble,' said Jones who, like Rodham had joined the huddle on the after end of the poop. 'Loss of face for the Chinks . . .'

'Yes. Yes, I know,' responded Kirton testily.

'Take her to Singapore, sir. I'll find her a job in domestic service . . .' said Rodham, eager to end this ridiculous scene as soon as possible as it was beginning to make Kirton look a fool.

At the second mention of the Lion City the woman again protested, but Ching soothed her by saying in what Rungus he commanded, 'Captain find you a good job at Singapore. You will be alright.'

'Put her back in my cabin,' Kirton suddenly said sharply, addressing Pritam Singh, 'and put a guard on her until I get back.' Then he turned to Rodham, 'I'm going ashore to see if there is anything further we can do for the villagers,' and with that he clambered over the ship's rail with his customary awkwardness, waving Ching to accompany him.

He was back within an hour and ordered some further materials to be landed. 'They have cleared the wreckage of the longhouse and are making good progress on a new one; they've also got a good deal of fish drying, and the headman tells me he needs nothing further except perhaps some paraffin,' he remarked to Rodham.

'I'll see to it,' the chief mate said, and Kirton turned his attention to getting the *Tethys* under way so that she was just moving under the last of the land breeze as the boat, after a hard pull, came under the derrick and was hoisted up and onto the hatch, to be snugged and lashed down on the chocks there.

Fate decreed that their passage back to Singapore would not be fast; they were delayed by a series of headwinds and calms after clearing the Balabac Strait in a black and screaming rain-squall. The unusual experience terrified the young woman as the *Tethys* dug in her lee rail so that sea water poured over it. Rodham failed to get the fore-topgallant off the ship in time and it blew out of the bolt-ropes, the first sail the *Tethys* had lost in her new reincarnation, and if its flogging and loss vexed Kirton, it caused the poor Rungus woman to cower under the break of the poop, for it happened near noon, though the sky darkened as though it was near nightfall.

But both *Tethys* and her passenger soon recovered, and in the somewhat idle days that followed the young woman began what Kirton realised was a determined attempt to make herself not merely useful, but—at least according to her lights—indispensable. She relieved the cook of the washing of his utensils and insisted on assuming the duties of laundress such that Kirton was made aware that she took particular care of his own *dhobi*. At first Ah Chuan resisted this, but after Kirton had said somewhat heartlessly, 'Leave girl to do this work, Tiger, must have something to keep busy and no make trouble.'

Ah Chuan was obliged to accept this as much as he had to accept that the Rungus woman still occupied the captain's cabin, a holy-of-holies that prior to her ever coming aboard was strictly the preserve of Captain Kirton and himself.

The morning the *Tethys* anchored off the Esplanade was dull and overcast, presaging rain, and heavy rain such that Kirton did not make the usual signal for a lighter to begin the discharge of their cargo. The boat was swung out, nevertheless, and Rodham and Ching, their ledgers and strong-box of cash bound up in oil-cloth, prepared to go ashore when one of the *jurmudis* reported a *sampan* bearing the flag of the House of the Green Dragon on its way out to the ship.

Ten minutes later Cha's chief *crani*, Lee, stood on the deck with doleful news. The head of the Green Dragon Hong, the Honourable Cha Lee Foo, had gone to join his ancestors. The news ran like a flame through dry-grass and Kirton's first reaction was to order the ensign worn at half-mast. Lee informed them that the old man had simply died in his sleep, but he had found papers, the existence of which Lee, Kirton, and Rodham knew about, indicating that Rodham and Lee should inherit the business. From that day, Lee said, the Chinese form of the company's name was to change; henceforth the business would adopt the title of Lee, Rodham & Co. in the European fashion. Rodham was briefly tempted to require that his own name took precedence until Kirton, pretending inconsequence, remarked 'very sensible doing it alphabetically.'

Under the enormity of the mantle suddenly falling about his shoulders, Rodham made no further protest, realising that he would require a close ally in Lee whose position as chief clerk was now as vacant as Rodham's as chief mate. The four men—Kirton, Lee, Rodham, and Ching—spent a long forenoon sitting round the saloon table discussing their combined future and were there when the saloon steward requested permission to lay the table for the midday tiffin.

'Come gentlemen,' Kirton said, 'let us go on deck and take a drink in respect of our old benefactor before we eat,' whereupon the conversation became reminiscent. After a moment Kirton drew Rodham aside, aware that their relationship had undergone a change with the news of Cha's death. Without broaching the subject directly Kirton took what old Cha would have called 'the path of the crab,' a sideways approach addressing obliquely the matter of succession and the future of the *Tethys*.

'I take it, Kit, that you would be happy to see Jones in your shoes aboard here; recruiting a new second mate will be easier than a chief officer.'

Rodham nodded. 'Of course, sir . . .'

'I think that you had better get used to calling me Hal now, after all, I'm in your employ from this day forth,' Kirton smiled.

Rodham flushed, 'Of course . . . I hope that you won't find that irksome . . . Hal.'

'Not in the least and especially so if you and Lee honour an undertaking that Cha gave me.'

'And what was that?' Rodham asked, his tone guarded.

'Cha promised to leave a half-share of *Tethys* to me, with a lien on the purchase of the remaining half-share in *Tethys* provided I retained the company as my agent. It would relieve you of half the running costs and assure me of my future, at least until you go into steam as you must and as the Old Man intended, and you will have more capital for that too.'

'How much . . . ?'

'You must discuss that with Lee. I'll offer a fair price but you could appoint the Lloyds Surveyor to give you a valuation.'

A heavy silence fell upon them at the direct mention of old Cha, then Kirton remarked, 'He was one of nature's gentlemen; a very superior type of man.'

'Yes,' agreed Rodham, 'he was. D'you know he had read most of Dickens's novels, claiming they had taught him to speak English.'

'I'm not surprised,' responded Kirton at this private revelation. 'That's more than I have.'

'Me too.' A companionable silence fell upon them for a moment before Rodham added: 'This last has been a most successful trip, you know, despite the disruption to the regularity of our usual track.'

'Or because of it, I suspect,' Kirton added shrewdly, then, lighting a cigar, he laughed and said, 'You must be one of the very few chief mates who left a ship without the need to secure a testimonial. I always thought old McClure on the *River Tay*, of whom you've heard me tell often enough, rather resented giving me mine. I imagine you are about to live out every young seaman's fantasy, suddenly becoming the boss of your captain.'

Rodham chuckled. 'You weren't that bad, sir . . . Hal.'

'Well that's good isn't it,' Kirton said smiling and patting his young colleague on the shoulder, 'because I couldn't possibly have given you one; you were so often ashore making money!' Rodham laughed and then Kirton added, 'Come, let's join the others . . .'

A few minutes later the gong rang for chow and down the companionway they went. In the saloon a surprise awaited them, for no less than three stewards stood ready to attend them, Kirton's tiger, Ah Chuan, the saloon steward, Wu Chien, and the young Rungus woman. Lee gave her a curious look but that was nothing to the shock shown by Kirton, for the woman appeared dressed not merely in the *sarong* she had worn since she had been found on the shores of Telok Marudu but wore besides a *kebaya*, the short Malay jacket, made in a fabric that Kirton thought vaguely familiar. But it was not the rig-out of *sarong kebaya* that chiefly knocked him sideways, it was her loveliness, for she had done up her black hair and her long neck and proud carriage as she followed the motions of the two Chinese stewards in a beguilingly graceful imitation that stole his heart.

Ah Chuan took good care that she served only those he considered 'inferiors' at the table, reserving Kirton, Lee, and Rodham to himself. He had heard on that magic telegraph that works on a ship without apparent electrical impulse, that the young chief mate was elevated to become a man of great consequence, a *Tuan besar* of importance. But this meant that the woman, awkwardly serving at the bottom of the table, was frequently in Kirton's line-of-sight without his having too obviously to stare at her. Whether it was the recent death of their employer, the unusual number of diners, or the presence of the woman, but the meal passed in a formal silence that—Kirton reflected later—the poor woman must have found intimidating, for she had been in the steward's tiny pantry often enough on the passage from Marudu Bay and must have heard the often loud banter between the brigantine's officers.

During the meal the rain had begun and Rodham and Ching put off their shoreward run until it eased. Kirton left the table calling Jones after him. The two men withdrew to the chart-room where Kirton asked Jones if he would be willing to serve as chief mate of the *Tethys*. It was clear that the poor man had been on tenter-hooks ever since the news of Cha's death had reached the ship and the smile that greeted the offer said it all. Kirton held out his hand and said, 'I can think of no better man for the job, Vikram, but I would not stand in your way if you sought your own command . . .'

'I have tried, Captain Kirton,' he confessed, 'and maybe if and when our friends establish a steamship company . . .' Jones let his dreams tail off, to be lost in the heavy drumming of the rain on the coach-roof, then he asked, 'What shall you do for a second mate?'

'Any ideas?' Kirton responded.

'One of the *jurmudis* might make a third mate, but I'm not certain . . . Let me think about it.'

'Well, I daresay we could manage for a voyage, you and I, but I don't want to leave it too long.'

'No, of course not.'

'By the way,' said Kirton, riffling through the small number of letters that Lee had brought out to the ship and lay neglected on the chart-room table. 'Ching is going to combine the job of *comprador* with that of *shroff*.'

'Very sensible,' Jones agreed, his head rocking in approval. Then seeing Kirton's attention had been taken by the letters, he said, 'Sir? There is one other matter . . .'

'Eh? What's that?'

'Why, the girl, sir.'

'Oh yes, the girl,' Kirton said wearily.

'Ching says she is desperate to remain aboard, sir.'

'Yes, she may, but she can't can she? I mean she may have made herself useful but where can we accommodate her on a long-term basis? And one woman in a small ship like this . . . one of the men is bound to try something on and she has been through enough already. Rodham promised to take care of the matter . . .'

'He's going to be rather busy in the next few weeks,' Jones observed. 'I'm not sure he quite knows what lies in store for him, though Lee is a very competent and loyal chap who knows which side his bread is buttered upon.' He paused and then, emboldened by his new relationship with Kirton, went on: 'Please forgive me, sir, if I am being forward, but the problem of the girl could be solved if you made her your *nyai*. All the men expect it and she would not object.'

'*What?*' Kirton, whose attention had turned back to the letters, swung back to the Indian.

Unsure of Kirton's reaction Jones said slowly, 'She could be useful. If she learned English, I mean, sir . . . It is not good for a man not to have a woman . . .'

Kirton betrayed himself by flushing red and blurted out, 'Yes, that's as maybe. Thank you Mr Jones, but I have no plans . . .'

'No, of course not, sir, please excuse me . . .' And with that Jones escaped onto the fresh air of the deck where the rain had stopped and the sun now shone with a withering brilliance.

Aware that he was setting aside a real problem, Kirton turned at last to the letters. There were five of them, all addressed to himself; three bore superscriptions in his sister's hand, two were local, one from Government House and the other from a firm of solicitors in Singapore. He stared at them, a quickening of his heart and a drying of his mouth presaging something being wrong. He shuffled his sister's into chronological order by post-mark then opened the first. He had not written to her in many months, not since he had heard of her engagement and predictably the first told him of her marriage. Although a man of no religion, Kirton was somewhat surprised to learn that her husband was a Roman Catholic. However, the announcement of her pregnancy in the second was, therefore not a surprise. The third told of 'the arrival of a fine boy named John Harry.' He had been given the first name after her husband, while the second was after himself, 'the second most admired of my male acquaintances,' she told him. Finally she concluded primly that he ought to consider coming home and marrying himself, at which point Kirton threw the letter aside with a curt dismissive comment:

'Bloody hell,' he fulminated, 'the whole world wishes me wed!'

Then his reluctant eye fell upon the other two letters and he cast about as to which of the two he should open first. While his sister's correspondence was old, these bore recent dates, so with a great apprehension he tore open the letter from Government House. 'After Compliments,' it informed him coldly that a complaint had been laid against him for his disrespectful conduct to the Spanish flag off Jolo; that the matter had been taken so seriously by the Spanish viceroy in Manila that a letter of protest had been despatched by a fast Spanish naval *aviso* from the colonial capital to Hong Kong and transferred aboard the mail steamer of the P & O Steam Navigation Company to be delivered in Singapore 'per favour of the Master.' Captain Kirton was warned that although it was well known that his ship sailed under Suluese colours, his own nationality remained British and his conduct should reflect the fact.

Kirton was swept by several emotions, the first of which was the high tone of the admonishment, the second was a feeling of dread that if his shooting of the Bugis pirate roused some sort of nationalistic reaction at the murder of a Dutch 'citizen' in Batavia he would be in very hot water indeed, and the third was a blind fury that a Spanish man-of-war could demand he hove-to by firing a shot across his bows when he was in Suluese waters. How much detail of all this had become public knowledge while he and the *Tethys* had been delayed by contrary winds and calms he could only guess, but the letter from the firm of Singaporean solicitors confirmed a good deal of it. The letter itself was innocuous enough, merely offering their services should Captain Kirton require them.

Deeply troubled, Kirton stumped his way on deck and began pacing furiously up and down the long poop, stopping every now and then to swear with a sincerity and vigour that warned everyone on deck to keep clear of him. No-one had seen him in this mood before, nor had anything so outrageous yet so terrifying happened to him. Neither falling off the yard in the *River Tay*, nor being under fire from the Bugis raiders had worked on his self-esteem as this official admonishment. Humiliated, shocked and exposed, he wastefully half-smoked two cigars before going below to write to the governor's secretary, explaining that the Spanish corvette had effectively invaded Suluese waters illegally, that she had fired three shots at the *Tethys*, at least one of which had been when he had

deliberately hoisted the British mercantile ensign to deter further harass-
ment, and that he fully intended to note protest himself as soon as he was
able and immediately following the despatch of the present missive. He
agreed that he had not dipped the Suluese ensign to the foreign warship
since his own ship was within the territorial waters of His Highness
Sultan Jamal ul-Azam, which she had every right to be, and which the
Spaniard did not.

Then, realising that Rodham and Ching had taken the boat and gone
ashore after the rain had eased, he sent for Pritam Singh, gave him some
money, and ordered him to hail a *sampan* and convey the letter directly
to Government House. The tall Sikh took the letter with great gravity,
saluted, and began roaring for a passing boat. Kirton then passed word
for Vikram Jones and his tiger, Ah Chuan. When the first appeared
Kirton told him to sit on one of the deck-chairs laid out in the sunshine
beside the steering-box, and when the second arrived a moment later he
ordered two gin-slings.

'I am not keen on strong drink, sir . . .'

'You will be. I've something to tell you, Vikram,' he began, taking a
long draught of the drink when Ah Chuan brought it to him.

'What a day,' remarked Jones when Kirton had confided the contents
of the two letters.

'You might not feel so inclined to remain in the ship,' Kirton said,
drawing on his cigar and calling for another drink.

'Please, sir,' Jones said, waggling his head, 'I would consider it most
dishonourable to abandon you and the ship now, and for such a paltry
reason.'

'Thank you,' Kirton said quietly, 'though I am not certain how paltry
a reason this is.'

'It is a storm in a tea-cup, sir.'

Most unusually for him, Kirton was rather tipsy when he went to bed
that night. The only truly sober thought he had as he turned-in on the
narrow chart-room settee was that he was damned if that bloody woman
was going to keep him another night from his own bunk. The drink
which sent him rapidly to sleep woke him just as surely in the small hours
of the night. His mind immediately filled with the deep concerns aroused

by the letters, and it was not long before he was padding lopsidedly up and down the poop in his bare feet, another cigar clamped in his teeth, nursing a mild hang-over and muttering about the injustices of life.

Not since he had had to come to terms with becoming a cripple had he felt so keenly a sense of the futility of a man's existence when the Fates turn against him. Why, he asked himself, had the governor's secretary not summoned him to give an account of his own side of the story? And what a piece of bad-luck that the Spanish corvette had had time to return to her base at Cavite, near Manila, and for word to get to Hong Kong and then to Singapore while he, quite innocently, was taking on some extra cargo and working his way back to Singapore by way of Marudu Bay. In the several years that he had commanded the *Tethys* he had never made such a slow passage from the Selat Balabac, and then to arrive in Singapore to learn that the one man who might have eased his awful sense of isolation was dead seemed a most monstrous imposition by an unkind and vengeful God. Not that he believed in the deity, of course, but whatever profound engine drove the universe, its ultimate heartlessness struck him that morning with a particular severity. He had, he realised, grown too accustomed to his comfortable life in his little ship; indeed, nursing the black dog that had come upon him after leaving hospital a cripple—how he hated that word and what it truly meant, almost as bad as *invalid*, which, enunciated slowly, could be rendered as *in-valid*—he had taken up old Cha's offer to bury himself among the islands and now the world had sought him out. But it was not just the Spanish corvette; there was also the matter of the Rungus woman.

In his misery that night he dearly wished she would come to him, spontaneously and consolingly, so that he might drown in her and forget his fate, if only for a few hours. But what use had she for him? She was, self-evidently, a free-spirit, but she knew nothing of white men, or their world. Nor did the *Tethys* give her many clues, composed as her ship's company was of several races. She had, Kirton judged, found a niche for herself and eventually would succumb to the blandishments of one or other of the men with whom she was now in contact.

He pitched his cigar over the side and went back to the discomfort of the chart-room settee from where, three hours later, he was woken by

Ah Chuan with coffee and the outraged information that, 'Woman make *kebaya* from the *Tuan's* spare settee cover!'

Kirton met his tiger's annoyance with a laugh. 'Never mind, Ah Chuan. I thought I recognised the cloth . . .' If only his own troubles revolved such simple wrong-doings.

After breakfast the large *sampans* came alongside and they began to discharge the deck cargo and by noon, as more rain clouds banked up over Pulo Bukum, they removed the hatch tarpaulin and broke bulk. By this time Kirton was ashore calling upon Lee and Rodham at the House of the Green Dragon.

'You will stay for tiffin?' Rodham asked after they concluded the ship's business.

Kirton nodded. 'Yes, thank you. There is something else that you should know,' he began, and told the two of them about the letter from Government House.

'That's ridiculous,' spluttered Rodham. 'We were surrounded by islands, well inside the sultan's waters. That bloody Spaniard was as much a pirate as those bastard Bugis.'

'Yes. And I strongly repudiated the charge. I sent Pritam Singh ashore before sunset last night with a letter to that effect.'

'You'll probably hear no more about it.'

'You might, though. Perhaps you'd keep your ear to the ground.'

'Yes, of course.' Rodham paused to take a sip of his pre-prandial *stengah*, then went on, 'Incidentally, Hal, I've arranged for the Lloyds Surveyor to take a look at the *Tethys* with a view to a valuation . . .'

'That was quick.'

'I happened by chance to bump into him on the Esplanade last night.' Kirton nodded.

'Now, what about this woman?'

'We'll sign her on as stewardess,' Kirton said almost without thinking and rather to his own surprise. 'I'll sort out some accommodation and she can return to her village whenever she wants to, otherwise, well, matters may get complicated.'

Rodham smiled slyly.

'This is not what you are thinking . . .' protested Kirton flushing and provoking outright laughter from his new and impossibly young owner.

'We'll see . . .'

Kirton returned to his ship, his mind in a turmoil. Naturally he sensed a watershed in his affairs: If all went well with the survey and Lee and Rodham were not too grasping, he might soon own a real interest in his ship, rather than a percentage of her voyage profits which—though both generous and lucrative—held him in thrall rather than gave him the freedom that he so desired. And this the more so since, all of a sudden, he desperately wanted to nail his place in the Lion City's shipping world, for on his way back to his boat at Collyer Quay he had once again bumped into McClure who was taking the air of the Esplanade. His ship lay alongside the new wharf of Keppel Harbour and McClure was strolling with a fellow master to whom he introduced Kirton as 'a former second mate of mine, now master of a country-*wallah*.' McClure's tone was vaguely disdainful and it was only later that Kirton learnt that as senior master in the Scottish River Line he had been dignified by the appellation of 'Commodore,' a conceit increasingly adopted by the growing number of British steam navigation companies.

'A sailing ship?' his companion had asked, whereupon McClure had interjected. 'Not a ship Dougie, a brigantine,' as though it made a great deal of difference, but appended the information—over Kirton's head—that: 'Captain Kirton wanders about the islands doing a good deal of lotus-eating,' then, turning to Kirton himself said smoothly, 'I hear that you almost provoked a war with the Spanish.'

'Hardly that, McClure,' Kirton snapped back with no pretence at respect. 'I'd have been ashamed to have acted differently.'

McClure flushed, harrumphed, wished him a cold 'good day,' and moved off with his friend. Kirton found himself shaking with rage after this unpleasant little encounter. So upset was he that he waved aside the waiting boat and stumped off to cool his heels along the Esplanade in the contrary direction from which McClure and his companion had taken.

Once again the disparagement inherent in McClure's words bit deep. The man had become insufferable and Kirton resolved to avoid contact with him in the future, if he could, and certainly not to attend the premises of Lee, Rodham & Co. if he discovered the commodore of the River Line was in the place.

By some sort of subconscious yet autogenous motivation, he found himself on his way to his bank where he quickly determined the exact extent of his wealth. The result of this spontaneous enquiry surprised him for not only was the balance more than he had expected—and he was casual about such matters, the ship providing him with most of his daily needs—but the sum far exceeded his rough-and-ready calculation. There was a large deposit that was, at first, inexplicable. On enquiry he made the discovery that it had been made by a transfer of funds from his old employer; there was, of course, no explanation, but Kirton thought back to the opinion of Jones that had he, Kirton, appeared on the scene before Rodham, he might have been now in Rodham's shoes, providing the European 'front' to the respectable business that old Cha had spent a good portion of his life building up. For a moment Kirton stared at the Chinese bank-clerk who had imparted this information as though the poor man was lying, or might evaporate at any moment, allowing Kirton to wake from his dream; but no, the small figure stood, a model of respect, while Kirton digested the news, bowing when Kirton took his leave.

He wandered back to the quay, his mind in a whirl. It was clear that Cha wanted him to acquire the *Tethys*, if only to make himself independent—if necessary—of any folly his son-in-law might bring about. But in Lee and Ching old Cha had two steady men alongside Rodham; the *shroff* was also a bastion of good faith, though everyone knew he made a comfortable sum raking off a percentage or two more than he was allowed in all his transactions. Not that Rodham had ever showed the slightest signs of fecklessness; he was devoted to his Chinese wife and his growing number of children, and was only too well aware that he had fallen upon his feet in a city where economic activity was ever-expanding. Kirton was in no doubt that Rodham would very soon have several small steamers under his house-flag, and that the *Tethys* would be pensioned-off.

Of course, while Kirton might assume that he would be offered the command of one of the new steamships, he was by no means certain. He had disguised his bad leg as much as he was able when passing for master, but he could not hope to do so in the future and the new house of Lee,

Rodham & Co. could not be expected to operate a steam-navigation company under the Suluese flag. Thus his part ownership of the *Tethys* remained his lifeline, and if the fortunes of the company prospered and they divested themselves of what was rapidly becoming an out-of-date asset, he needed the little old brigantine for himself.

When he finally regained the busy deck of the *Tethys*, where cargo-work was in full swing, he had recovered his equanimity. He had even resolved to solve the problem of the young Rungus woman, although explaining his solution to her would have to wait for Ching to return from the shore where he had been busy with his ledgers and a consultation with Lee.

Stumping aft and below to the saloon where he called for a pot of coffee, he found her being instructed by the saloon steward, Wu Chien, in laying up the table; clearly some means of communication had been established between the two of them. The realisation of this caused an upwelling of intense jealousy in Kirton; it took him utterly by surprise, but it was so powerful that all he could do was to retreat to the chart-room and light a cigar, his hands shaking. Had he been a hard-drinking man he would have called for a whisky, but instead he waited for the appearance of coffee, intending to reoccupy his own quarters and throw the woman out.

He decided to have the two youngest *jagas* accommodated in the same cabin and had plans for a second bunk to be fitted whilst one of them was on leave and before the ship sailed, thereby providing a berth for the woman, but it was she who brought him his coffee, and his strange and conflicting emotions ebbed from him as she laid the silver salver with its pot, cup, and saucer on the chart-table with a motion that was at once naturally graceful and oddly awkward.

'*Tuan*,' she breathed obsequiously, in obvious awe of the *orang puteh* whom she wished to serve, though Kirton perceived nothing of this, merely feeling himself a lumbering oaf in the presence of her simple elegance as she met his gaze with a hesitant smile upon her face.

Fortunately he was rescued from this situation by the appearance of Vik, who scooted the girl away and, wagging his head, handed Kirton a letter.

'This was brought out by a government messenger, sir,' the new chief mate informed him with some pomposity.

Kirton took it and turned it over. He was reluctant to open it but any sign of weakness would not play well with Vee-Jay, so he picked up the chart dividers and used them as a paper knife.

'Sit down,' he commanded Jones, reading the letter. It was brief and to the point. 'Sir,' it read,

> *your response to mine of the 19th instant has been noted and it is considered by Government that in the hoisting of the British ensign you acted impetuously. The presence of the Spanish man-of-war within Suluese waters has also been noted and, as a Master holding a British Certificate of Competency, you are requested and required to ensure that in future your actions are circumspect and that you act with more caution. You are also requested and required to keep Government informed of any further movements of Spanish war-ships in Suluese waters wherever these may be observed. Yours faithfully, etc. etc.*

It was signed with an illegible flourish.

So there it was: an admonishment and an instruction—requested and required being as mealy-mouthed a way of giving an order as he could conceive—but the latter clearly let him off the official British hook, howsoever he had upset the viceroy's government in Manila. Nevertheless, such was the state of his mind after the travails of that morning, that even the mild rebuke stung him. He was, at the bottom of it all, a servant of His Highness Sultan Jamal ul-Azam and the *Tethys* flew the sultan's colours. That the vessel had been indisputably within Suluese waters—surrounded by the islands that littered the approach to Jolo road, as he had been constantly reminded—remained the chief plank of his defence. His hoisting of the red ensign had, in fact, been intended to warn the Spanish naval commander that the *Tethys* was something of an anomaly, and that opening fire on her, even firing a shot across her bow to bring her to for boarding, would quite possibly implicate the British authorities at Singapore, but the Spaniard had fired two more shots, disdainful of even this warning.

He handed the letter to Jones, who read it and then looked up smiling. 'Then that's that, sir,' he remarked conclusively.

'I sincerely hope so,' Kirton responded, 'but it may not be the case if we encounter either that or any other Spanish man-of-war in the eastern islands.'

Jones shrugged. 'As we say, sir, let us cross that bridge when we come to it.'

Kirton blew out his cheeks, his mood lightening. 'Yes, now, let's change the subject, Vikram, this woman. She wants to stay aboard. We'll sign her on as stewardess . . .'

He went on to instruct the chief mate of the alterations he required to be made to one of the after cabins.

'The *jagas* won't like that, sir,' Jones said.

'No, but they won't turn down a hard-lying allowance.'

Jones chuckled, 'No, that's true. They'll be fighting for the privilege of sharing a cabin!'

'*Bagus*,' said Kirton, shortly, 'now to our next voyage, Vikram, we missed out seven places last voyage and they may well be wondering why. We'll cut-out Jolo next trip and concentrate on running south from Marudu . . .'

The two men discussed the coming voyage until the gong sounded for tiffin when a considerably happier Kirton followed the chief mate down into the saloon to be served his curry by an immaculately attired stewardess who attended them under the watchful eyes of Ah Chuan and the saloon steward.

As they rose from the table Kirton remarked, 'If the girl is to sign-on we had better get it done sooner rather than later. We'll need a name and a date of birth.'

'Leave it to me, sir,' Jones responded.

Kirton went on deck. It was blisteringly hot, even though Tan had rigged an awning over the after part of the poop. Two deck-chairs were set out on the counter and Kirton eased himself down on one of them and lit a cigar. The curry and the general relief of the letter from the governor's office soon sent him into a brown study as he contemplated his one remaining problem, his lack of a second mate. In the end, his problem unresolved, he pitched the stub of the cigar over the stern and slipped into a pleasant doze.

Chapter Ten

The Disgrace of Wu Chien

THE *TETHYS* LAY OVER TO A SPANKING BREEZE AS, ON THE STARBOARD tack, she ran down the coast of Sarawak, homeward-bound for Singapore after a successful voyage. They had taken in cargo as far south as Tamaran, well into the Dutch East Indian territory of Kalimantan where they had done a lively traffic in pots, pans, knives, paraffin-stoves and lamps, and the oil that powered them, besides numerous other British manufactures much in demand by the local people. Their only failure in delivering items the headmen wished for were guns and ammunition. When Ching ruefully explained this deficiency in their trade-goods, Kirton shook his head.

'No, Ching; I nearly started a war with the Spanish. A war with the Dutch would be far worse and end all our prospects . . . you savee?'

'Ah, so, *Tuan*,' the *shroff* acknowledged resignedly, 'Ching savee, but velly sad, guns make plenty money and the brown barbarians hate the white men with square heads.'

The two men were in the saloon studying the *shroff's* ledger prior to their arrival at their home port, pouring over the accounts with a good deal of satisfaction. Tamaran had yielded a good crop of rattans, gum damar, coir, and copra and as Kirton sat back, Ching said:

'*Tuan*, if we had steaming-boiler-ship we able to run *ulu*; much more-better than trade only on coast.' The Chinaman's finger traced a wiggly line across the saloon table as though proceeding up a long river, a long and profitable river.

'That is true, Ching, and maybe in due time, after tomorrow's tomorrow we shall try that.'

'That make old Ching ver' happy, *Tuan*.'

'We shall have to see what the gods decree,' Kirton remarked just as the pantry door opened and the woman appeared in her *sarong kebaya*. Kirton was aware that Ah Chuan was half concealed behind the pantry door and had some part in her approach, for she came up to him, leaning against the heel of the brigantine and gave him what seemed very like a curtsy, enunciating quite clearly:

'Would *Tuan* like *chai* now?'

Concealing his astonishment Kirton inclined his head and responded. 'That would be most kind,' at which the woman retreated and Kirton half-heard Ah Chuan say that the *Tuan* had said 'yes.'

'You treat girl too good, *Tuan*. She cause trouble by'm'by . . .' said Ching who, as a Chinese regarded the Rungus, and all Malays, as an inferior race. Even Kirton, though the overlord of the ship, remained a *fan kwei*, or red barbarian in his eyes.

Shortly thereafter the woman reappeared and set the silver salver down on the saloon table. Along with the tea she brought them some sweetmeats and said slowly and with great deliberation, 'I make these special for *Tuan* . . .' As she disappeared into the pantry Kirton heard Ah Chuan congratulate her.

'*Bagus, bagus*, good, good,' the satisfaction in his voice like a purring cat.

'Maybe this proper way to treat woman,' Kirton remarked to Ching with a broad grin as he indicated the *shroff* should enjoy the treat.

Ching merely grunted, then said, 'Forgive me, *Tuan*, but you velly young man. Later you understand more better.'

Kirton was rescued from the turn the conversation had taken by the consumption of the sweetmeats and the refreshing cup of tea. The appearance of the woman and the odd gesture of her production of both tea and the little cakes had propelled him into an exceptionally good humour which was in no way diminished by the ringing of one bell, a signal that the watch was about to change at four o'clock. They had failed to ship a second mate in Singapore and Jones and Kirton had stood watch-and-watch during their sea passages, though Kirton had had Tan keep him company and was teaching him the rudiments of coastal navigation and cabotage, since the man knew well enough how to handle the brigantine.

He rose from the table and before reaching the companionway ladder turned back to Ching.

'We still have a little space in the 'tween deck, Ching. What you say we see if any cargo can be got at Matu?'

Ching shrugged. 'Maybe, better we tly than come homeside with cargo-space.'

'Just what I was thinking,' replied Kirton and almost leapt up the ladder to relieve Jones.

'We'll put in to Matu, Vikram,' he said easily, 'just on the off-chance we can fill up what remains of our space.' The uxorious Indian looked crest-fallen. 'Come man, we'll only be a few hours later getting home,' Kirton said with a smile. 'Think of the bonus!'

'Of course, *Tuan*,' Jones replied obediently.

'Give me a course then, on your way below.'

Ten minutes later the *Tethys*, her yards braced to the new course, seethed along. If they were successful they could make the anchorage by nightfall tomorrow and be away long before sunset that evening.

The *Tethys* came to her anchor off Matu just as the breeze failed and the last of the daylight faded behind the low mangrove headland of Tanjong Sirik. It was too late to investigate whether or not the *kampong* could offer anything in the way of trade, for it was known for its oranges, so having set the *jagas* to their nightly duty when at anchor of maintaining the watch, Kirton came below to join Jones, Ching, and Pritam Singh at the saloon table. They had yet to persuade Tan to join them, he being highly suspicious of the food that was served at the officers' table, though Ching—who ate only Hokkien dishes—told him that a selection was always served so that none might be offended. It was one of the minor achievements of the ship's cook, though, Ching explained to Tan; the lord of the ship—being a barbarian—ate indiscriminately.

Under the watchful eye of Ah Chuan at the pantry door, the saloon steward and the woman served the evening meal with an unusual formality. The woman caught all their eyes, and those of Kirton in particular, as she moved about the panelled saloon, softly lit by the oil lamps. After Kirton and Jones had retired to the deck to smoke their cigars and drink their late-night *stengahs*, the chief mate said in his inimitable, old-fashioned way, 'That was quite, quite splendid, Captain Kirton.'

Two hours later Kirton lay in his own bunk, drifting into oblivion. He was smitten with the young woman but felt helpless in his passion. He nursed a vague hope that she might be married off somewhere and remove herself from his dreams, and he cursed his disability with a quiet venom that achieved nothing other than a venting of his feelings. He might have lain thus all night, suspended between waking and sleeping, for it was hot and airless in the anchorage, and beyond his mosquito net the insects were busy. Shortly after midnight he finally drifted off into a fitful doze, one leg thrown inelegantly out of his bunk. He had heard eight bells rung before his consciousness shut down, along with the *Jaga*'s low cry of 'all's well.'

Nothing much could happen to them at the anchorage. The sea breeze would not disturb their anchor, for Matu lay on a northern mouth of the extensive deltaic estuary of the Rejang River, a vast area largely of mangroves, and the holding-ground was perfect. A ship-master could slumber gratefully under such benign circumstances.

Suddenly Kirton was jerked awake; something was wrong, very wrong. He lay for a moment listening to the sounds of the brigantine but she lay as quiet as when he had slipped into a deep slumber. Then he heard the noise again, a scuffling sound, a muffled cry and he was out of his bunk in a trice. They had been boarded by *orang laut*, the same Bugis pirates that he had last encountered in Marudu Bay! Perhaps the very same, seeking revenge for the headman he had killed! Grabbing his Colt he checked the chambers and hauled himself up on deck but a moment's survey told him that the decks were quiet. They were too far from Telok Marudu and even further from the Bugis' homeland of Sulawesi, he thought with some relief. He caught sight of the *jaga* forward, leaning over the foc's'le rail checking the cable. He shook the remnants of sleep from his brain; had he dreamed of something? Then he heard the noise again; it came from below.

Kirton dropped back down the companionway into the saloon with as much agility as he could muster. Jones was up now, rubbing the sleep from his own eyes, but Kirton pushed past him and plunged down the dark alleyway. It turned a right angle along the forward end of the poop and as Kirton came round the corner he was confronted with an unpleasant scene, one of writhing bodies only half glimpsed in the gloom. Wu Chien, the saloon steward, had the woman by her neck and was attempting to drag her backwards along the alleyway to his own cabin at the far end. His purpose was clear enough.

Just as Kirton brought the big Colt up with a bellow, the door of Ah Chuan's cabin opened. Ah Chuan had lit his cabin lamp and the light, weak though it was, played on the sordid little struggle. Kirton could see that the woman's eyes were bright with fear and fury, just as he had seen her on the beach at *kampong* No. 5.

'Let go!' Kirton roared, cocking the revolver. 'Wu Chien! Let go, I said!'

At the same time Jones and then Tan appeared at Kirton's back; there was little they could do in the narrow confines of the alleyway but they buttressed their commander and Kirton saw Wu Chien's eyes flicker from one to the other. For a moment he seemed hesitant in his resolve, as though changing tack, and Kirton sought to gain the upper hand, roaring again, 'Let go!'

But Wu Chien suddenly increased his grip on the woman's neck with the obvious intention of strangling her. At the same time Ah Chuan released a torrent of Cantonese to which Kirton paid little attention, advancing very quickly, the Colt held high and pointing directly at Wu Chien's forehead. The steward tried to jerk the woman's head round to cover his own as he backed away, but Kirton's shuffling advance was too quick for him and he suddenly found he had passed his own cabin door and was hard up against the bulkhead at the far end of the alleyway. Deprived of the refuge of his cabin the wretched man's resolve collapsed. He thrust the woman away from him with a gesture of disgust.

'She try rob me, *Tuan*,' he pleaded in a desperate attempt to exculpate himself, despite the circumstances clearing indicating otherwise.

Kirton was not inclined to remonstrate over these, but before he had a chance to say anything Ah Chuan launched himself into another tirade of abuse at his erstwhile colleague. Still pointing the Colt at Wu Chien, Kirton bent and helped the gasping woman to her feet. Her *sarong* was torn and she was all but naked so that he could feel the heat of her body and its aroma, both of which roused a deep anger in him at the infamous conduct of the steward.

'Mr Jones,' he said with a dreadful formality, 'take her to her cabin and get Ching to ask if there is anything we can do for her, anything, otherwise leave her to compose herself.'

'Aye, aye, sir,' responded Jones, and Kirton released the poor woman who was now trembling violently and almost limp in his arms.

'Ching all'eady here, *Tuan*,' the *shroff* announced, but Kirton was not listening; his eyes were fixed on Wu Chien, fearful that the steward had a knife and would attempt some desperate measure. He passed the woman to Jones without removing his glare from Wu Chien's own eyes, saying 'Mr Tan, go to chief mate's cabin and fetch handcuffs.'

Now only Ah Chuan remained with him to confront Wu Chien, who now played his last card. Deprived of his prize, his back against the bulkhead, the steward was a cornered animal. From behind his back he suddenly produced from his belt the saloon's long carving knife, and jabbed it viciously at Kirton.

Ah Chuan shouted a warning and Kirton gestured with the Colt. 'Drop that or I'll blow your head off!' Kirton said with a primitive purpose that matched that of his opponent and was all too clear.

Then, quite suddenly it was all over. The carving knife was dropped to the deck and Wu Chien followed it on his knees, pleading for his life in his native tongue.

"What's the bastard saying Ah Chuan?' Kirton asked his tiger.

'He say now that Captain Kirton is a just man and he will understand. Girl velly beautiful, his miserable servant Wu Chien could not help himself. The lying son of a pig whose mother is a goat is no good, *Tuan*. Better you shoot him now and call accident later.'

'No, the moment for that is past . . . Ah, Tan, you have the handcuffs,' said Kirton as the new second mate returned. 'Put them on him . . .' Kirton had lowered the Colt and turned away; he now felt very weary. Something within him had snapped and he sensed that some turning point in his life and the life of his little ship had been reached. He turned away, intending to see the woman, but Tan called after him:

'What do with pig, *Tuan?*' Tan asked.

'Shackle him to a ring-bolt on deck. I will deal with him tomorrow morning.'

He found that Jones had taken the woman through into the saloon and wrapped her in a large cotton bed-spread. Ching had made *chai* for them all and offered a cup to Kirton as soon as he arrived.

'Thank you Ching, that is most kind of you.' Kirton's gratitude was heart-felt. The old *shroff* had been his right-hand man on so many occasions that Kirton had come to both trust and like him. With Cha gone, Ching was his last personal link with that old Confucian China that was fast disappearing under the imperatives of capitalist expansion—so eagerly embraced by ambitious Chinese in Singapore.

He sat and regarded the woman; she had stopped shivering and as he eased himself wearily down into his chair at the head of the saloon table she suddenly threw herself at his feet, taking his hands in his, kissing them.

'Please, please,' he spluttered, trying somewhat feebly to disengage himself, 'there is no need for this.'

'*Tuan, Tuan,*' she breathed, lowering her brow onto the backs of his captive hands. Then great sobs wracked her body and he finally withdrew one hand and, seeking to soothe the distressed soul, he smoothed her oiled hair which shone in the lamplight of the saloon with a deep and alluring lustre.

'There. There,' he said, hearing the inadequacy and banality of his own words. Ching placed a cup of tea on the table in front of him and he smiled and nodded his acknowledgement.

Ah Chuan entered the saloon. 'Pig bastard tie-up to iron ling deckside, *Tuan,*' he said. Tan followed him, adding, 'I've told the *jaga* on watch to cut the pig's throat if he gives any trouble.'

Kirton smiled wanly, still stroking the woman's head. She suddenly looked up and began to speak, the words tumbling from her so that all of them—Kirton, Jones, Ah Chuan, Ching, and Tan—stared at her. Kirton thought he heard Jones mumble something about women always being trouble aboard ship, but Kirton looked up at Ching.

'What is she saying?'

Ching listened for a moment and then his usually impassive face seemed riven by conflicting expressions that Kirton read as astonishment, then amusement, then something that looked like pleasure.

'Well?'

'She say, you save her life, so she your slave *Tuan*, she happy to become your *nyai* . . . *nyai* belong concubine, velly honoulable.'

Kirton looked at the woman in bewilderment, taken completely aback. 'I . . . this . . .' he spluttered, moved by a visceral temptation but unable to act in any way other than honourably, especially in front of the saloon full of curious observers, all of whose faces bore varying expressions that mirrored those of the *shroff*. He finally mastered himself, and said, 'This is unnecessary, please tell her Ching,' but the old man had hardly uttered a word of his version of the woman's native tongue when she turned her face up to Kirton's, the tears running down her face and uttered the words 'please, *Tuan*,' with such an immensity of piteous supplication that he could do nothing other than raise his head and address them all.

'I think we should all go to back to bed. Tomorrow is the time to deal with the matters arising from Wu Chien's behaviour. Please Ching, tell her this and that she is safe now and I will talk to her in the morning, after seeing what Matu has to offer in the way of cargo.'

Then, tenderly lifting her to her feet he escorted her to her cabin and went on deck. Walking forward to the break of the poop he looked down and regarded his prisoner. Wu Chien lay on his side, his face turned away from Kirton. Pritam Singh sat on the corner of the hatch, a *parang* by his side. It gleamed dully in the starlight, as did the Sikh's teeth as he looked up at Kirton. Kirton nodded his satisfaction, turned, and went below to his bunk.

Matu, they discovered, had dried fish and copra to trade and it was late in the forenoon before Kirton had come to a conclusion regarding Wu Chien. He had considered having him arraigned before the courts in Singapore, but was mindful of the years of good and faithful service the wretched man had rendered, and was moved by the notion that his crime had been one of passion. There could not have been one man dwelling aboard the *Tethys* that had not, if only in his imagination, conjured up an image of lying with the Rungus woman. That the unlikely figure of the saloon steward had translated this lust into action was a mark of the man's weakness of character and by the time his tiger brought him his morning coffee, he had made up his mind.

As he set down the silver salver with its pot and cup, Ah Chuan asked the question that was clearly troubling the entire crew: 'You send that pig before Magisllate Singapore-side, *Tuan?*'

Kirton stared up at him and smiled. 'Go speak Mister Jones, Mister Tan. Ask them to join me. And you too, you come see that I give Wu Chien fair justice. You savee "fair justice"?'

'I savee, *Tuan,*' the tiger replied, hurrying off on his important errand.

Gunny sacks of copra were being hove out of the ship's boat by the derrick on her mainmast, the whip running to the capstan by the main fife-rail round which the duty watch of seamen tramped to the wailing work-song. The bale was followed by Ching who laboriously clambered over the rail and came aft to report that they would finish cargo with one more boat-load.

'Thank you, Ching,' Kirton nodded. 'Please, you fetch woman and bring her here, I am going to deal with Wu Chien.'

'Yes, *Tuan,*' Ching complied somewhat breathlessly. When Ah Chien returned from his mission, Kirton had him bring a saloon chair on deck, and fetch the red ensign from its place in Kirton's cabin, then he got to his feet and walked aft. Ah Chuan set the chair right aft where Kirton was lowering the Suluese ensign. In its place he hoisted British colours, but not to the peak, only high enough for it to float lazily behind the chair.

A moment or two later, flanked by two *jagas*, both bearing arms, Wu Chien stood arraigned before the master of the *Tethys* and his officers. Ching and the woman stood off to one side and Kirton invited her to sit on the steering-box which provided a long seat on either side. Thereafter she did not take her eyes off Kirton, a fact that he was aware of and puzzled him. He thought she would have stared at her assailant.

Kirton cleared his throat. 'Wu Chien,' he began, his voice as stern as he could make it. 'What have you to say about your conduct last night?'

The man looked shrivelled, cornered, terrified, barely comprehending what was going on after spending the night on the hard planking of the deck with nothing to eat and only a bowl of water to sustain him.

'Does he understand the question, Ah Chuan?' Kirton asked the tiger, and Ah Chuan exchanged some words with Wu Chien. 'Yes, *Tuan*,' he responded.

Wu Chien hung his head. 'Velly sorry, *Tuan*,' he mumbled at last.

'You have no more to say?' Ah Chuan translated and Wu Chien shook his head.

'I have three options, Wu Chien, three choices—translate Ah Chuan—number one is send you to British court in Singapore. I will charge you with attempted rape. Number two, I will send you ashore at Jolo to the court of the sultan, His Highness Jamal ul-Azam, and number three, I will deal with you myself. Which do you choose? Ching, please explain what I am saying to his victim.'

Wu Chien had visibly shrunk at the mention of the sultan's name and, after a few moments of gabbled Chinese dialect, it was clear that Wu Chien fell upon Kirton's mercy, for he was on his knees and bowed to the lord of the ship. Insofar as he himself was concerned, Kirton preferred the choice the steward had made. He did not wish for *The Straits Times* to carry a court report of trouble aboard his brigantine and he would be unhappy to release the man to what little he understood of Sharia Law as administered in Sulu. On the other hand he was not certain if such a conclusion would satisfy the victim of Wu Chien's lust.

Turning to Ching he asked, 'Have you explained to the Rungus woman what is going on?' Ching inclined his head in the affirmative.

'Very well. You will remain in shackles until we reach Singapore, Wu Chien. Then you will be dismissed from my ship. The house of Lee and Rodham, which you remember as that of the Green Dragon, will not employ you again, ever. By your conduct you have dishonoured your ancestors and brought shame upon yourself. You go from my presence as under a dark cloud and I am sorry for it. Have you anything to say?'

Wu Chien shook his head. 'Then I dismiss the case.' Kirton banged the deck with his cane and brought the proceedings to an end. Five minutes later the shout came that cargo was completed and that dinner was served.

On the run to Singapore the woman was established as saloon steward and, or so it seemed to Kirton, no-one gave the matter further thought. Wu Chien eked out the last of his time in utter humiliation and could not wait to get clear of the ship and disappear. But on the evening they dropped anchor in the road off Tanjong Pagar Jones came aft to speak with Kirton, requesting a personal interview.

'What is it Vikram?'

'Sir, please take the woman as your *nyai*. If you do not I fear someone else will act foolishly. Besides, she is much in love with you . . .'

'How the devil d'you know that?' asked Kirton in utter astonishment.

Jones laughed, rolling his head, then struck off the reasons on his fingers. 'One, sir, I am a married man and understand something of the ways of women. Two, you are very young, sir, and need a woman if only to relieve us of any anxieties as to the otherwise.' Here he paused to let the implication take effect; then he resumed: 'Three, the whole crew expect you to do this and know that it is right for the *Tuan* to have company in bed. Four, she is devoted to you, you saved her life twice! What else must convince you?'

'But I cannot speak her language, I do not even know her name . . . why she could barely master a cross when she signed-on . . .'

'Give her a name of your own, sir,' remonstrated a somewhat exasperated Jones, whose pragmatism seemed to tear through the fog of Kirton's confused emotions like a shot through gun-smoke.

'You sound as if you have this planned,' he managed to say after a moment.

'No, no, not me, sir,' Jones responded laughing, 'it is in the stars, the gods ordained it, it is written, it is Fate . . .' He threw off this evidence as though it was entirely reasonable. 'You admit that she is beautiful and very pleasing to the eye, eh?'

'Well yes.'

'Then what are you waiting for?'

'But my leg, Vikram. Look at the bloody thing. It gets worse by the month . . .'

'Ah so. It is that which holds you back is it? Well, that is no reason. In her eyes you have acquired an honourable wound.'

'How do you know that?'

'Because old Ching tells me things he does not tell you. He did not explain the three options to her, he merely said that the Tuan was lord of the ship and that he was a fair administer of justice and that his sentence would lay her attacker under a deep shame worse than death itself.'

'Good God!' Kirton was shocked, but a moment's reflection showed the wisdom of the old Confucian *chin-chew*.

'I leave the matter with you, sir. But if you decide you cannot bring yourself to, er, how shall I put it? take advantage of your good fortune, then we must seek some way of finding the woman employment ashore, perhaps in the household of Mr Rodham before she causes more trouble aboard.' Jones rose and smiled. 'I think that I have heard Ching call her something like "Sharimah," sir, if that helps.'

Kirton watched him go, his thoughts in a whirl; suddenly he could not imagine the *Tethys* without the Rungus woman.

Chapter Eleven

Sharimah

The ending—at least as far as Kirton was concerned—of the woman's anonymity seemed to present him with a further milestone in his life. During the *Tethys*'s routine sojourn in Singapore he felt that he ought not to sleep aboard, because with most of the officers enjoying the joys of family life, Kirton and the woman he now called Sharimah were almost alone in the officers' quarters, sharing it with the duty *jaga*. That first night they anchored after the discharge of Wu Chien he lay unsleeping in his bunk, mulling over what Jones had said. Deep in his heart Kirton was a romantic; his experience of women, though limited, was not negligible. The little adventure in Yokohama that had got him into hot water aboard the *River Tay* was no casual affair. The girl, Mitsuko, had been making herself available to Kirton ever since he first called at that port and bought her a drink in a house of pleasure on a previous voyage. But though he tumbled onto the *tatami* matting readily enough, neither he nor Mitsuko thought there was anything other than carnal pleasure in their encounters, though the false notion of having his 'Geisha' appealed to his inherent gallantry.

The appeal of Sharimah was something quite different and in the wake of Jones's words he realised that he had been smitten from the moment that he first set eyes upon her, and that his personal denial was a complex matter of a natural reticence and a strange respect for the young woman whose natural grace had beguiled him from that instant. That she displayed spirit and fortitude and had declared her intention of staying aboard the *Tethys* seemed to somehow weave its way into the mythology of the little brigantine's lotus-eating existence among the islands. For the first time Kirton realised that from the moment that she had come on board she had to remain, that she had at the very least to be part of his existence as he lived out his otherwise lonely life commanding his beautiful little ship.

But if the woman felt spurned by notions of the white man's disdain, Kirton did not wish to use the power that had seen Wu Chien lose his livelihood to bring the Rungus woman to a state of submission; that, he felt, would have been improper, marking him as a scoundrel of the worst type. Since taking command of the *Tethys* under the name of the House of the Green Dragon Kirton knew that he had compromised his position in white society. Although he had not quite 'gone native' in the eyes of some in Singapore, in that of others he as good as had. And although taking a *nyai* was perfectly acceptable among the white population, Kirton was strangely reluctant to rush into such a union, inhibited by the difficulties he knew attended a real intimacy with someone whose name was half guessed, whose age uncertain, and with whom he had hardly a word in common. Besides there was the problem of his leg; he was a cripple and there was no gainsaying the fact.

Rising the following morning he resolved to remove himself that evening to the hotel that he had used during the week he sat for master, but when the other officers went ashore to their homes and the prospect of leaving the *Tethys* solely in the hands of the duty *jaga* along with the woman impacted upon him, he dithered, procrastinated, and put his departure off until the following evening. Instead he ordered dinner alone in the saloon, only to find that it was the woman, Sharimah, who brought in a tureen of soup.

'Soup, *Tuan*,' she said simply, bobbing a sort of curtsy before withdrawing into the pantry. The 'soup' was a fish stew that he had never tasted before, and when he had finished his second helping the woman appeared without his summoning her and, without thinking, he asked, 'Where is Ah Chuan?'

'Ah Chuan, go shore-side,' she said as though picking her words carefully. Then she placed her hand on her breast and said carefully, 'Tonight I serve you.'

Kirton stared at her and she smiled. He seemed about to speak to her. '*Tuan?*'

'Who teach you speak English?'

She smiled again but the question must have baffled her. Kirton launched himself into a complicated mime show which did little to answer his questions, though it made her laugh and she cut across his gesticulations by putting her hand on her breast again and saying, 'Me velly happy, *Tuan* . . .'

'Very happy,' he said in an attempt to rid her of the Chinese failure to enunciate the letter 'r'. She caught the difference quickly then asked, 'More chow-chow now?'

Kirton nodded, kicking out Jones's vacant chair so that when the woman returned with his *pilau* of rice, he commanded her—with appropriate gestures—to 'sit down here.'

She complied, and between mouthfuls of rice he pointed round the saloon to various articles of furniture, the port-holes and the door to the companionway, giving each its proper name. She repeated each in turn and then, having exhausted these, he made two fingers of his right hand walk across the table-cloth. 'Walk,' he said, whereupon she looked puzzled and imitated him.

'No, no,' he said grinning and dragging himself to his feet to limp across the beam of the ship. 'I . . . walk . . .' then he returned to his chair and stood behind it. 'I stand . . . now I sit down.'

She clapped her hands and repeated his actions and his words. After about half an hour of this delightful tomfoolery Kirton declared: '*Bagus!*' Rising from the table she astonished him by saying: 'Now you stand up.'

'Yes, Sharimah,' he said, delighted. 'Now I go on deck . . .' he pointed towards the companionway ladder, 'You bring me coffee and two cups . . . *two* cups, you savee?' He held up two fingers.

'Yes, *Tuan.*'

By the time she arrived with the coffee he had arranged a pair of deck-chairs side by side facing aft and looking astern, out over the twinkling lights of the anchorage and the Esplanade as *Tethys* swung gently to the conflicting influences of the wind and tide.

'Now,' he said, indicating the second deck-chair and lighting his cigar, 'you sit and we shall learn some more words.' It rapidly became clear that Ah Chuan had been busy teaching her a good deal more than she had at first admitted to knowing. Inhibited by natural shyness at so close and unusual an encounter with the *Tuan*, it took a while for her to relax in circumstances that were utterly alien to her, the more so when *he* poured *her* a cup of coffee and handed it to her.

Kirton did not return to the hotel the following evening or any other evening. He spent almost all his time teaching Sharimah English, or at least a heavily English-biased version of pidgin, finding in her a ready and willing learner. The duty *jaga* duly reported the captain's antics as he frequently rose to his feet to act out some little scene of his own imagining to explain some phrase to her, and by the time the *Tethys* was discharged and had taken on her next lading of outbound goods, Sharimah was sharing his bed.

———

'So,' said Rodham mischievously on the eve of the *Tethys*'s next sailing, 'what are you going to do with this *nyai* of yours, Hal?'

'Do with her? She isn't a bag of copra Kit,' Kirton snapped back, irritated by the younger man's cool presumption. 'Anyway I would have thought the situation vis-à-vis Sharimah and myself is pretty obvious.'

They were sitting on the veranda of Rodham's house not far from Mount Faber. It was a small but rather lovely bungalow with a view over the western approaches to Singapore with distant shipping darkening forms against the approaching glory of a flaming sunset. The still air was full of the noise of cicadas and the scent of a myriad of flowers. Rodham offered Kirton a cigar. 'This used to be your only vice,' he chuckled. 'They're best Deli leaf.'

'Thank you.' Kirton helped himself, got out his knife, pared the rounded end, twirling it appreciatively alongside his ear, set a Vesta to it. 'Vee-Jay would love one of these,' he remarked inconsequentially.

After blowing the first blue cloud into the evening air, Rodham remarked, 'So, at the end of next voyage we will close the sale of *Tethys*. That should give you a good deal of satisfaction but, Hal, I'm determined to move into steam. Small at first, hundred, hundred-and-fifty tonners to start with but we can move *ulu*, upstream in so many rivers, doubling our trading hinterland. There may not be much for the *Tethys* to lift, so unless you come over into a steamer alongside Vee-Jay . . .'

'No, Kit, you well know my mind on this. There will still be trade for the *Tethys*, even if it lies further east.'

'Well, you won't get anything from the Philippines; your name is mud in Manila . . .'

'You know that for a fact?'

'Oh, yes,' Rodham said emphatically. 'We have a trading partner in Zamboanga and one consequence of your encounter with that bloody gun-boat is that it has cost us a good deal in *cumshaw* to maintain friendly relations with them. They ship us quite a bit of stuff, mostly in their own bottoms . . .'

'I wasn't thinking of the Philippines,' Kirton said, 'I was looking further south-east at the old East India Company's anchorages of Port Dorey and Geelvinck Bay.'

'That's a long way from home.'

Kirton shrugged. 'The *Tethys* is my home,' he said simply.

Rodham stared at him curiously. 'You know when I sailed with you I never really thought of you as a romantic, but now that our positions and our perspectives have shifted I do see what they say about you.'

'What the hell d'you mean by that? Who is saying I am a romantic? I hardly ever speak to another white-man beyond the demands and business of the ship . . .'

'Old Vee-Jay comes over for dinner occasionally while he's on leave, brings his wife; lovely woman, just like my Suki . . .'

This last remark was addressed to the young woman who approached them with two glasses on a small silver tray, placing one down in front of Kirton as he struggled to get to his feet.

'Please, Captain Kirton,' she said, her voice smooth, 'do not trouble yourself.'

'You are most kind, Mrs Rodham.'

'Suki, please.' She had something of her father's smile, though there was more angularity in her features compared to old Cha's moon-face.

She was undoubtedly a beauty, Kirton thought, and Hal Rodham a lucky man.

'Thank you.' He felt large and lumbering, with his crippled leg and his ungainly attempt to slip easily to his feet, but Suki had turned away and was setting the second glass beside her husband. She smiled and he reached out and touched her outstretched arm. Kirton heard her say in a low voice. 'Do not be too late, darling.'

'Where were we?' Rodham asked as his wife glided away in her soft slippers and the sussuration of her silk robe. It was dark now and the cicadas were falling silent, so that the night was pierced by the occasional and curious call of the nightjar. 'Oh yes, old Vee-Jay considers you a true romantic.' Rodham chuckled. 'He's a curious cove; full of book-learning, apparently thanks to some school near Calcutta. More English than many Englishmen ... I should like to make him master in his own right.'

'Why don't you do that? I think that he's more than half expecting it and might, if offered a chance elsewhere, leave your service and grab the first command that offered. He seems to suffer from some sense of being second-class and not worthy, though I suppose that's inevitable watching the antics of some of our cloth hereabouts.'

'Oh, buggers like McClure, you mean?'

'Him and others. McClure's the only man I know who can make the words "command of a country-*wallah*," sound like something only a little elevated above a rickshaw boy.'

'I expect he'd be horrified by your present establishment.'

Kirton harrumphed. 'Thank God I don't have to associate with his likes any more ...'

'You have gone native.'

'Well, that's what romantics do, isn't it? Anyway, how did Vee-Jay come to his conclusion respecting myself?'

'To be candid, I forget,' Rodham said, grinding out the stub of his cigar, 'but he marked your card all right.'

Kirton abandoned the subject and took a second sip of the whisky. Suki had made it far too strong for his puritan taste and he gave an involuntary shudder.

Rodham did not notice as he changed the subject. 'About the Spaniards, Hal.' His voice was uncharacteristically serious. 'There is a rumour that they are preparing a military expedition to work their way down the Sulu archipelago and annex the territory, leaving the sultan a puppet. That is something you may need to keep an eye out for. Until we get our steamers and you get to Port Dorey we have great need of you and your brigantine.'

'Well, thanks for the warning.' Kirton said, surreptitiously emptying his whisky glass onto the decking of the veranda. He made as though to toss the contents off and hove himself to his feet.

'How's the leg?'

'Bearable until the bloody rains come,' Kirton replied curtly.

'I'm sorry for you . . .'

Kirton shrugged. 'Others have bigger crosses to bear,' he responded philosophically. 'I must get back to the ship. Many thanks for the dinner, I greatly enjoyed my evening.'

'Next time bring your *nyai*; the cutlery won't embarrass her and I hear her English is pretty good.'

'Thank you,' Kirton said with genuine pleasure.

'Suki would like it . . .'

'Really?' Kirton was not so sure. Suki was a cultured Chinese lady and Sharimah remained a Rungus woman, an aboriginal in the eyes of most Chinese, even those of the rickshaw boys on Collyer Quay.

'Well have a good voyage.' Rodham got to his feet and shook his friend's hand. 'I'll call for a . . .'

'No, no, it's a lovely night for a walk.'

'As you wish,' said Rodham, watching his former commander limp off, leaning on his stick, hiding his disability under the cloak of the tropical darkness.

For some seven months the collective life of the *Tethys* ran smoothly alongside the expansion of Lee, Rodham & Co. Rumours that Captain Kirton's payment for the purchase of the brigantine had been remitted to Glasgow for the laying down of two small inter-island steamers proved true. For the *Tethys* and her close-knit little ship's company, their captain's adoption of the lovely Rungus woman resolved any problem that having a single female on board might otherwise have provoked. They approved of the liaison; not only was it expected of the white *Tuan*, but it settled a strange air of contentment over the brigantine, besides giving the *Tethys* a certain *cachet* among the gossiping observers along the Esplanade at Tanjong Pagar.

The only man who might have found it an imposition was Ah Chuan, Kirton's tiger and the lord of the ship's personal servant. But Kirton, being the man he was, and sensitive to the potential loss of face Ah Chuan might have suffered from any sense of displacement—public or private—was shrewd enough to compensate him. In the first place Kirton made it gently but firmly clear to Sharimah that while she might occupy his bed, she was never to give orders to Ah Chuan or act with presumption in regard to any other member of the ship's company, whatsoever their rank. Hers was unequivocally that of saloon stewardess. In this she appeared utterly content, her simple ambitions being to serve her lord who continued to feed her mind by a constant teaching of English.

As for Ah Chuan himself, Kirton promoted him to purser, increased his pay, and, since the *Tethys* now had two vacant cabins under the poop, gave him the job of finding more and regular passengers requiring passage to the destinations from which the brigantine had made her regular run. Ah Chuan was allowed all profits from this aspect of the vessel's voyaging, less 10 per cent which was remitted to an account from which annual good-conduct money was paid to every member of the crew at the Christian *Tuan's* Christmas-time.

By these measures the *Tethys* acquired a reputation along the waterfront the chief component of which was that her master was quite mad. In those years, on the eve of the coming of rubber production throughout the Straits Settlements, the Lion City was continuing its marvellous expansion, an ever-more brilliant jewel in the British crown, open to trade, a polyglot city of several races and faiths whose socio-religious diversity was so complex and integrated that they only rarely spilled over into violence. Of course, when diversity became division the disorder was rapidly and heartlessly crushed by the authorities, but the reputation of the rule of British colonial law when compared to that of the neighbouring Dutch served to maintain a peace under which money might be made in a port free of restrictions.

Nevertheless, howsoever rosy the picture might be painted generally, nor—specifically—how the reputation of the old-fashioned brigantine might be regarded along the waterfront (and there were plenty who regarded her as an anachronism despite her ability to turn over a steady if modest profit), the upper echelons of British colonial rule watched her with a suspicious curiosity. It had long been recognised that her master was a maverick and there were hints that his persistence in flying the Suluese ensign had a far deeper significance than mere commercial expediency born out of a past that related directly to her commander's gammy leg. 'Captain' Kirton—he was afforded the rank with a distinct air of disdain—was well known for nearly having caused a war with Imperial Spain. As time passed the simple details of this were forgotten, or embellished, and associated with other rumours hinting at his indiscriminate use of firearms. There were those among the British hegemons who considered his Sikh *jagas* to be a necessary body-guard and that his limp was the result of some unknown skirmish in the riverine jungles of Borneo or Kalimantan. He was rumoured—particularly among the *mems* who appreciated his good-looks—to have been richly rewarded for unspecified 'services' to His Highness Sultan Jamal ul-Azam, even given the rank of Datu. That was impossible, others scoffed, but all agreed that he was an *orang kaya*—a rich man.

Among the British Establishment there were many who, when they thought about it, had a growing feeling that Kirton was letting the side down by going native. Perhaps it was only to be expected of a British merchant seaman, they opined, who had forfeited the glories of a proper shipping line. It was, of course, puzzling that he did not drink to excess, this being the chief characteristic of the waterfront wastrels and feckless seafarers which circumstances had cast up in Keppel Harbour for one reason or another. But Kirton's long association with what had once been the House of the Green Dragon spoke volumes; he was probably an addict to opium as that old Chinese devil Cha Lee Foo had been. As for the inter-racial familiarity that was well-known to be the way this madman ran his ship—well that was down-right dangerous.

Others pointed to his *nyai*, whom it was said, was a common Rungus woman he had carried off a beach 'somewhere to the east' in some sort of piratical raid. She was indisputably beautiful but nothing but a fisherman's daughter, and the manner of her acquisition gained her the cognomen of the 'Ruckus' woman by the wits over their gin-slings and whisky *stengahs*. Others, usually lower down the social scale of colonial society, affirmed that she was a Suluese princess, that she had been seen on her occasional visits ashore, dressed sumptuously and with a huge Suluese pearl at her throat.

Rumour and conjecture swirled wildly about the *Tethys* and her commander who was himself largely oblivious to most of it beyond a vague notion that there were places he would not be welcome. Happily the remarks of Nurse Trimm and others in the British Military Hospital all those years earlier had cast him loose from the conventions of colonial life. Kirton had no desire to belong to a club and had taken his chief pleasure outside the matter of running the *Tethys* in first preparing for his examination as master-mariner and afterwards in acquiring books from London, ordered through his sister with whom he corresponded increasingly diligently, anxious about the progress of his distant nephew.

Despite the contentment on board the brigantine, it was against this background mixture of disapproval, misunderstanding, envy, and unsatisfied curiosity that Kirton, the *Tethys*, and her ship's company now plied their trade.

Chapter Twelve

Teniente Espina

'*Tuan! Tuan!* Wake-up, *Tuan!*'

Kirton eased himself out of the bunk, trying not to disturb Sharimah, but it was impossible to ignore the thundering on the cabin door and she stirred beside him. Re-tucking his *sarong*, Kirton limped to the door and opened it. He was confronted by a wild-eyed Pritam Singh.

'Are we dragging our anchor. . . ?'

'No, *Tuan*, but there are many Spanish men-of-war offshore!'

'God damn! Call all hands!'

Dressing quickly Kirton reached the deck, picking up the long glass as he emerged on deck. The *Tethys* lay off the little township of Jolo with just over half of her homeward lading taken up from the place, but instinct told him not to await the remainder. The sudden appearance of a number of Spanish men-of-war was not something that would encourage trade. It was only just growing light and he cast about the seaward horizon for a sight of what had alarmed Pritam Singh.

It did not take him long to see the Spanish squadron, lying at anchor beyond Pulo Tulian. They must have arrived after sunset last night, he thought, for they were well offshore and that distance and the arrival of the morning's sea-breeze offered him the only chance of escaping their attention.

By now the ship was seething with activity as Kirton told Jones to heave short and Tan to cast off the sails in their gear ready to hoist.

'Hoist boat, *Tuan?*' Tan asked suggestively.

'Yes!'

Kirton hobbled forward to see how Jones's fo'c'sle party were getting on with the anchor cable.

'There are thirteen of them, sir,' Jones said nervously, straightening up from the rail over which he had been leaning to count the white-painted shackles as they came out of the water. 'Is this wise, sir?'

'What? To get out before the Spanish seize us? Surely it's our only option; God knows what those bastards intend but it won't be to the advantage of the state of Sulu, I'll lay money on that . . .' Jones seemed unconvinced and merely grunted. 'Come on, Vikram,' Kirton said encouragingly, 'd'you want to see your wife in Singapore as usual or what?'

'There's no wind,' Jones said, the exasperation clear in his voice.

'There will be,' said Kirton, more in hope than anger and, turning aft, offering up a prayer that the Fates would prove him right.

By the time Kirton returned to the poop he found Sharimah had a pot of coffee on the coach-roof, Tan was shouting '*arriah!*', and the boat was being lowered onto its chocks. From forward Jones now called that the cable was 'up and down,' awaiting only Kirton's order to break the anchor out of its muddy bed, but there was no wind.

Kirton stared to seaward. There was no change in the aspect of the Spaniards, no smoke betraying a flashing-up of boilers. He wondered on what standing-orders their naval officers worked, and whether or not they had noticed the green-hulled brigantine lying close inshore, and if so, whether they knew her identity? Was the corvette that had previously attempted to bring the *Tethys* to, part of the squadron? It seemed impossible that she was not.

Not a breath of moving air stirred the surface of the water. He gratefully took the cup of coffee Sharimah held out to him. Perhaps he should have left the boat in the water to kedge the *Tethys* down the coast to Bwansa, an anchorage about three miles from Jolo itself, but dismissed the idea; the very movement might attract the attention of the Spanish. Instead he called Jones aft and handed the ship over to him.

'*Saya pergi makan,*' he said with a feigned aplomb, using the Malay. 'Keep everything ready and send the port watch to breakfast as soon as the cook's ready. Oh, and get the ensign bent on the flag halliards.'

'The British one, sir?' Jones asked archly.

'No, the sultan's,' Kirton replied shortly.

And with that he went below and called for something to eat, for he was suddenly very hungry. Sharimah brought him half a papaya and some slices of cold dolphin meat from a fine specimen they had caught the day before.

But he had hardly finished this before an extremely anxious Jones appeared in the saloon. 'They've seen us, sir. They're sending a boat . . .'

'How far off?'

'A mile or so.'

'Time to finish *makanan*,' Kirton said nonchalantly, almost amused at the consternation on Jones's face.

'She's a steam-launch, sir.'

'Very well. I'll be up in a moment.'

Kirton tarried as long as his nerves allowed him to and was privately shocked when he reached the deck to find a Spanish officer shouting for a ladder to be lowered over the side. Tan was looking aft for orders. Kirton nodded. He did not like the look of the small gun mounted on the picket-boat's bow. It was manned and its muzzle traversed the length of the *Tethys*.

Kirton leant on the binnacle and lit a cigar as the Spaniard came aft, led by Tan and followed by a second Spaniard, a midshipman by the look of him.

'*Buenas dias, señor*,' Kirton said. 'I hope you speak English. I have exhausted my Spanish . . .'

'Indeed Captain Kirton, I do. I am Teniente—Lieutenant—Miguel Espina of the Spanish Navy,' the young man announced, 'and I am charged by my commodore to search your vessel for contraband.'

'And what contraband could I possibly be carrying, Lieutenant?'

'Guns, perhaps . . .'

'The only guns I have on board are those breech-loaders,' Kirton pointed at the elderly brass cannon at the hances, 'a handful of rifles borne by my *jagas*, a shotgun for shooting wild-fowl and a Colt revolver. These all either belong to the ship or to me personally.'

'Nevertheless I shall require you to open your hatch even though I see you have made preparations to sail. That has nothing to do with our arrival I presume?'

'You speak excellent English, Lieutenant,' Kirton hedged.

'Thank you. I spent some time on the River Tyne where our corvettes were built; you may have noticed the excellent Armstrong gun on my launch. Now please give orders to open your hatch.'

Kirton passed word for the corner of the hatch to be opened up, summoning Jones to go below with a lantern 'and afford our visitors every courtesy.'

Espina rapped out a few words to the midshipman, whose name seemed to be Bustamente. He went with Jones while Espina made a second request for the ship's papers.

The sun was up now burning the low mists off the land which rose behind Jolo town, but the sea remained smooth as silk. He would have to play for time.

'Pray come below, Lieutenant . . .'

Kirton led the way and ensconced the Spanish officer at the saloon table where he offered him coffee. At first Espina was disposed to refuse but at the appearance of Sharimah in the pantry doorway he changed his mind and Kirton withdrew to his cabin to bring the log of the brigantine, calling for Ching to produce the cargo-manifests.

Having laid the papers before the Spaniard, Kirton took a surreptitious look up the companionway. He had pushed the sliding cover fully open and could clearly see the ensign at the peak of the gaff. There it hung, lifeless, indistinguishable from a rag.

Suddenly Tan's face blocked out Kirton's view; he was about to speak when Kirton, taking a cigar from the case he kept in his pocket, asked conversationally 'How's the mate getting on in the hold?'

'Velly well, *Tuan*, you wantchee me. . . ?' Kirton put a finger to his lips then pointed upwards, blowing a plume of cigar smoke vertically so that Tan withdrew his head and stared aloft. As the blue smoke rose above the companionway it began to drift away to port. Higher up the fly of the ensign lifted, then fell. Kirton swore beneath his breath. He turned to look into the saloon. Espina was still scrutinising the manifest which old Ching had laid before him. Kirton caught Sharimah's eye and made a gesture indicating he wished Espina's coffee-cup to be refilled. She smiled and nodded.

Then he turned back to Tan, but Tan was unceremoniously pushed to one side as the Spanish midshipman descended the companionway to make his report. Kirton drew aside and, as the officious young man entered the saloon, blocking Espina's view of himself, Kirton hauled himself half-way up the companionway.

With his head just above the sliding hatch he stared about him; there was the slightest whisper in the air. He again looked aloft. The ensign was lifting, unmistakably lifting; he stared about him once more and noticed to seaward, one of the corvettes, presumably that from which Lieutenant Espina had come, was under way, a cloud of black smoke pouring from her funnel. He made up his mind.

Beckoning Tan to his side he said quietly: 'Masthead the fore-topsail, let fall the course and get the fore-topmast staysail and jib hoisted.'

'Yes, *Tuan*.'

'And while you're forrard, break out the anchor.' Kirton turned to the *jurmudi* waiting by the wheel. 'Stand by the outhauls ...'

Just then Jones came along the deck, having resecured the hatch. 'Let the spanker brails go, Vikram. Get the ship under way chop-chop.'

Jones was about to remonstrate, but Kirton had withdrawn his head and retreated to the saloon where he made a great show of affability, asking if Espina had had enough coffee and if the ship's papers satisfied him. It was coolly done, but as soon as the Spanish crew of the picket-boat bobbing alongside realised that the brigantine was getting under way, they shouted with alarm. It took a moment before a red-faced Espina forced his way past Kirton and ran up on deck.

'What are you doing?' he asked furiously as Kirton hauled himself out after the Spaniard, still smoking his cigar.

'Getting under way, Lieutenant. Now that you have seen my ship's papers and the manifest I cannot waste time with a fair wind,' Kirton dissembled.

'But you have not finished loading your cargo.'

'I've shut it out, Lieutenant, a master's prerogative and ...'

'But I'm detaining your vessel . . .'

'You have no authority to do so, sir,' snapped Kirton. 'I am within the territorial waters of His Highness . . .'

'The port of Jolo is under full blockade, Captain, and a declaration to that effect is on its way ashore this morning. You will please come to an anchor again.'

Beneath his feet, Kirton felt the *Tethys* stir as above his head the sails caught the zephyr and the brigantine gathered way. He uttered another private prayer and said, 'I think it is time you left my vessel, Lieutenant. It has been a pleasure meeting you . . .'

But Espina was staring past Kirton, his eyes suddenly round with astonishment. Kirton turned to see Pritam Singh lining his *jagas* up; each carried his rifle and a bandolier.

'Captain Kirton, how *dare* you!' objected a furious Espina.

'For inspection, *Tuan*,' Pritam Singh explained, ordering his men to present their weapons with a smart and very military clickerty-clack. From over the side came more shouts as the *Tethys* gathered a bone between her teeth. She can only have been making three knots, but already she was giving the Spanish picket-boat a rough ride.

'Come sir, we don't want to tow you all the way down to the Balabac Strait, do we? And I have special instructions from Singapore not to get involved with local politics or become a *casus belli* between our two great nations. Let us part like gentlemen . . .'

'May the devil take you, *Capitano*,' Espina spluttered, reverting to his native tongue as he made for the rail, the midshipman following him. Here Espina motioned Bustamente to embark first, then, glaring at Kirton, he followed, pausing only to call out, 'We know you and your ship, Kirton. You are an insolent Englishman and most certainly no gentleman!'

Two minutes later the picket-boat was bobbing in the wake of the brigantine and the corvette was still sufficiently distant to give them a reasonable chance of escape, for she would have to bring-to to recover her launch.

'Give her the topgallant, the gaff-topsail and the main topmast stay-sail,' Kirton ordered, and went aft to stand beside the *jurmudi* at the helm.

'You go topgallant yard, look-see for rocks—*batu*—and reefs . . . I take helm; send Mr Tan aft. We go inshore . . . close . . .'

In response to the *jurmudi*'s instruction, Tan and then Jones joined him.

'Get aloft Tan; Vikram, you go forrard to the knightheads. I'm going as close inshore as I dare. My reckoning is that the Spaniard won't risk his ship.'

Tan was already on his way when Jones remonstrated: 'They are not going to like this, Captain Kirton,' Jones said, his face full of concern. 'We have lost cargo too . . .'

'Damn the cargo; they've declared the coast under blockade. They know we're registered here and can detain us for as long as they like. Now, neither you nor I want that, do we?'

Kirton looked up; the Suluese colours streamed from the gaff and the *Tethys* was bowling along. Was Jones pusillanimous or merely cautious? He had no idea, nor had he time to analyse the state of his chief mate's mind.

'*Batu, Tuan*! One point port bow.'

'Get forrard, Vikram, and see us clear of these dangers!'

Best give the poor fellow something to do than let him worry, Kirton thought; worrying was Kirton's job. He had got away with something like this once, surely he could do so again. He eased the helm and the brigantine came up a little. Tan, God bless him, was signalling from the weather fore-topgallant yard-arm that all was now clear ahead, shouting down to the seamen in the waist in a torrent of Cantonese to trim the braces. The *Tethys* was sailing like a witch, flying along with the increasing of the breeze.

Kirton allowed himself the luxury of looking astern; the corvette was following, a great bone in her teeth, but her course was further out to sea, diverging from that of the brigantine, unwilling to hazard her greater draught in the unfamiliar and reef-strewn waters along the shore. Even as Kirton observed her, she lobbed a shot into the wake of the flying *Tethys* before turning back towards Pulo Tulian and the rest of the squadron above which there now hung a pall of smoke as they raised steam.

Kirton passed a sigh of relief and found that his knees were knock-ing, then he saw Sharimah's face smiling at him from the companionway opening. 'You are a great lord of the sea, Hari,' she said. He smiled back; it beat being a mere gentleman. But then her smile faded; a puzzled expres-sion crossed her lovely face as her gaze fastened astern, not to seaward, but inshore. She pointed. 'Hari . . .' she said, *'perahu, perahu besar . . .'* and Kirton twisted round.

It took him a moment to see the boat, but he recognised it instantly. It was that of the sultan's *shawbunder*, his customs officer and harbour-master, Mohammad bin Yusuf.

'Come Sharimah, take wheel,' he gestured as she leapt on deck.

'Hari, I . . .'

'You know how to do it. I've taught you and you've done it before. Just keep her going as she is. Watch the compass and do not follow the lubber's . . . never mind, just keep her steady like I have told you.'

Handing the helm over Kirton bent into the companionway and picked up the long glass, turned aft, struggled down onto his good knee, and levelled it on the *perahu*. It was the *shawbunder's* all right and the fat old official was standing up in it waving his arms frantically, his crew dipping their paddles with a furious precision that implied tremendous effort. Kirton hauled himself to his feet and looked again at the Spanish corvette. She was already several miles away.

'Let fly the sheets!' he bawled. He could see faces turning aft in dis-belief. 'Let fly the sheets! Chop-chop, d'you hear me!'

Returning the telescope to its nest Kirton cast off the spanker sheet, then took the helm from Sharimah. He met the brigantine as she rounded-to in a thrashing of ropes and thunder of canvas, every spar in her shaking.

'Stand-by to heave taught again!' he roared above the din. 'Mr Jones! Mr Tan! Any dangers close by?'

'No sir,' came from the knightheads.

'Not close, sir,' from aloft where Tan and the *jurmudi* clung on for their lives as they worked their way off the yard-arms in towards the foremast.

'Lay aft, both of you!' Kirton shouted. 'Leave the *jurmudi* aloft!'

'When the two mates reached the poop Kirton ordered them to brail up the spanker between them, then, explaining that a *perahu* was chasing them and he intended to find out why, he handed the helm over to Tan with an apology. 'I didn't mean to shake you off the yard, Tan.'

Tan grinned, his high and ruddy cheekbones red with excitement. 'You not catchee Tan that way, *Tuan*,' he laughed.

Kirton grinned back then turned his attention to the *perahu*. 'Get Ching up here,' he called to Sharimah, who had not left the deck. 'We do not have much time.'

'No sir, we do not; we are making leeway . . .' An anxious Jones was at his elbow, regarding the already dangerous proximity of the coastal shallows upon which they inexorably drove down.

'Give the *perahu* a line once she is alongside and we find out what the *shawbunder* wants, then haul all aft and put her on the other tack while I talk to him.'

'Aye, sir . . .'

'And in the meantime, get that ladder over the port side . . .'

In the next half an hour, after what seemed an age waiting for the near-exhausted Suluese to bring the *perahu* up with them, things happened very fast. The tubby *shawbunder* struggled up the boarding ladder and stood panting on deck for all the world as though it had been he who had laboured at the paddles of his *perahu*.

Kirton, casting a quick glance at the still retreating Spanish corvette, immediately drew the official into conference with his *chin-chew*.

Words tumbled out of the *shawbunder* who, at their conclusion, handed Ching a letter, the superscription of which was in Chinese characters. Ching turned to Kirton and told him that the *shawbunder* was disappointed that they had not stopped to load all the cargo but understood Captain Kirton's desire to escape the Spanish. The Suluese had, Ching reported, known of the approach of the Spanish squadron which had left Zamboanga and stopped off at several of the islands in the Sulu archipelago. He had hoped to see the *Tethys* loaded before their arrival before Jolo.

Kirton nodded, then took a quick look round. Jones had the big *perahu* in tow now and was shouting orders that got the brigantine under command again. As soon as she had gathered way, he ordered the helm over and brought her round onto the port tack, standing out to sea, away from the dangers of the land. Kirton returned his attention to Ching. 'Please go on, Ching.'

Ching resumed his narrative: however, now that Captain Kirton had escaped they wanted him to bring them guns, because the Spaniards meant war and the destruction of the sultan's power. His Highness therefore desired that he returned to Singapore and brought them guns and ammunition as quickly as he could. His ship, so the *shawbunder* said, flew as fast as an eagle and could be back within ten days . . .

Kirton grunted; the expectation was utterly unreal, but he said nothing.

'Sir! The Spaniard is putting about and making sail!' Jones's anxiety was contagious.

Kirton spun round, his bad leg almost tripping him ignominiously. He did not need the long glass to see how the situation had changed. As the *Tethys* stood offshore on the port tack she reduced the distance between herself and the man-of-war and the Spaniard had turned about to resume her pursuit. Now she came at them belching smoke and with a fluttering of canvas along her yards.

'Very well, Ching, tell our guest if he wants guns he will have to pay heavily as it is illegal, but I will see what I can do, though I make no promises . . .'

Datu Mohammad bin Yusuf burst into another speech which was accompanied by some passionate beating of his breast and at the conclusion of which the patient Ching translated. 'He say he leady to fight and die for fleedom, *Tuan*, like all Suluese. He not want to be slave of Spaniard, to be forced to become infidel and worship dead man on cross . . .'

'Yes. Yes, I understand.' Kirton smiled and bowed at the *shawbunder*. 'I come back soon honourable *Datu*,' he said to the official, 'now you go or we will both become prisoners . . .' he pointed to the Spanish corvette which had now set her big topsails and whose single funnel belched a cloud of black smoke that sullied the glory of the morning. 'Now you must go . . . Ching . . .'

Ching translated as Kirton turned away to order Jones to heave-to and bring the *perahu* alongside. It seemed an age before the *shawbunder* had regained his seat in the *perahu* and the craft had let go and swung away. The last Kirton saw of the *shawbunder* he had collapsed upon his cushions and his slaves were fanning him under his large parasol.

Jones already had the *Tethys* coming up into the wind, bringing her back on the starboard tack. 'Sharimah!' Kirton called.

'Hari?'

'Fetch me my sextant, if you please.'

When she handed him the instrument with a strange reverence he turned to the Spaniard and set the angle between the corvette's main truck and her waterline.

'Shall I stream the log, sir?' Jones asked.

'No, this will tell us all we need to know. You and Tan sail the ship as you never have before, Vikram, and I'll keep you in cigars for a month if we get away safely.'

Kirton stood on the long counter, bracing himself against the after end of the steering-box and observed the angle made by the Spaniard. As he slowly turned the index wheel of the sextant he did not need to take the instrument from his eye and read the scale: he could tell the angle was increasing, meaning that the Spaniard was gaining on them.

'Come two points to port, mister,' he called out to the chief mate, 'and trim the braces accordingly . . .'

That should bring the wind further round onto the brigantine's beam, increasing her speed. He returned his attention to the Spaniard. Judging by the great bone in her teeth she was making her best speed. 'Come on *Tethys, come on,*' he muttered lowering the sextant to wipe his eye. Sharimah was by his side.

'Who belong Tethys, Hari?'

'A white man's goddess from the oldest times,' he explained patiently, almost glad of the didactic diversion. 'She was the mother of all the rivers and seas in the world, or so they thought in those days . . .' How much of this explanation Sharimah understood he did not know for he was again focussed on his sextant. The exchange with Sharimah had been long enough to make quite a difference to the two images in the sextant telescope; he adjusted them and suddenly realised he was turning the index wheel in the other direction.

Kirton bit his lip, eager to inform them all that they were losing their tormentor, but cautious not to raise hopes too soon. He stood, in a lather of anxiety, feeling the brigantine heel over. He took another observation, then another. There was no doubt about it, unless the wind suddenly failed . . .

Then he saw what he had hoped for: The Spaniard turned away for the second time. He was not the only one to observe the change. A ragged cheer went up from the deck and Kirton swung round, a grim smile cracking his features. Jones was striding towards him, his hand outstretched.

'Well done, sir,' he said.

'Well done you,' Kirton responded crisply. 'Now I think you may stream the log . . .'

Relief flooded Kirton's body with adrenaline and he swallowed hard. It had been a close run thing, by heaven!

'*Tuan?*' he turned to find Ching at his elbow. At sea Ching rarely appeared on deck, though to be sure this was an exceptional forenoon, good enough to break any habit, but Ching, being the diligent man he was, had the letter brought out by the *shawbunder* open in his hand. 'You must know what this speaks.'

'Tell me,' Kirton said brusquely.

'It is from our agent in Jolo, *Tuan*,' Ching reported, referring to old Cha's nephew, Ban Guan, who still managed the business affairs of Lee, Rodham & Co. in Jolo. 'It belong letter, many compliments to you, *Tuan*, but he ask for guns; rifles, many rifles and as soon as possible. He say he can fix a good plice, maybe even gold . . .'

'Huh,' grunted Kirton, 'but does he offer any advice as to how we can actually land any contraband like that? Or where? I mean those steam-boiler Spanish men-of-war will prevent any chance to trade at Jolo . . .'

'Yes, *Tuan*, he suggests we go seclet place to unload . . .' Ching referred to the letter. 'He say there is place among the islands he can send many *perahu* to . . . there is drawing . . . He say more things too.'

Kirton took a look at the sketch-map Cha's nephew had drawn.

'He say he up all night,' Ching went on, 'velly much worry, try and make best drawing-chart for Captain Kirton.'

Kirton shook his head. 'I'm not sure I understand this, Ching. Come below to chart-room. Let us make puzzle work for us, eh?'

CHAPTER THIRTEEN

Captain Kirton's Dilemma

'GUNS? BUT WHERE?' RODHAM TURNED TO LEE. 'D'YOU KNOW ANY-thing about this?'

Lee shook his head and Rodham swung back to Kirton. 'We don't know what Ching is talking about,' he said conclusively.

'I should have brought him with me, but he has ship's business to attend to. Anyway, I'm not certain if Ching knows about it first-hand, or was simply translating what Bam Guan had to say in his letter.'

They were in what had been old Cha's private quarters, which were now not only the official offices of Lee, Rodham & Co, but those of the Eastern Steam-ship Company, as yet something of a conceit, but with two small steamers on the stocks in distant Port Glasgow.

'Well we need to know before committing ourselves to such a rash act as gun-running, for God's sake,' said Rodham. He seemed to have grown much older of late, Kirton thought wryly. Gone was his former frivolity; Kit Rodham was now a serious business-man. As if reading his thoughts Rodham went on.

'In fact, Hal, if we do find anything in this, we may have to detach the name of our house right out of it and leave the enterprise entirely to you,' he said, running his hand through his hair and drawing attention to the fact that this was thinning. 'Of course, if we find out—and I don't quite know how we can now—if all this is true, we'd have to sell them to you first . . .'

Kirton was about to remonstrate when Lee suddenly interjected. 'Wait! I think I know som'ting . . . Long time ago . . . I get ledger . . .'

Lee hurried from the room and Rodham and Kirton exchanged glances; Rodham shrugged his shoulders. 'D'you think . . . ?' Rodham began, leaving the sentence unfinished.

'The old *towkay* was capable of anything,' Kirton remarked ruefully. 'The Chinese plan long-term . . .' He too left his words hanging in the air.

Rodham clapped his hands and when the serving-girl came in he asked for '*chai*, chop-chop.'

After a long silence and in the failure of Lee to reappear, Rodham said with a doubtful shake of his head, 'Even if there was once a cache somewhere, I can't see it still existing now . . .' He shook his head. 'I mean what could the old devil have been up to?'

'I've no idea . . .'

At this point Lee rejoined them waving a small file. 'I find this in the old safe, right at bottom.' He laid an ancient-looking cardboard folder on the low table in front of them. The securing tapes were already loose and he flicked it open. It contained only a few sheets of yellowing paper but, even though it was Rodham who turned the papers over, and Kirton viewed them upside down, it was Kirton who enunciated the words that were embossed across the top: 'The Spencer Repeating Rifle Company, Boston, Massachusetts!'

'Stone the bloody crows,' breathed Rodham, almost reverentially. 'One thousand repeating rifles and fifty thousand rounds of ammunition . . .' Rodham flicked over to the second sheet, which appeared to be a receipt. 'That's enough for a whole bloody regiment, but where the hell are they? There's no indication here . . .' Rodham laid the pages down and opened both hands in a gesture suggesting he ought to have been holding this consignment of arms in their palms. 'Any ideas, Lee?'

Lee frowned, looking lost in contemplation, then a slow smile passed across his face. 'I lemember one time, long time gone, when he build this honourable house, the Honourable Cha saying to me "good godown meant for plosperous business always need gold in loof".'

'What the hell does that mean?' Rodham asked sharply.

Silently Lee pointed upwards.

'Good God! You mean we're sitting underneath it . . . ? All these years . . . ?'

Kirton was laughing.

'What's so amusing?'

'I don't know,' Kirton responded, 'but you're going to find it difficult to play Pontius Pilate now, since the stuff will have to come out of your godown!'

'What on earth . . . ? I mean how . . . ? Well what were they for?' A puzzled Rodham went on, the dark shadow of a rebellion against the British Crown swimming into his imagination.

'What's the date of the invoice?' Kirton asked.

'Eighteen sixty-four,' read Lee, then looking up his eyes brightening with comprehension. 'Ah so, big tlouble in China jus' then; many wars . . . Red Turban . . . Panthay but biggest the Heavenly Kingdom Movement.'

'Was that the Taiping Rebellion?' Kirton asked.

Lee nodded. 'Yes, velly bad man Hong Xiuguan think himself brother of Jes' Chris'. War last longtime, maybe fourteen, fifteen year, not ended until Blitish General Gordon come to help of Empelor Qing.'

'And it ended in 1864. Old man Cha missed the boat!' exclaimed Kirton. 'Got lumbered with a thousand rifles!'

'Well, I'll be jiggered!' added Rodham.

'They were fighting when I came out in the old *Cormorant*,' Kirton said.

The mood of reminiscence must have triggered another memory in the mind of Lee, for he added, 'I think Ching made deal.'

'Well, never mind that Lee, let's go and see what we've got in the attic.'

'Attic?' queried Lee, unfamiliar with the word, whereupon Rodham mimicked Lee's earlier gesture of pointing vertically upwards.

They gained access to the roof-space via a trap-door and a ladder concealed in an adjacent cupboard. Fetching a lamp the three men ascended into the gloom. Here and there a sun-beam shone in slant-wise through the tiles, motes of dust dancing in its slender rays. The roof of the godown covered a large area, criss-crossed by heavy beams of Siamese teak, the scent of which filled the heavy air, and floored by a softer timber more like Borneo *seraya*. At first it seemed empty apart from a few chests of personal and household effects. Idly opening one, Kirton lifted some elegant silk gowns.

'They belong Madame Cha. She die longtime ago,' said Lee, pushing further into the gloom.

'How much room do a thousand rifles take up?' Rodham asked rhetorically.

'Look-see!' Lee called, holding up the lamp to illuminate what lay stacked neatly at the far end of the space, against the gable wall. Lee quickly counted the wooden crates as they were neatly stacked in piles of five. 'One hundled, ten gun in each box . . .'

'And here's the ammunition,' Rodham said almost stumbling over a number of smaller cases. One of these had been broached, presumably to check the contents and in the flickering lamp-light Kirton saw a neat array of small boxes labelled 'Blakeslee Cartridges.' One of these had also been broken open and the three men gathered round. It contained ten tubes each holding seven cartridges, the extent to which the repeating Spencers could be fired without reloading.

'Well, I'll be jiggered,' Rodham said again, shaking his head. 'We've been sitting on a bloody fortune.'

'I think the fortune has been sitting on you, Kit,' Kirton said solemnly reviewing the pile of arms before he asked, 'how the hell are we going to get this lot out to the ship?'

'Are you sure that you want to, gentlemen?' Lee asked. 'Plenty dangerous if Customs find out. Do big damage to our new *Hong*.'

'It's too good an opportunity to miss,' Rodham said decisively. 'Captain Kirton will carry them to Jolo . . .'

'Are you sure about that, Kit?' Kirton said, reining in the younger man's enthusiasm. 'As Lee says it is both dangerous and illegal.'

'Well let's go and discuss it over some *samsu*,' Rodham temporised.

They returned to the floor below and resumed their seats. Shortly after sitting down and when Rodham had summoned the serving girl Ching arrived. Lee rapidly brought him up-to-date with their find, at which the *shroff* looked somewhat peeved that they had made the discovery without his help, but he confirmed that the firearms had indeed been intended to equip the Taiping rebels.

'So, Ching,' pressed Rodham, 'I don't know how you, or whoever it was, got them up in that roof-space, we need to get them down and out to the *Tethys*.'

'Take topside one-by-one, night-time. They come from Amelican ship but have coconut matting all lound. Customs no find out . . .'

'Well we can bung some generous *cumshaw* . . .'

'No, Kit, no bribery. I won't have it. I don't mind having them disguised and declared as hunting guns. We've taken firearms to Sulu before, though not in such numbers, but let us have a degree of propriety in all of this. After all, I shall be taking most of the risk.' Kirton's tone was emphatic.

'More better small truth than big lie, Mister Kit,' Lee said to his partner. 'I aglee with Captain Harry.'

Rodham made a gesture of slightly exasperated acquiescence but asked, 'What do you think, Ching?'

But Ching surprised them all in his reply. 'Ching want no part in this business.' He turned to Kirton. 'Velly sorry Captain Kirton but Ching too old for such game. Go shore-side this voyage; may-be no come back.'

'You're going to retire?' Kirton asked incredulously.

'Maybe, maybe not. I tell you if you come back.'

'*If*, I come back . . . ?' Kirton queried.

'Spanish Admilal not like what you do; perhaps he catch you this time.'

A silence fell on the four men, broken eventually by Rodham. 'Well, Hal, what d'you intend to do about it? Bam Guan's letter said payment could be made largely in gold.'

Kirton rubbed his chin and after a moment replied, 'I'll sleep on it . . . One whiff of this being in support of the sultan and I'm in trouble with Government House, having already been accused of almost starting a Hispano-British War.' With that Kirton rose to go, gathering up his hat and cane when a thought struck him and he paused.

'What is it?' Rodham asked.

'Nothing,' Kirton dissembled. 'I'll see you gentlemen in the morning, at ten o'clock. Good evening.'

'Won't you stay to dinner?' Rodham called after him.

Without turning his head Kirton replied. 'When I get back, if and when I have delivered those illegal guns *you* have over *your* head.' As a Parthian shot it was both well-made and well-timed.

Once on the street outside Kirton, recalling the matter he had thought of a moment or two before, also noted that the evening was well advanced. The sun had set and only a faint crepuscular light gleamed dully in the west. He looked at his watch; he was already late for his own dinner and Sharimah would be worried. His boat's crew would also be wondering about him, for he was normally a model of punctuality. But the matter could not be put off, not if it was to have the effect he most desired. So, instead of ordering the rickshaw boy to take him to Collyer Quay, he peremptorily ordered: 'Government House, chop-chop!'

After some difficulties gaining access to anyone of importance, Kirton was received by a disgruntled secretary unwillingly dislodged from his dinner table. The official's frown deepened when he recognised the man responsible for the disruption to the digestive process, for the limping figure who turned towards him immediately revealed his identity.

'Captain Kirton,' he said, wiping his mouth with the spotlessly white napkin he held in his hand, 'I wish I could say this was a pleasure, but I have guests for dinner and ...'

'Well sir,' Kirton said disingenuously, 'I am acting upon your explicit instructions.'

'How so?'

'You requested and required that I reported any unusual movements of Spanish men-of-war around the Sulu Archipelago. Well, there are a dozen of them and they have placed the Sultanate under blockade. I cannot say for certain, but judging from the appearance of so formidable a force I would say that the viceroy has charged the flag-officer in command with the job of annexation to the Crown of Spain.'

He had the secretary's attention now. 'You think so?'

'I do, sir.'

'Hmm,' the secretary responded ruminatively. 'We had heard something coming out of Manila about the suppression of piracy, but not territorial aggrandisement.'

'Well sir. They chased me again after telling me I was under blockade
. . .'

'You didn't hoist the British flag . . . ?' the secretary asked, suddenly
anxious.

'No sir.'

'Then how . . .'

Kirton shrugged. 'I out-manoeuvred them,' he said simply.

The secretary nodded. 'Well done,' he conceded, albeit reluctantly.

'Then I'll wish you a good evening and hope that I have not spoiled
your dinner.'

Kirton turned on his heel and left, watched by the secretary who was
still digesting the intelligence. 'Curious bugger,' the secretary muttered to
himself before returning to his guests. 'Perhaps he's not such a bad sort
after all.'

That evening Kirton sat alone on the poop of the *Tethys*, his mates
both at their respective homes ashore. He had dined late, very late from
the silent reproach in Sharimah's dark eyes. Even Ah Chuan had allowed
himself a single cluck over food he considered spoiled by his master's
tardiness. Now he sat with his cigar and his *stengah* staring out over the
anchorage but seeing little, his gaze inwards, searching his conscience.

'Is something the matter, Hari?' She came to him silently and, as was
her wont, she knelt at his feet and gazed up at his face.

'I am a little like Hamlet, my lovely, though it is a matter of "to do or
not to do?" rather than "to be or not to be?"' he sighed.

'I not understand.'

'No, of course you don't,' he said, brushing his hand over her sleek hair.
'You tell me?'

He took a deep breath, pitched the cigar overboard and looked at
her. 'Very well. You remember the Spanish ship that chased us off Jolo?'
She nodded. 'Well she and other Spanish ships impose blockade—stop
trade—and I think they mean to take all of Sulu from the sultan, make
it part of the Spanish Empire. No more trade for *Tethys* at Jolo, no
more freedom for your people . . .' She was frowning and he was sure
she did not follow him. The realisation came as a reminder that he was
going to have trouble without Ching, not merely in his more nuanced

conversations with Sharimah, but with everyone he dealt with. 'D'you understand?'

'*Freedom* . . . what it mean?'

Kirton delivered himself of a huge sigh; how could he explain the concept to her? He wracked his brains for the Malay word, then entered into a pantomime such as they had first relied upon to communicate. Crossing his wrists as though they were bound and wriggling in his deck-chair with such vigour that she began to giggle, he announced: 'Not freedom!' Then throwing his arms wide and embracing the air, he cried: 'This freedom!'

She frowned a moment and then seemed to understand, but they were interrupted by the duty Sikh *jaga*.

'*Tuan*, a boat is coming alongside,' the man reported.

'What? At this time of night? Very well, I'll be there in a moment . . .' He made to get up, reaching for his cane, then asked the *jaga*, 'by the way, d'you know the Malay word for "freedom"?'

'Yes, *Tuan*: *merdeka*.'

Kirton turned to Sharimah but he did not have to ask her, she was already on her feet, ready to assist him as he struggled to stand. 'Ahh, *merdeka*, yes I savee, Hari.'

'I must go and see . . .'

'Yes.'

He limped to the waist to find Rodham clambering on board.

'What the devil brings you out here at this time of night, Kit?' There was exasperation in Kirton's tone of voice, but Rodham either did not notice it, or did not heed it.

'I've been thinking . . .'

'So have I and I haven't yet finished. I told you I would give you my answer tomorrow at ten o'clock.'

'I'll cut to the chase, Hal. This is far too good an opportunity to waste. Payment, even in part, in gold, would secure us a great future, steamships . . .'

'Secure *you* a great future, I know . . .'

'Look Hal if anything happens to you we'll get you out . . .'

'Providing I'm not dead and providing that I have secured the gold first . . . Earlier today you were loading all the responsibility on me, content to sit back and cream the profit. Come Kit, I'm not a fool. I stand on the deck of the only thing I own in the world and I'm not going to throw her away to ensure you have your steamships quickly . . .' Kirton held up his hand. 'And I don't want any promise that I can have command of the first one or the biggest one. As far as I'm concerned I'm not sure I want to penetrate *ulu*; thus far I have avoided any of the serious diseases that attack our race up rivers. Anyway, you can't come aboard here and attempt to cajole me. I'm still the master under God here so, good chap that you are, I am going to throw you off, to the sharks if you won't go peaceably.'

Seeing it was no good Rodham emitted a sigh. 'Well at least promise me that you'll give it really serious consideration. It would make you a rich man, Hal. A seriously rich man.'

Kirton grinned in the darkness as the pallid oval of Rodham's face turned away to scramble back into his boat. 'You could not possibly understand, my old friend, how I could never be richer than I am now,' he murmured to himself as he swung round and returned to the poop.

He had expected Sharimah to have gone below but she sat, waiting patiently on the spotlessly clean teak deck-planking and looked up expectantly as he approached.

'I thought you would have gone to bed,' he said, easing himself back into the deck-chair with a groan.

'Your leg?'

'Uh-huh. But also our visitor, Kit Rodham.'

She began rubbing his leg. 'What he want?'

'What he want, my darling, is for me to load cargo of guns for Sultan of Sulu so that he can fight for Suluese freedom . . .'

'And freedom of Rungus people?'

'Yes, I suppose so.'

'You are Englishman, no?'

'Yes.'

'You are free under your *Rajah Perampuan*, Vic . . .' she stumbled over the name. 'Victoria?'

'Uh-huh.' He smiled.

'If bad Spanish man come take away your freedom and I come and trade you guns . . .'

Kirton chuckled. 'It happened once,' he said. 'A long time ago, but no-one offered us any guns.'

'But you . . . you . . .' she searched in vain for the right word.

He made his hands into fists and gently pummelled her; 'Fight?', he suggested.

'Yes, fight,' she answered, hitting him—not so gently—in return.

'But if we take guns, Sharimah, we break law. If Spanish men find out what we do, they very angry . . .' He resorted to mock fisticuffs of pretended increased violence. He cut short his mime. 'Maybe we are all killed.' He threw himself back in the deck-chair as if shot. Then he sat up straight. 'Not just me, Sharimah, but all the ship's people. And what would they do to you if they got hold of you? Worse than the Bugis pirates . . .'

'No. no, Hari!' Now she was kneeling and beating his breast in earnest.

'Stop! Stop!' he gasped. 'Alright, so you think *merdeka* worth the risk . . .' He struggled to express himself so that she could understand. '*Merdeka* good; Spanish . . .'

'Spanish men hurt.' She made a gesture like twisting her wrist. 'All people in Sulu know that. Sultan good man; make life good for Rungus people; you come with good things. Spanish men come with . . . with . . .' she made a gesture of distaste, then flung her arms wide and hung her head. Kirton took a moment to recognise her parody of the crucifixion of Christ.

'How do you know about that?' he asked.

'Long time ago, Spanish men come into my country with . . .' and here she repeated her mime. 'They have black book and men in . . .' she knocked against her chest.

'Armour. What happened to them?'

'We kill them and take heads. Hang longtime in longhouse; now all gone in fire. Cannot tell little people that come from us . . .'

Kirton smiled and reached into his pocket for one final cigar. 'Get me one last small whisky . . .'

'No, Hari; you come to bed.' She reached up and drew the cigar from his lips to kiss him. 'You smoke too much tonight. You smoke again tomorrow.'

CHAPTER FOURTEEN

Merdeka

KIRTON SLEPT BADLY THAT NIGHT AND WAS CAUGHT IN A SHOWER OF rain as he was pulled ashore in the boat the following morning, neither of which circumstance put him in a good temper. Normally a man of equable temperament, he was deeply conflicted about the shipment of arms, realising that he alone put his honour on the line over the whole business. True the good name of the house of Lee, Rodham & Co. might suffer, but it was too well established to lose much by a single aberration. The new steamships would soon repair such of its fortunes as were damaged by one gun-running episode by that wayward eccentric Kirton and his anachronistic brigantine, of which all Singapore knew he was now the sole owner. Indeed, Kirton suspected all Singapore, or at least all European Singapore, would delight in his downfall by such means. He could hear the words murmured behind the palm leaves on the verandas over-looking the clipped and watered lawns: 'only to be expected . . . maverick . . . arrogant . . . damned bounder went native, you know . . . not really one of us . . . gives us all a bad name. . .' And so on and so on.

What he was contemplating doing was illegal and indubitably so; gun-running was as egregious a traffic as carrying opium, or was it? Sharimah's simple plea for *merdeka* could not be denied. The people of Sulu had always seemed to Kirton happy enough under their sultan, so why stand-by and allow the Spanish to annex the territory? And if the Spaniards did not take the archipelago, then the Dutch were as likely to attempt something similar. Neither nation was known for the benignity of its colonial rule . . .

But all that rhetoric about freedom meant that he, Captain Henry Kirton of the brigantine *Tethys*, a British master-mariner to boot, would have to misdeclare his cargo when he cleared his ship outward at the custom-house. While shotguns had not infrequently appeared on the ship's manifests, claiming that one thousand repeating rifles were not what they were, that they were more of the same, weapons for hunting, amounted to perjury of a sort. And he was damnably uncomfortable with that. If he was discovered he might lose his certificate, his ship, his livelihood, everything.

And his leg was getting worse, of that he was in no doubt . . .

On the other hand he could chuck it all in. He had, he calculated roughly, a sufficiency to live on for a while which, wisely invested in—among other things—the Eastern Steam-Ship Co.'s new vessels, would see him out. He could, he thought, secure himself a position on the board if he wanted to, or at worst as marine superintendent of the company and eke out his days in a modest bungalow out near Seletar or Changi, keeping a small boat on the Johore Strait, happy enough with Sharimah and perhaps some children.

But he had involved her with the decision as to whether to do or not to do what was proposed. He gave a bitter little laugh which caused the nearest oarsmen to look at him. He would fall from grace in her eyes if he did not aid 'her people,' even though the Rungus, as one of many tribes in Borneo, were regarded by all others—and especially His Highness Sultan Jamal ul-Azam in his *istana* in Jolo—as primitives.

Was it right to be swayed by a woman, he kept asking himself with every stroke of his boat's crew's oars? Or was he not man enough to decide for himself? Hitherto old Ching had carried out most of the formalities of clearing inwards and outwards, his own attendance being minimal and confined largely to the signing of the ship's papers. The *Tethys* had become such a regular feature of the inward and outward traffic of the port of Singapore, that colonial bureaucracy had touched her only lightly, for it had had no need to do otherwise. Ching, that wise old *chin-chew*, knew when a palm required a little light lubrication to expedite matters, and Kirton had never previously broken the law in the manner he now contemplated. But Ching was not with them this voyage;

could Kirton dissemble by simply sending Vee-Jay ashore as his deputy instead? He had not discussed their next lading with his chief mate, nor with Tan, his second. He had sworn Sharimah to secrecy and she had pledged it in love.

Kirton cursed under his breath. All the while he pondered the matter, he knew, at a sub-conscious level, what he intended to do; that if he did not, he would regard himself a moral coward, whatever European society might say about him. At the end of the day he commanded a vessel that wore the sultan's colours; if the sultan or his agents paid for the arms then His Highness had every right to defend his state and his people against imperial expansion on the part of the aggressive Spanish. There, that was it!

'*Tuan?*'

The boat had arrived and he had not noticed. Kirton levered himself to his feet as the boat's crew held her as steady as was possible to allow their commander to disembark at Collyer Quay. As he limped towards the waiting rickshaws he had to acknowledge the deterioration in his leg. Perhaps he had not got long, he thought. Well, to hell with it!

He turned his mind abruptly and decisively to how they were going to get those cases of Spencers out to the anchored ship.

At the offices of Lee, Rodham & Co. the two partners were waiting for him, the tea ready and their faces expectant. Kirton sat down, recalling the late-night visit of the junior of the two, which he had dismissed as soon as he had seen Rodham off the *Tethys*.

Neither man spoke as Kirton raised the bowl of *chai* to his lips. They watched, the older with imperturbability the younger with impatience, as he replaced the bowl on the low table in front of him.

'Very well,' Kirton said, 'we'll do it, and here's how . . . '

Before he returned to his ship Kirton had two matters to attend to. The first was a visit to Gurney, Gurney & Jago, the firm of solicitors who had offered their services to him upon the occasion of his first encounter with the Spanish Royal Navy. He spent two hours ensconced in the private office of the senior partner, David Gurney, from which he emerged ready for a meal on the Esplanade. From here he sent a boy to an address furnished by Gurney senior, with a short letter he had written in the solicitor's office, and awaited a reply that came just as he finished his post-prandial cigar. Tipping the boy generously he read the note. 'Come at once,' it read. He could not read the signature but Gurney's assurance that this fellow Gareth Lloyd was the best man then in Singapore for such private matters, removed any anxiety. Not that Kirton felt much anxiety now—about anything. He had made up his mind. Extinguishing his cigar he hauled himself to his feet, calling for a rickshaw. Giving the address to the rickshaw-*wallah* he settled back on the grubby cushions, allowing his mind to wander to thoughts of Sharimah. She and she alone formed his destiny he concluded, after the troubled hours of the night and the decision he had announced to Lee and Rodham during the forenoon.

The doctor's premises lay out on the Tanglin Road and he found the physician to be a short, pot-bellied Welshman, six or seven years Kirton's senior, who introduced himself as having: 'An appropriate name to check out your timbers, Captain Kirton,' the little man chuckled as he ushered Kirton into the cool of his consulting room. 'Please, take a seat and tell me your problem.'

Kirton recounted his medical history from his fall from the yard in the *River Tay*, after which Lloyd invited him to strip-off and lie down on his examination table. Lloyd gave him a thorough going-over, labouring his jest by declaring that there was no point in getting a ship into dry-dock without carrying out a proper survey.

'Well now,' Lloyd said as he concentrated on Kirton's gammy leg, probing the muscles with surprisingly strong fingers and taking a magnifying glass to the skin of the offending limb. 'Generally speaking, you are in excellent condition, which ought to be expected for a man of your age, but is not often the case in Europeans who have been out here for some time. Do you drink much?'

'Usually one or sometimes two whisky *stengahs* before I go to bed.'

'The whisky's habitual is it?'

'Yes, but only when my ship is at anchor. I rarely drink when she is under-way at sea. . . though it would not be true to say never.' Kirton paused. 'Look, let me make myself clear, I am not a soak.'

'Good,' the physician said after listening to his chest. 'But you smoke far, far too many cigars—that you cannot deny.'

'No, I can't,' Kirton replied ruefully.

'What about fevers? Quotidian? Malarial? Have you been afflicted?'

'Not really. The occasional rise in temperature and feelings of being off-colour; but nothing as serious as the conditions I have heard others suffer from. My trading has largely been offshore from open anchorages. I have never been *ulu* . . .'

Lloyd nodded. 'That has undoubtedly preserved you to a remarkable degree. Very well, get dressed and come through when you are ready. I won't be a moment.'

Lloyd withdrew, Kirton dressed and returned to the chair in Lloyd's consulting room. The doctor was absent and he sat there for a moment before Lloyd called him out on to his veranda, indicating a brace of rattan loungers.

'Do sit down Captain. Would you care for a gin? This isn't a test of either your sobriety or your veracity, I'm going to have one,' Lloyd said with a smile. 'You rely heavily upon your cane, I see,' he added.

'Increasingly,' Kirton admitted, 'which is the chief reason for my desire to consult you. I came on the recommendation of Mr David Gurney.'

'Oh, David sent you did he? How is he? I haven't seen him for a while.'

'I was with him this morning; he seemed fit enough.'

'Good, good.' Lloyd called for two gins and when his Chinese servant brought them he contemplated his glass with a grin. 'Did you know the Chinese call this *gweilo chai*, white man's tea,' he chuckled.

Kirton nodded. 'Yes, I did know that. I have a Chinese crew.'

'Ahhh . . .' Lloyd sipped his gin and Kirton waited with increasing impatience for some sort of diagnosis. He was on the point of prompting the physician when Lloyd said: 'You have a serious condition, Captain, an infection of the bones in your bad leg located chiefly in the femur and probably by now the pelvis. It's called osteomyelitis and can be caused as far as I know by a number of agents, the bite of an insect or small animal for example. In your case, examining your skin, I'd lay money on it being a fungal infection. Such a mycosis is not uncommon in the humid latitudes in which you and I have spent much of our adult lives. Is it worse during *landas*—the rainy season?'

'It used to be; now it is more-or-less permanent . . .'

'That's the chronic form and, to tell you the unpleasant truth, it doesn't usually get better. It may have been simmering for some time and I'd say your body had put up a good fight, but . . .' The doctor shrugged, then went on: 'Unfortunately the bones do not appear to have knitted very well owing either to bad setting in the BMH or to over-use, particularly in the early days after your discharge; putting too much strain on the whole shebang, if you grasp my meaning.'

'Only too well, I think,' Kirton said grimly. 'I take it there is no treatment?'

'Not really. I've known cases where a fit man with a fit body overcomes the infection naturally, but he usually goes home to do it, improving on the voyage.'

'That's not an option,' Kirton said curtly.

'I see.' Lloyd paused. 'Although I can't be certain, but I'd say the infection has spread to the pelvis, which—sadly—discourages me from recommending a high amputation . . .'

'That's not an option either.' Kirton cut Lloyd short.

'No, I guessed not.' Lloyd paused, taking his measure of the younger man before adding: 'I'm sorry to be the bearer of bad news; of course you could live with it for several years, but . . .'

'But?'

'Well, my dear fellow, if it has infected the pelvis, months is the likelier prognosis.'

Kirton nodded and then gave a short laugh. 'Well, Doctor, my thanks. What is your fee?'

'Oh, I'll waive that in the circumstances.'

'No, no, I insist . . .'

'There's no fee, Captain,' Lloyd said firmly. 'I would not dream of charging a man in such a situation as you now find yourself.'

'Are you certain?'

'Absolutely. Now, come and dine with me next time you are in Singapore. I shall want to know how you are getting on.'

'You think I'll live that long?' Kirton asked wryly with a lopsided smile.

'Undoubtedly,' Lloyd said, assisting Kirton to his feet and seeing him to the door where the rickshaw-*wallah* waited.

'Until next time, Captain. And bring your lady . . . I assume you have one?'

Kirton waved his thanks and settled back into the rickshaw. Anyone seeing the young mariner on that journey back to the waterfront that afternoon might have remarked that his face wore a curious expression of resolution and a strange contentment. And those few interested in, and capable of interpreting it, might have concluded that Captain Harry Kirton knew exactly where his future lay.

CHAPTER FIFTEEN

A Cargo of Rifles

THE *TETHYS* LAY AT HER USUAL ANCHORAGE FOR A WEEK AS HER NEXT outward cargo came aboard, carefully managed by Lee so as to leave room for the forbidden lading. That was to be loaded in the small hours of the morning on which the brigantine was scheduled to depart from Tanjong Pagar.

'Outward cargo's a bit short, sir,' Vee-Jay remarked to Kirton, his face anxious. 'I suppose that is due to the absence of Ching.'

'I guess it must be,' Kirton remarked disingenuously. 'I do know a couple of the Copenhagen steamers are late . . . I don't know why . . . Anyway, we cannot wait,' Kirton said with an air of finality and, as he thought privately to himself, that of a commander of a first-class mail steamer.

In the meanwhile a gang of Chinese Triad members, sworn to secrecy and generously paid, carefully removed the crates and cases from the loft of the godown, and wrapped and sewed them into burlap. On the afternoon prior to the day the *Tethys* was due to sail, two *lorchas* left Singapore Creek and headed out to sea; passing Tanjong Katong they disappeared over the horizon.

Kirton had given Jones and Tan an extension of their leave. 'You needn't come aboard until tomorrow forenoon,' he had said with a smile. 'I have some private papers to deal with before we sail,' he added, by way of explanation, determined that neither mate, but Jones in particular, knew what he was up to before they were at sea and it was all too late. Tan would go along with it, for he intended paying the entire crew a generous bonus, but Jones was a different kettle of fish and required careful handling.

Kirton did not sleep properly that night, though he dozed in his deck-chair, leaving the duty *jaga* to ponder on his commander's unusual behaviour. Perhaps he and his *nyai* had had a row; the *jaga* chuckled to himself.

Kirton had gone no-where near the godown of Lee, Rodham & Co. since giving his instructions as to how the cargo of contraband was to be loaded. He now waited anxiously, for there was little wind and the Chinese *lorchas* must deliver their lading long before dawn, even if their crews had to move them through the water with *yulohs*.

He need not have worried; shortly after six bells in the middle watch—three o'clock in the morning—an alarmed duty *jaga*, keeping the anchor watch woke him. '*Tuan*! *Tuan*! I think pirates come alongside!'

Kirton was on his feet in an instant as, out of the gloom loomed the batwing sails of a *lorcha*. 'This only special cargo,' he said briefly. 'You take forward mooring rope, I catch after one.'

The first *lorcha* was soon secured on the offshore side of the *Tethys* and a dozen Chinese came over the side and stared about them. Then Kirton recognised one of Lee's confidential *cranis*, a man who spoke good pidgin and who had been charged with overseeing the clandestine operation. He quickly explained how to man the capstan and swing the derrick over the side. Kirton himself went down on the main deck and peeled back the loosely secured hatch tarpaulin, revealing the hatch-boards. These were soon removed and the first sling of crated rifles was lifted over the side and lowered into the gloom of the hold. Kirton went to the companionway and brought out the two lanterns he had prepared, one of which he lowered into the hold and the other he hung over the side. They gave just sufficient illumination to enable the loading to go smoothly, but without showing an excess of light betraying to the shore what was going on. The coolies worked furiously; the first *lorcha* was discharged within an hour; the second, which contained chiefly the ammunition, before the false dawn began to show. Under the lamp-light Kirton checked the cases of ammunition bearing the newly stencilled marks 'Condensed Milk,' chuckling at the deception. The last tier was composed of a few crates of rifles, all of which bore the words: 'Shotguns; 12-bore.'

Calling the duty *jaga* aft he said, 'You help me, we put one of these in my cabin. Maybe make good sport.' The Sikh grinned knowingly.

By two bells in the morning watch, five o'clock, the portable boards were replaced and Kirton dragged the tarpaulin over the hatch, leaving it to the *tomelo* to secure after sunrise. Half an hour later Kirton stood on the poop and watched as the second *lorcha* followed the first back into Singapore Creek. With a sigh of relief, Kirton settled in his deck-chair where, an hour later, Sharimah woke him with a pot of coffee.

'Everything *bagus*, Hari?' she enquired in a low voice.

'Everything very *bagus*, my lovely,' he responded with a smile, taking her outstretched hand.

There was only one last hurdle to get over he thought as he wearily sipped his coffee.

———

That too proved to be easy. He had cleared his ship inwards and outwards so often that the bureaucratic process flowed with a natural efficiency. Indeed the clerk aided this by asking Kirton the question: 'The usual, Captain?'

'Pretty much,' Kirton responded, 'though we're a little light this voyage, my *shroff* having retired.'

'You'll miss him,' the clerk had chuckled, indicating Ching was a familiar figure. 'God knows how old he is.'

Kirton limped back to his boat, wryly aware that had he been a fitter man he might have betrayed himself by cutting the occasional jaunty caper. However, his good mood was almost destroyed as he gained the deck of the *Tethys* when a concerned Vee-Jay accosted him.

'I understand we took in some cargo during the night, sir.'

Kirton nodded. 'Yes, we received a late consignment for Jolo; some unmarked consignment for the sultan,' he dissembled, hurrying on to ask, 'Are we ready to weigh?'

Jones might have been about to press Kirton about the nature of goods for the sultan, but Kirton's query threw him. 'Er, more-or-less, but we've one boat-load of stores to come,' Vee-Jay admitted, 'I forgot to expedite it last night.'

'No matter,' Kirton said magnanimously, stifling a smile. 'I'm going to have a coffee, let me know when you're ready. In the meantime Tan can cast off the sails and let them hang in their gear before sending the hands to the capstan.' Kirton deliberately left Jones to his tasks, thereby avoiding any further questions that, as chief mate, he had every right to ask.

Having divested himself of the ship's papers he called for coffee and ensconced himself on the poop, drooping with fatigue. In fact he had dozed off by the time Jones reported the vessel ready to sail. Kirton looked up at his chief mate and with a friendly smile said: 'Get her under-way, there's a good fellow, Vee-Jay, and take her out. I'm dog tired after last night's interrupted sleep.'

Jones visibly brightened at the prospect. 'Aye, aye, sir,' he said, punctiliously.

And so the *Tethys* slipped out of the anchorage off Tanjong Pagar and stood away to the eastward watched from the roof-top platform of the godown of Lee, Rodham & Co. by the two anxious partners.

'Well, that's a relief,' remarked Rodham as he headed for the ladder, his head full of dreams of the sultan's gold.

Lee lingered a little longer, waiting until the brigantine was hull-down before he ventured below. A small but persistent doubt lingered in his mind. He had not enjoyed a good night's sleep any more than Harry Kirton, but his had been full of disturbing dreams and Lee did not like disturbing dreams, for they boded ill.

⸺•⸺

Kirton pored over his chart, tapping his dividers on the small island of Siasi which lay about fifteen nautical miles to the south-south-west of the south coast of the island of Jolo itself. This was the landing spot indicated by Ban Guan in his letter and Kirton was attempting to work out the best approach. Though he had scant knowledge of naval tactics, he thought that the Spanish would have most of their squadron close to the main island of Jolo and its open roadstead of the same name. Since the place was the principal *entrepôt* for the region, it was the logical place to invest in order to inflict the maximum economic harm. However, he was equally certain that the Spanish flag-officer, be he commodore or admiral, would have some of his men-of-war cruising through the islands and a few on particular stations such as the Sibutu Passage. If so it would prevent Kirton passing into the Celebes Sea to approach Siasi from the south, his only real option. And if the Spanish entertained any suspicions that succour might come to the Suluese from the west they might also have a picket watching the Balabac Strait. If that were to prove the case and they attempted to stop Kirton's vessel and board in force, he would be caught out before the game had begun. On the other hand Kirton doubted the Spanish would act so rashly in international waters, and the Balabac Strait was too wide for a single man-of-war to effectively close. Moreover, with a fair wind, he was confident he could take the *Tethys* through under the cover of darkness and tuck her directly into Marudu Bay before the Spanish knew he was anywhere near them.

But what did he know? He was no naval strategist . . .

The question was, knowing his ship spelt trouble, would the Spanish be on the lookout for her? It seemed sensible to assume so, in which case they would have a rough idea when and where she might be encountered, for the *Tethys* had followed roughly the same track for years now. Sure there had been variations, forays south along the coast of Dutch Borneo, for example, but her presence in the Sulu archipelago, for example, had been almost as regular as clockwork, her calls at Jolo as important to the economy of the place as the diurnal quests of its fishing fleet.

Kirton flung the dividers down and eased himself onto the chart-room settee. The truth was, now that he was embarked upon it, his voyage was an entirely foolhardy mission, for whatever clever plans he might lay, he was entirely at the mercy of the wind. Should that fail at a critical moment the *Tethys* would lie at the mercy of a steam corvette. Perhaps then, it would be best not to make too neat a plan but to use his knowledge of the localities and the optimum wind conditions for passing any possible choke-point on the basis of 'as-and-when.' He got to his feet again and gave the chart one last glance before laying it back in the drawer, straightening up that on which they currently relied as the brigantine made her way up the coast of Sarawak somewhere over the horizon to the south. They would not be in the approaches to Marudu Bay or the Balabac Strait for two more days. And first he would have to take his officers into his confidence.

This he did the following evening, sending Pritam Singh to keep a deck-watch while he detained the two mates in the saloon. The irregularity offended Vee-Jay Jones, but Kirton pacified him. 'I shall only keep you a few minutes, gentlemen, but before I do I want your assurance that what you hear now stays between the three of us.' He felt Jones bristle, but ploughed on. 'Under hatches we have a consignment of rifles for the . . .'

'Rifles?' expostulated Jones, wagging his head, 'I knew it, by damn! What do you intend to do, compromise us all? By all the stars of heaven, Captain Kirton, I never thought that you would do such a thing!'

Kirton ignored the outburst, and resumed his speech. 'This has been ordered and is consigned to the sultan at Jolo and is, insofar as we are a vessel belonging to the Sulu state, a legitimate cargo. Whether the sultan intends issuing them to his guard to preserve the freedom of his people from the imminent incursion of the Spanish, or using them as hunting guns is, I suppose, a matter for the sultan himself. My own view is that the former is His Highness's most likely intention, though I am sure that for anyone with scruples the latter reason will serve.' Kirton looked meaningfully at Jones. 'Our consignors have obtained an excellent price for the goods and an equally good freight-rate which includes a generous bonus for all hands—that much I secured in lieu of your good opinion, Mr Jones. All we have to do is land the goods on the island of Siasi from where fishermen will carry it across to Jolo . . .'

'Carry?' scoffed Jones, 'you mean smuggle.'

'Put your own interpretation on it if you wish,' Kirton said, keeping his temper.

'And if we're intercepted?' an angrily truculent Jones retorted.

'Well, I'll tell them that's it's nothing to do with you, you're a passenger and are taking no reward from our lading . . .'

'That is not an answer . . .'

'We'll fight,' snapped Kirton. 'After all we have two cannon and one thousand repeating rifles under hatches. I am sure the *jagas* would be only too willing to get their hands on a few of them . . .'

'*One thousand*? You could not pass that number off as hunting guns!'

'No, but the manifest says we have one hundred. We have carried that number before.'

'Cheap single shot percussion-lock shotguns, but not repeating rifles.'

'No, but *if* we are boarded, and I do not intend that we should be, the boarding officer will find the upper tier—all that he can see easily—marked quite openly as such. That is all I have to say, gentlemen, thank you for your attention. I believe it is your watch, Mr Jones, unless you intend retiring to your cabin?'

'Please, Captain,' Jones responded, rising with a pained look on his face.

'Thank you,' said Kirton, adding, 'would you be kind enough to send Pritam Singh to my cabin.'

When the senior *Jaga* reported to him Kirton indicated the lower drawer under his bunk. 'Help me get this out . . .'

The two men struggled for a moment, working against the heel of the ship, but once the drawer was laid aside Kirton said: 'Oblige me and get out what's underneath that burlap.'

With a frown Pritam Singh knelt down and fished in the void below the drawer-space and the deck. As he withdrew the first of the five Spencers Kirton had concealed there, the *jaga* looked up at his commander, his expression curious.

'Yes, they're for you,' Kirton said with a smile as Pritam Singh almost caressed the American guns, his eyes glowing. 'Repeating rifles, better than your old Enfields. I want you to issue one each to your men and quietly get to know how to use them. Don't let the Chinese see them, do it in your cabin, understand? Then put them in the arms rack. Then I want you to wrap the Enfields in this burlap, open the hatch and put them in the top tier. Oh, and add these to the bundle.' Kirton handed Pritam Sigh his two Boss shotguns. 'Make sure they are on top—*de atas*—you savee?'

The Sikh smiled. 'Yes, *Tuan*.'

'Good. Then get some black paint and dab the corner of the crate under the burlap. Now, there's ammunition here too for the Spencers, one hundred rounds each . . . I'm going on deck, now and I leave all this to you. Do it as if it was just normal.'

'Very good, *Tuan*.'

The two men exchanged conspiratorial smiles, Kirton picked up his cane and disappeared.

'There, *Tuan*.' Tan pointed to the distant horizon, about three points on the port bow.

'Got it,' responded Kirton, levelling the long glass at the faint smudge of smoke that disfigured the rim of the world. Through the powerful lens he could just see two masts and a scrap of sail, though the Spanish man-of-war was hull-down. It was an hour after dawn and already the sun was climbing up the sky, in all probability catching the canvas of the brigantine, for there were rain clouds massing on the western horizon.

'Lie her off a couple of points to starboard,' he ordered the second mate, who called his watch-mates to the sheets and braces, settling the *Tethys* on her new course, while Kirton dodged down into the chart-room.

His heart thumped in his chest, for this was the moment of decision. The Spaniard lay just to the north of the island of Balambangan; their nearest refuge, Telok Marudu, lay ahead and to leeward. If he tucked the *Tethys* in that great bay the corvette, or whatever she was, could easily blockade her there without technically entering the sultan's waters. But if he could slip past the entrance of the bay in the shelter of the off-lying islands, pass through the Sibutu Passage before it was closed to him and then sail south, beyond Tawau, then he might lose a pursuer, idling in Dutch waters. The gap between Balambangan and Banggi was narrow and they would be extremely unlucky if they lay on the Spaniard's line of sight, if he had judged her cruising station correctly. Between Banggi and Malawali they would remain entirely concealed. So, he calculated, their nearest approach would be between seven and ten miles and, if the wind held, the *Tethys* would make eight or nine knots. He doubted the Spaniard could better that, but of course he could not be sure.

He busied himself for a few moments with parallel rulers and dividers before returning to the deck to stand beside the *jurmudi*.

Having finessed the course he called Tan. 'I've brought her round a little more; we will run inside Balambangan, Banggi and Malawali,' he said, indicating the three islands, 'with this wind freeing us off all the time.' He indicated the nearest island, Balambangan, before going on: 'Once we settle on course and are behind Balambangan, set the flying jib and the main topgallant staysail and trim everything just right. You savee, Mr Tan?'

'I savee, *Tuan*,' grinned the second mate.

'*Bagus*. Now I go below and *pergi makan*.'

At first Kirton thought they had slipped past the Spanish man-of-war, but as they exposed themselves in the narrow gap between Balambangan and Banggi, Tan called down to the saloon that the Spaniard was making sail. Jones had just come into the saloon and as Kirton rose from the table, he said, 'We've been sighted by a Spanish man-of-war, Vee-Jay. It could be a long day . . .'

'D'you want me on deck?'

'No, no, have your breakfast first.' Kirton gave both his chief mate and an anxious Sharimah who stood at the pantry door a smile and hoisted himself up the companionway.

After he had gone Jones looked up at the Rungus woman and said, 'Your *Tuan* either *orang besar* or . . .'

'The *Tuan*,' Sharimah cut in, 'is *orang besar*.'

'That is what worries me,' Jones murmured, reaching for the kedgeree.

On deck Kirton again stared in the direction Tan was pointing; although still hull-down, the Spaniard had hoisted topgallants and the hidden funnel now belched clouds of black smoke, clear evidence that she was in pursuit of them.

Kirton cast his eyes aloft, then hobbled aft to stare into the compass-bowl before turning to the *jurmudi*. 'You no look astern,' he ordered the man crisply. 'You make best course; savee?'

'I savee, *Tuan*.'

Kirton did not need his sextant to see that the Spanish man-of-war was gaining on them, for two hours later she was hull-up, but to maintain a speed faster than her quarry she needed to burn coal, and judging by the amount of filthy black smoke pouring from her, her wretched firemen must have been having a dreadful time in their stokehold. Even as he watched her as Jones took bearings to establish their position at noon,

Kirton saw the corvette clew up her sails as of being no use, acting as a drag on her.

For the umpteenth time that forenoon he looked aloft to see if they could improve the set of their own canvas, finding himself wishing that the little brigantine still carried studding sails, but this was no time for wishful thinking. He caught sight of Sharimah's face in the companion-way entrance and smiled at her; she smiled back, but she could clearly see the 'enemy' astern as the *Tethys* rose and fell, scending as she drove along.

Turning back to the corvette, for she appeared to be the same vessel as had twice attempted their apprehension off Jolo, he judged that if she could maintain her present speed she would overtake the *Tethys* before nightfall. If that happened he would have to bluff his way out of trouble again, or fight. He heard the gong for tiffin but he lingered on deck, unwilling to go below, as though sheer will-power could retard the advance of their tormentor.

He would be a fool to fight with his two brass pop-guns; in truth his desire to preserve his ship and his crew ruled that out despite what he had said earlier, so bluffing was the only option. And what were his chances of that? He had been more than lucky on those previous occasions.

'Tiffin, Hari,' Sharimah called and with a sigh of resignation Kirton went below.

CHAPTER SIXTEEN

The Spanish Corvette

THE CORVETTE SURGED UP ON THE PORT QUARTER OF THE *TETHYS* HALF an hour before sunset. She was flying a flag signal indicating the brigantine should heave-to and followed this up with a shot across the merchantman's bows, at which Kirton gave the order for the helm to be put over, the fore-topgallant and fore course to be clewed-up, the spanker to be brailed, the main topsail to be dropped to the doubling, and the fore-topsail to be backed as the brigantine came round.

As the *Tethys* was brought to the wind Kirton studied the Spaniard. She was the same corvette as had intercepted them before and he read her name as she circled her quarry, sending a cloud of sulphurous smoke across their deck as she did so: *La Reina*. A grand name for a small man-of-war, he thought inconsequentially.

As he watched as the Spaniards lowered their steam picket-boat, Jones came up to him. 'Foretops'l laid to the mast, sir,' Jones reported frigidly.

'Very good, Vee-Jay. Now listen carefully. When you go down into the hold with the boarding officer I am going to send Pritam Singh with you. You tell him what to do, preferably in Malay or Urdu, then let him expose the required items. Don't interfere with him, whatever you do. Understand?'

'No, sir, I do not, but I shall do as you order.' Jones's tone was icy.

'That's all I ask of you. Thank you.'

The picket-boat was in the water now and preparing to cast off, smoke rising from her small brass funnel. Kirton ducked his head into the companionway and called for Sharimah. Giving her some instructions, which included asking her to bring him his cap, he resumed his watch on the approaching boat as it rapidly closed the distance between the two vessels.

He called for Pritam Singh and raised his eyebrow, at which the Sikh nodded.

'The bastards have guns trained on us,' Jones said nervously.

'I suppose that means we must frighten them,' Kirton remarked drily.

A few minutes later Lieutenant Espina stood again upon the poop of the *Tethys*. As before he was accompanied by the same midshipman.

'Good evening, Lieutenant,' Kirton said politely. 'I hope you have made a note of our prompt compliance with your signals to heave-to.'

'We have had to chase you, Captain,' Espina almost snarled.

'Well, sir,' Kirton replied, 'for that I apologise but we did not think you were chasing us, merely exercising or something.'

'Don't fool with me, Captain. Your papers please, and open your hatch.'

'Of course. Mr Jones, call Number One *jaga* and the *tomelo* to open the hatch and take the young man below. Come with me sir . . .' Kirton led the way down into the saloon, remarking conversationally, 'I have coffee, or would you prefer whisky? Also I do not have a *comprador* aboard anymore.'

Espina said nothing until he entered the saloon where a smiling Sharimah offered him coffee or tea and Kirton presented his humidor of cigars. He observed that the Spanish officer hesitated, and then settled with coffee and a cigar to examine the *Tethys*'s manifest, his eyes flickering to the graceful figure who flitted in and out of the pantry.

After a moment Espina said, his finger on the papers before him, 'These guns, Captain. . . ?'

'Twelve-bore shotguns, Lieutenant, along with a trifling amount of ammunition consigned to a Dutch merchant in Tarakan,' Kirton answered, trying not to sound glib.

Espina grunted. 'And you have no plans to call at Jolo?'

'None whatsoever,' Kirton responded with perfect honesty, 'though I shall be trading down the coast of Borneo and Kalimantan as usual. Mostly paraffin and domestic utensils, as you can see . . .'

'Utensils . . . ?' queried the Spanish officer.

'Oh, pardon me, er, pots and pans for cooking, oil lamps and lanterns, some mirrors—they are very popular—good Sheffield steel knives, that sort of thing, plus some earthenware bowls, English china cups and saucers, the Dutch colonists like them . . .'

'Yes, yes, thank you,' snapped Espina testily.

After a few minutes more he pushed the papers aside and stared at Kirton who had eased himself into his chair at the head of the table. 'You have a bad leg, Captain,' he remarked, with a kind of relish.

'Unfortunately yes, Lieutenant. Not something I would wish on my worst enemy.'

'That bad?'

'That bad.'

'I am sorry to hear it,' Espina responded smoothly, leaning back and scrutinising the Englishman as Kirton inclined his head graciously. 'These,' Espina indicated the documents before him, '*appear* to be in order but somehow I have the suspicion that you are trying to trick me, Captain Kirton.'

'Unfortunately, Lieutenant, we did not hit it off at our last encounter, when I undoubtedly did so. I felt,' Kirton paused and blew a smoke-ring at the deck-head above them, 'that you had taken an unfair advantage of me but since then the promulgation of your blockade has become common knowledge . . .'

'But you are not wearing an ensign.'

'We rarely do at sea, Lieutenant. Perhaps I should have hoisted one when you ordered me to heave-to, but I forgot . . .'

'You do not look like a man who forgets such details.'

Kirton shrugged. 'A year ago I should have agreed with you; today, with my leg, I am less of a punctilio.'

'I'm sorry; a what?'

'Less smart, Lieutenant. Constant pain makes one forget such matters,' Kirton said, his tone full of candour.

Espina grunted again, his eyes distracted by Sharimah who lent alluringly over the table and offered him more coffee. The Spanish officer shook his head and turned again to Kirton. 'Captain, if we find out that you have tricked us in any way—any way, you comprehend?—you must not expect any leniency or mercy. My commander's orders are explicit: Any vessel found carrying contraband as per our declaration thereof will be taken as lawful prize. You command an armed merchantman and wear, or should wear, the ensign of Sulu ...'

'That is not quite so, Lieutenant,' Kirton interjected. 'Owing to your blockade, I am in the process of reverting this vessel to the British registry. Now I ask you, am I going to compromise this by carrying contraband in the face of your previous warnings?'

'But we know that the *shawbunder* at Jolo requested you to bring guns, Captain,' Espina said.

Kirton forbore to think of how the Spanish had gained that intelligence, though perhaps it was not so very difficult. Instead he laughed. 'He certainly did!' he replied. 'And offered me a fair inducement too, but I am not the fool you take me for, Lieutenant,' Kirton dismissed the presumption, silently praying that things went according to plan in the hold. If they did not, he was lost.

Espina regarded Kirton with a jaundiced eye. He seemed about to speak but any further conversation was interrupted by the appearance of Midshipman Bustamente who entered the saloon to make his report. This was verbose, which set Kirton's heart a-thudding in his breast. The young man had brought below one of Kirton's own shotguns and threw it on the saloon table in front of Espina with a decided air of exasperation.

Kirton did not understand a word of the Spanish but his relief at what appeared to be the success of his stratagem turned suddenly to anger and he stood and, leaning over, lifted up the shotgun and handed it to Espina, barking at the midshipman, 'Have a care for my polish you damned imp!'

The three of them stood for a long moment, with Kirton glaring at the younger man, until the silence was broken by Espina who jerked his head, whereupon the midshipman withdrew. As the young man left humiliated, he stumbled on the companionway steps, letting out an oath before resuming his ascent to the deck. Espina ignored the outburst. Instead he was looking at Kirton, who was running his finger along a deep scratch in the polished surface of the table, swearing under his breath.

'My pardon for that, Captain,' an embarrassed Espina said, to Kirton's surprise.

Kirton nodded, his expression suddenly dark. 'There was no need for that, Lieutenant, no need at all. Now, may I continue my voyage?'

Espina sighed, looking like a man who had lost a game of cards. 'I do not see why not,' he assented and rose from his chair. As the Spanish officer withdrew he turned again at the saloon door. 'I hope I shall not find you have deceived me, Captain . . .'—then he was gone, clattering up the companionway, his sword scabbard dragging behind him. Wearily Kirton followed, the effort almost too much for him after half an hour of intense dissimulation.

As soon as he gained the deck he was confronted by both mates and Pritam Singh. The picket-boat was already a few yards off the side of the *Tethys* and heading for *La Reina*. He turned back to the expectant little trio. The sun had almost set and their faces were thrown into sharp relief. 'All well?' he asked laconically, and both Jones and the Sikh nodded. 'Very good. Will you be so good, Vee-Jay, as to lay the ship before the wind and resume our course.'

For a moment or two Kirton watched as the picket-boat rounded-to alongside the corvette, hooked onto her falls and was lifted from the water. Slowly *La Reina* swung away from them, a roil of white water appearing under her stern as she headed north, back to her cruising station. Then he went below and lay down. His leg was suddenly giving him great pain and he drifted off into a fitful sleep so that it was not until he was woken by Sharimah an hour later with an enquiry as to whether he wanted dinner that he learned what had transpired in the hold. All, it appeared, had gone according to plan. The case containing the old Enfields and Kirton's sporting guns had been broached and the two shotguns, lying uppermost, had been taken out by Pritam Singh and handed to the midshipman who held them under the small square of fading daylight filtering down into the gloom to look at them. He had tried the action with some enthusiasm and remarked in broken English that 'English shotgun very good. Boss very good.'

Jones pointed at the port of discharge, neatly stencilled on the burlap wrapping: Tarakan. 'For Dutchman,' he said curtly.

With a pretended enthusiasm, Singh had also pulled down a case of 'Condensed Milk' in which the young Spaniard showed little interest, for he seemed for a while beguiled by the 12 bores.

'Not Egg Durs,' he had remarked inconsequentially, and Kirton had to explain that the young Spaniard knew the name of another British gun-maker.

After a few minutes more, during which Bustamente dutifully poked and prodded around in the semi-darkness, he withdrew, brushing his immaculate white uniform down with a muttered anger at the filth it was accumulating in the hold of a merchantman. Covered with dirt and dust he made for the ladder.

'He had had enough,' concluded a much relieved Jones, accepting one of Kirton's cigars as Sharimah set two tumblers of Scotch down on the table before them.

'Well, thank goodness for that,' remarked Kirton, staring at the Scotch. 'Under the trying circumstances I think we might indulge ourselves.' He raised his glass to his chief mate. 'Now, let's proceed to Tarakan, then lose ourselves in the Celebes Sea before attempting an approach to Siasi from the south.'

— ◆ —

But that is not what happened. Kirton would never quite know why, but when he went on deck three mornings later he was disconcerted to see astern the smudge of black smoke besmirching the horizon. No-one else had yet spotted it, but Kirton knew he had not deceived Espina and that, having debriefed his boarding party, *La Reina*'s captain had decided to keep an eye on the *Tethys*, allowing her a period of grace before again showing himself.

'Damnation!' Kirton swore, stumbling down to the chart-room in so much haste that he almost fell. The noise brought an anxious Sharimah to the foot of the companionway by the saloon door.

'Hari? You feel pain?' She need not have asked; he was as white as a sheet, his eyes closed in agony.

'I'm alright,' he gasped, opening his eyes and staring at her. 'I'm alright,' he repeated, recalling the reason for his precipitate descent. 'Get me a whisky.'

'Hari?' she cautioned.

'Get me a whisky,' he said again, abruptly, turning away to enter the chart-room.

She brought him the drink which he knocked back and caught his breath. 'I'm alright, my lovely,' he said with a wan smile as she stood by his side while he stared down at the chart, a great swathe of which was uncharted in all but the most superficial detail, showing the dotted lines of an incomplete running survey. He leaned over it, running his finger down the stuttering line which marked the dynamic edge of seemingly endless mangrove swamp.

'Please God,' he whispered to himself, and then he saw them, four words which offered hope. He circled them with his pencil and picked up the parallel rules, laid one end on the last plotted position, then swung the other round to lay it on the four words, read off the course, juggled a few figures for compass error, and went back on deck.

'Steer west a half south,' he said to the *jurmudi*, calling for Tan and the watch to stand by the braces. As the brigantine answered her helm he hauled in the spanker sheet himself and saw the *Tethys* settled on her new course. When Tan came aft to enquire the reason for the abrupt alteration of course, Kirton said nothing. Instead he merely pointed to the north.

Tan let fly a torrent of Chinese oaths and Kirton went below. Half-way down the companionway he paused and looked about him, frowning.

'No,' he muttered, wondering to himself. 'Surely not . . . that cannot possibly be the reason . . .'

Chapter Seventeen

A River in Borneo

To Kirton's intense relief they passed safely over what proved to be only a slight bar in the estuary and ghosted into the mouth of the river with leadsmen in the fore-chains port and starboard, a man at both topgallant yard-arms and both anchors catted and ready to let-go. Gradually the mangroves closed on either beam, but the stream ran deep and true, as if powered by head-waters eager to burst their way into the Celebes Sea, lifting Kirton's flagging spirits.

Then the first bend turned them to windward, arresting their progress and Kirton let the port anchor go. The *Tethys* brought up to her cable, the strong current digging the anchor well into the ooze of the river's bed.

As soon as he was satisfied that the anchor was holding against the strength of the current, Kirton ordered the fore-topgallant sent down, yard and sail to be stowed on deck, ready to run aloft if required. He could do nothing about the brigantine's long topmasts, for the top and topgallant masts were all-in-one, but at least two bare poles were more difficult to spot from seaward than a yard crossing a pallid sail. Just to be certain he had the main topsail dropped on its jackstay below the main cross-trees where it normally nestled when not required. He also ordered that no ensign would be worn at the peak of the gaff until further notice. By this time the entire ship knew that the Spanish corvette had resumed her chase and that—at the very least—the *Tethys* was to be kept under observation, even if it meant a Spanish man-of-war penetrating these nominally Dutch waters.

It was a calculated risk, of course, but this corner of the Dutch East Indies was remote, and he doubted if, even should word reach Batavia, a Dutch man-of-war could arrive on the scene to dispute matters with *La Reina* before they had come to a head with the *Tethys*.

'We will lie doggo here for a day or two,' he told his officers at tiffin. 'I want full watches on deck and the *jagas* doubled-up with their rifles on deck.' This last directed at Pritam Singh, who nodded. 'Mister Tan, the two breech-loaders are also to be charged, loaded and primed. Charges to be drawn and renewed every morning. We don't have more than a score of shot, so I want some bags of iron scraps—old shackles, rubbish from *tomelo*'s shop . . .'

'We've a good number of nails loaded on spec in the hold, sir,' Jones added, his face working nervously.

'Yes, you get the idea. And each officer to be issued with a rifle; we'll take them from the cargo too. They're repeaters, seven shots. Pritam Singh will show you how to handle them. I hope none of this will prove necessary, but I'm damned if I'm going to let the Spanish loot my cargo or take my ship.'

'Sir . . . ?' began Jones anxiously.

'If there are issues of conscience rest-assured I shall do my best to avoid anyone being put in a position of extreme danger or insist on anyone's unconditional loyalty, but I shall expect a degree of obedience, at least until I can no longer bluff matters out . . . Now you will have to excuse me, I'm going to get the *tindal* to rig me a bosun's chair and get myself hoisted aloft.'

'Is that wise, sir?' asked Jones, who in his fretfulness could not resist a comment of some sort.

'No, Vee-Jay, it is not wise, but needs must when the devil drives.'

Being hoisted to the near-naked fore-masthead was an unpleasant experience, reminding Kirton all too readily of the last time he had been aloft and the consequences thereof. True, he had on a couple of occasions hauled himself laboriously up to the main cross-trees, but he did not count such minor expeditions. Now he swung about the mast truck, his leg plaguing him like the devil. He knew he was running a temperature and feared the sudden onset of a serious fever.

He steadied himself before casting his eyes round. Ahead of the *Tethys* the river stretched for about half a mile before a second bend took it round to the west again, flowing through dense mangrove swamps. He noted, with some satisfaction, that the *Tethys* herself was sufficiently tucked round the first bend to conceal her from seaward, though of course her masts rose some way above the mangroves, giving him his vantage point. And from this he could see *La Reina* about a mile to seaward of the river's mouth.

Gingerly, using his good leg hooked round the pole of the mast to steady himself, he levelled his pocket-glass. It shook a good deal, partly from his mild fever, but also due to his precarious position, so it was impossible to be certain, but there seemed to be some activity on the corvette's deck. He compelled himself to wait patiently, taking the opportunity to take another look round, concentrating on the river as it wound itself into the green hinterland. In the distance, hills rose, the extensive foothills which culminated somewhere to the far north in the magnificent peak of Gunung Kinabalu. He could hear the chatter of monkeys, and here and there a flock of birds would suddenly rise *en masse*, whirl low over the canopy before resettling. His eye was caught by a distant speck wheeling high-up against the sky; an eagle soared just below clouds pregnant with rain.

Then he studied the river itself, as it flowed steadily past. Such was the speed of the stream, doubtless influenced by the first rains falling on the distant mountains, that the *Tethys* lay with her head directly upriver. Along the edge of the mangroves, where the entangled branches dipped into the water and in many places had caught streamers of vegetation and small branches, a myriad of eddies and counter-currents ran.

Transferring his attention to the deck of his little ship, he stared down at her with a feeling of immense pride. He felt light-headed and swallowed hard. 'Not now, for God's sake,' he muttered. Lloyd had been right; his plaguey leg was more now than a mere inconvenience. Suddenly he heard old Ibrahim, the *casab*, telling him to look after the *Tethys* and was almost choked by emotion at the recollection.

'My God, Hal,' he said to himself, 'this is no place to be wobbly . . .'

But there was no gainsaying the sweep of her deck . . . He waved at the two faces of the seamen tending the gantline by which he was suspended in his bosun's chair, then he raised his eyes and twisted seawards again. He did not require a telescope to see what was happening now. Smoke billowed from the corvette's funnel and she had at least four of her boats in the water. Clearly *La Reina*'s captain was going to creep further inshore and cover a major boarding party with his guns! At the same instant he realised something else: as the *Tethys* lay, in the grip of the river's stream, her broadside guns could not be trained far enough aft to command the width of the river astern of her.

For a second he felt the wings of defeat and despair touch him and the emotion that had almost unmanned him at the recollection of old Ibrahim again swept over him. Then two extraordinary things occurred: A shadow passed over him, not once but twice, and—greatly daring—he looked up to see, about a hundred feet above him, the silhouette of the sea-eagle wheeling overhead against a patch of sapphire blue sky through which the sun shot its shadow. As the great bird swept away, low over the canopy, the monkeys stilled their chatter. 'Ibrahim?' he found himself saying, quite involuntarily, at which the great bird screeched its call and soared away, leaving the monkeys to resume their relieved babble.

Kirton, felt a powerful stiffening of resolve. Taking one more look to seaward to confirm the Spaniards' design was as he had surmised, he transferred his attention to the deck again and shouted, '*Arriah! Arriah!*'

As he began his jerky descent, half-spinning and kicking himself free of obstructions, the second strange event happened. Swung so that he faced aft he suddenly caught sight of Sharimah. She stood at the companionway staring upwards, her right hand shading her eyes as she watched Kirton dangling inelegantly from his gantline. And then she smiled. He was sure she smiled, though her face was partially shaded by her hand, but the very thought of it brought Kirton to a high-pitch of nervous energy. Adrenaline flooded through him and his usually quick wits came to his aid as, reaching the deck and casting off the encumbrance of the bosun's chair, he took the cane one of his seamen offered him and stumped rapidly aft.

He almost leapt onto the low poop and limped his way towards the companionway.

'Sharimah, go see Cookie with Ah Chuan. Make plenty *makanan* for all crew: cold rice and dried fish, last all day.'

As soon as he was sure she understood he roared for Jones, Tan, and Pritam Singh, rapping out orders to put the *Tethys* in some sort of posture of defence.

'The Spanish are coming in force this time,' he explained when they had gathered about him. 'My guess is that they intend taking the ship as a prize and I'm not going to let them. With the strength of the river's outflowing stream they'll take some time getting here, even though their bloody picket-boat is towing the pulling boats, so we make best of a bad situation. There will be a big bonus for everyone if we pull this off. Let the hands know that . . . *gaji besar* . . . big wages . . .' Kirton stared about him to see they all understood what he was saying. Pritam Singh and Tan were already half-smiling, though Jones looked dour and apprehensive. Kirton ignored his chief mate, alternating his glance at the others. 'Now, this is what we are going to do . . .'

He began by a rapid briefing of the chief *jaga*. 'Get more Spencer guns up and show both mates how to use them. Then, if we have time, spread the weapons among others in the crew, petty-officers first. Otherwise tell 'em to get their seamen's knives ready . . . Oh, and no shots until I say so. Savee?'

'Yes, *Tuan*.' The *Jaga* hurried off, calling out orders.

'Tan, I want you to get a good rope secured to the anchor cable just outside hawse-pipe then bring it aft down port-side, outside everything, run inside after leads and take to after capstan; you'll need a snatch-block or two and there'll be a lot of strain on it.' This was accompanied by an energetic mime-show. 'Then, when I say, we pay out some cable, heave on rope and swing ship across river so that starboard cannon sweep *sungei* . . .'

'Ah, I savee, *Tuan*,' the ever intelligent Chinese officer responded with a cruel grin.

'You make big guns ready, take best sailormen, but don't fire until I tell you . . .'

'I savee, *Tuan* . . .'

'Very good, see to it, chop-chop.'

Kirton turned to Jones. The chief mate's eyes were full of misgiving so Kirton relaxed and smiled at him, saying, 'Trust me Vee-Jay, just trust me. I know you have a wife and children.'

'Captain Kirton . . .' Jones began. But Kirton over-rode him. All along the deck men were already being given orders by Tan and Pritam Singh, and Kirton was aware of a buzz of activity which showed no lack of compliance with his orders. Somehow he was deeply affected by this obedience and Jones's part in all this was not important.

'I don't mind if you sit down below and keep out of all this,' he said kindly, 'but if you are prepared to carry out orders, please take charge of the waist. You heard what I said to Pritam Singh and Tan: No wild firing, everything is to be controlled. Now make up your mind. I'm going below to get myself ready.'

He did not wait to see what Jones would do, leaving the man to his own thoughts, but as he made to return to the deck after arming himself with his Colt and several clips of ammunition, Jones had not come below. Kirton paused for a moment, then went back into the pantry where Sharimah was preparing fruit. Putting his arms about her he whispered in her ear, '*Saya sangat sayangkan awak,*' meaning 'I love you so much,' adding in English 'you give me great courage, my lovely.' Then, without waiting for a response he returned to the foot of the companionway. For a moment he stared at the now empty arms rack where first the Enfields and latterly the Spencers had nestled.

'It has to be that,' he said to himself before hauling himself up on deck.

From the poop Kirton could see that preparations for receiving the Spanish were well advanced. Tan had the rope spring round the after capstan and on the hatch an array of a score of Spencer rifles lay, with Pritam Singh watching over them, explaining the mechanism of loading seven cartridges into the magazine in the butt-stock to the *tindal* and *tomelo*. To his relief Jones was hanging close-by and Kirton judged he was gathering nerve to join in the defence of the ship.

Kirton turned aft; at any moment, he judged, the Spanish picket-boat with its towed cutters would come round the bend. Then he found

Sharimah at his side. She slipped her hand in his, saying, '*Saya sayang awak*, Hari.'

He smiled at her. 'I know my lovely,' he said simply, turning his head to smile at her. 'And now you must go below and stay there.'

A second later the picket-boat came into sight. 'Go!' he commanded her, raising his voice. 'Stand by the spring, Tan!' Kirton called, then shouted at the carpenter at the windlass: 'Veer cable *Tomelo*!' As the half shackle rumbled out through the hawse, and before the river had the slack in its grip, he shouted to Tan. 'Now heave away, Tan!'

Tan, who was knelt at the breech of the starboard gun which was trained as far aft as possible, waved his hands at the seamen gathered round the after capstan. They threw their weight against the capstan bars.

Kirton watched as the ship's head swung to starboard, praying that the rope would take the strain, then he turned his attention to the approach of the Spanish boats. He could see Espina standing up in the stern of the picket-boat, the white uniform of his tunic crossed with a bandolier, a sword at his hip catching a gleam of pallid sunshine that shone through a break in the massing clouds. His side-kick, Midshipman Bustamente, commanded the picket-boat with other junior officers in the pulling boats that trailed astern on their tow-lines. These were crammed with seamen, some presumably detailed to take the oars when required, those further aft with muskets or rifles upright between their knees. At the bow of the picket-boat the mounted Armstrong gun was manned, the sun catching this too, glistening briefly on the brass cartridges in their long belt.

Against the strong current they approached slowly, giving Kirton time to go to the flag halliards and hoist the sultan's colours to the peak of the standing gaff. He then removed from the flag-locker the British red ensign, walked forward, and bent it to the mainmast flag halliards. After running this aloft he returned to the stern and stood, completely exposed on the long and elegant counter, leaning on his stick, a lonely figure in white nankeen trousers, a short, blue, brass-buttoned cotton jacket and white shirt with a white silk cravat round his neck, its tails fluttering in the light breeze. He stared at Espina who stared back.

When he thought Espina could hear him, he challenged the Spanish officer. 'What are your intentions, Lieutenant?'

'I intend to board and thoroughly search your vessel, Kirton,' Espina bellowed back in his near-perfect English. 'We know you have a large consignment of contraband arms on board.'

Kirton hoped he was bluffing, though if he had guessed correctly it was a fair presumption on the Spaniard's part.

'Boarding me here would be an illegal act, Lieutenant, I am in Dutch territory and I reserve the right to defend myself and resist your boarding party!'

'He's casting off the boats,' Jones observed sharply, appearing at Kirton's side.

'I can see that! Go back to the waist, Vee-Jay. You may have to take command if they pick me off,' Kirton's dismissal was abrupt. He was more concerned with the approaching enemy. 'I'll sink your boats, Espina!' Kirton shouted, conveying his intentions to those with arms aboard the *Tethys*, 'and you are in the field of fire of my cannon . . .'

Then all hell broke loose. The Armstrong fired an intimidatory burst which, aimed low, struck the brigantine's counter in a sweep of nasty explosions of splinters and ran a line of splashes across the river's grey surface. Ironically, owing to the extreme pain in his gammy leg, Kirton could not step backwards quickly, so he appeared to stand his ground defiantly, leaning on his stick whereupon Tan, without orders, fired the starboard breech-loader. Furious, Kirton hauled himself about to where Tan pointed at the rope-spring; it was already stranding where it passed through the lead. In another moment it would part and the *Tethys* would swing to her cable again, head upstream, her starboard cannon useless.

But then, presumably at some prearranged signal, there was the noise of an incoming shot, and with a whine a round from *La Reina* passed somewhere over-head and buried itself in the mangroves on the far side of the river.

Meanwhile, having dragged his charges as close as possible, Espina had cast off his boats and they were struggling under oars to get alongside at as many places as they might to confuse the defence. Free of her encumbrances, the picket-boat suddenly gained ground and surged up under the

Tethys's counter just as the spring parted with a crack like that of a rifle. The flying end whipped past Kirton, missing him by a hair's breadth.

Pritam Singh's *jagas* needed no other encouragement. As the Spanish pulling boats fanned out and were caught by the river's powerful stream, they levelled their Spencers. The boats were sitting ducks.

Seeing this, Kirton bellowed, 'Aim at their hulls! Sink the boats!'

The combined fire of the starboard breech-loader and the Sikhs' rifles created havoc; Spanish seamen could be seen gesticulating and bailing their boats; one had already drifted so far off as to be on the point of disappearing round the bend in the river. Only one still came on close enough to offer real support to Espina's picket-boat which had gained shelter under the brigantine's stern. Now the Armstrong was fired in earnest and Kirton stepped backwards, the bullets going over his head.

He beckoned Tan and shouted at him, 'Get a couple of shot and be ready to drop them into any boat that makes it alongside! Savee?' Tan acknowledged the order and made for the starboard garland, hefting a black sphere appreciatively.

Espina lacked neither courage nor persistence; using the cover of the *Tethys's* long counter he ordered the picket-boat edged up close enough to get a grapnel over the rail without anyone noticing until, preceded and then assisted by two energetic young Spanish seamen, a gasping Espina himself appeared alongside the *Tethys's* steering-box.

'Get off my ship!' Kirton roared at him lugging out the Colt, but a second later a bullet, fired by one of the sailors, smashed into Kirton's weapon sending it flying and a smiling Espina was advancing along the poop, throwing an order over his shoulder. It proved his undoing, for he had told the second seaman to slash the Suluese ensign's halliards and in that moment of distraction, a furious Kirton had unscrewed the hilt of his sword-stick, made a shuffling lunge and had the point at Espina's throat. Roaring for support, Kirton pressed his advantage, jabbing his sword-point into the high neck of Espina's collar so that the poor man involuntarily retreated, unable to catch his balance and bring up his own revolver.

Kirton did not look round, but he knew the *jagas* were now behind him and he kept jabbing the sword-stick as Espina and the two seamen who had gained the deck, faced by the fearsome Sikhs, retreated on either side of their chief. One of the Sikhs drew his own short sword and slashed the grapnel line, whereupon one of the Spanish sailors fell into the river, causing confusion in the boat, the occupants of which had no idea what was going on above them.

It ended in farce. As a second shot from the corvette whined overhead, Espina and his two compatriots ran out of deck. The lack of a taffrail that had vaguely troubled Kirton all those years ago when he had first boarded the brigantine and which he had never bothered to rectify, now proved Espina's undoing; he tripped and fell overboard, followed by one of the sailors; the other turned and jumped.

A moment later the crew of the *Tethys*, all of whom had gathered aft, watched—chattering like monkeys—as the picket-boat drifted astern, dragging Espina and his escort out of the water. Ten minutes later the entire Spanish flotilla of boats had vanished round the bend.

'I fear they'll try again under cover of darkness,' Kirton said as he sat at the head of the saloon table, his right hand in a bowl of cool water. The lucky shot that had knocked the Colt flying had caused heavy bruising and sprained his wrist, a situation made worse by his brandishing his sword-stick. Jones, Tan, and Pritam Singh were ranged about the table and Sharimah and Ah Chuan were clearing away their evening meal of cold rice and fish.

'What can we do to stop them?' Jones asked.

'Move the ship,' Kirton said.

'You mean run the blockade? That'll never work. Even if you get past the corvette she'll chase us and now we know her commander is willing to use his main guns, I don't see how we can escape. I think, sir,' Jones concluded, 'we should give up and surrender on terms.'

Kirton looked at Jones; it wasn't his fault that he lacked the enthusiasm for extending this ignoble squabble. Neither he nor any of the others deserved to suffer further. He suddenly felt guilty, taking them all down to hell because he had no future. He called for whisky, indicating they should all take a slug.

Since Kirton did not immediately round on him, Jones pressed what he conceived to be his advantage. 'They know we have a contraband cargo on board. I don't know how, but we heard what that Spaniard said . . .'

'I think I know how,' Kirton said wearily. 'I'm guessing but you said that young midshipman took an interest in my shotguns in the hold, did you not?'

'Yes, that's true.'

'Well, let us suppose he has an interest in firearms. He knew about Egg Durs, and he's a young man after all . . .'

'But I am sure he did not see a single Spencer in the hold,' Jones retorted.

'He didn't need to. There was a rack of the damn things at the foot of the companionway ladder. The last time he was aboard the Enfields were there, and when Pritam here mustered the *jagas* on deck with their arms all those months ago, they bore the Enfields. Suppose that young midshipman spotted the difference? It's possible and I'm inclined to think that he did and that when he got back to the corvette he told Espina . . .'

'Why didn't he point this out when he was aboard us the other day?'

'I don't know, perhaps he needed an hour or two to work it out; perhaps his relationship with Espina required him to gather some courage . . . I simply don't know, but I cannot think of any other explanation . . .'

Kirton looked round the table at the end of his dialogue with Jones during which Tan and the Sikh had remained silent.

'Now look,' he said at last, 'I'm going to ask you all to do one last thing for me and then I intend to discharge you. You will all have every prospect of getting back to Singapore and Vee-Jay you will have command of your steamer, but we've got a long night ahead of us first. After that . . .' Kirton paused and shrugged, 'well, we'll see . . .' He cleared his throat, tossed off his whisky and said, 'Now listen carefully, because we are going to move the ship *ulu*, upstream . . .'

As soon as the ship's company were fed they were mustered and began to implement Kirton's plan. One watch was detailed to get the kedge anchor over the side with a rope cable bent on to it. The other was ordered to send up the fore-topgallant, mast-head the fore-topsail, and let the upper square sails hang in their gear. The afterguard of the *jagas* got the main gaff-topsail up ready to hoist.

Then that part of the watch tending the sails now manned the boat and brought it under the bow where, by this time, the kedge anchor was over the side awaiting it. With the kedge lashed across the stern of the boat, the oarsmen struggled manfully upstream, towing its rope cable, to let it go after they had stretched the cable as far as they could. The other part of the watch immediately manned the capstan and, hauling in the cable, drew the *Tethys* slowly upstream. The spare men drew in the slack on the rope cable and they began the slow and laborious kedging of the brigantine upstream against the current. It was back-breaking labour, necessitating frequent changes of oarsmen, but Kirton was determined to work the *Tethys* up, beyond the next bend if it was humanly possible. Somehow, he hoped, the Spanish, discovering the brigantine had been moved, would demur from penetrating so deeply into Dutch territory. Whatever the outcome, the swift onset of the tropical night aided them. So too did a generous issue of spirits, broached from the cargo.

At first there was no wind, but after a couple of hours, by which time it was almost as black as pitch, a gentle zephyr stirred in the mangroves and lifted the red ensign which had been left at the main truck and could just about be seen from the poop against the clouds. Somewhere beyond the cloud-cover sailed a rising moon.

Kirton ordered the upper sails clewed down and trimmed, for the wind, gusting and fluky in its direction, now came over the port quarter; gradually the *Tethys* began to overhaul her boat. Fortunately it was in the process of running out the kedge, not the bower anchor. He ordered the cable buoyed and slipped, shouting into the darkness for the boat to drop the anchor and return to the ship as the wind slowly filled in.

'My God,' he breathed as he stood by the helm, conning the ship and holding her in midstream for fear of shallows inshore, 'if only this holds . . .'

For half an hour the *Tethys* crept through the water, gradually gathering way over the ground. Kirton had had the binnacle light doused; the compass was of no use here and he needed to see the flat, steel-bright surface of the river as it reflected the pallid, diffused light on the unseen moon as the turbulent cloud-cover now thickened and thinned. His heart rejoiced as they approached the next bend and he ordered the helm over.

Forward, Tan trimmed the yards; aft, Jones tended the gaff-topsail. 'Give her the spanker Vee-Jay,' Kirton called. He could not quite believe it, but the wind was backing in their favour as a squall gathered. They crept on; the sky grew darker and some drops of rain fell.

'All hands, stand-by!' roared Kirton. 'Squall coming!' The Fates, so recently in his favour were, he felt, about to punish him for his audacity.

The wind suddenly increased; from no-where a heavy rain fell but the wind held steady, though stronger, and suddenly the *Tethys* was seething along, over-canvassed, her *jurmudi* struggling at the helm.

'*Tuan*, I cannot hold her!' Kirton gained the grating beside him and the two of them held the brigantine steady. Someone on the fo'c's'le cried out: 'Starboard, *Tuan*, starboard!' and Kirton put the helm over a spoke then met the swing.

'Steady as you go, sir!' That was Jones's voice now, up in the knight-heads, conning the vessel in her wild charge upstream. God alone knew how many knots they were doing, but the opposing flow of the river enabled them to retain some measure of control until the wind and rain eased. Kirton blew the droplets of water from the end of his nose, relinquishing the helm to the *jurmudi*. They were far enough upstream now to deter any deep penetration of the river by the Spanish that night; of that he was certain. Now he must make preparations for re-anchoring. As if acting for his convenience, the wind dropped away as the rain ceased.

And then it happened. The wind suddenly veered and struck them with the full force of a second terrific squall. It was accompanied by a rolling thunder and then lightning, great sheets of it, reaching high, high up into the towering clouds. Once again the *jurmudi* lost control of the helm as the *Tethys* again gathered a furious way. Like a great horse, throwing off the constraints of her rider, she paid-off, charging headlong into the mangroves on her starboard side. For what seemed like an age she crashed her way through the outer growth, tearing at branches and sending a parcel of roosting birds into the air and a pack of gibbons into a terrified and howling frenzy. She seemed to come to a stand-still, her sails still drawing, her decks swept by the mangroves, wind, and torrential rain; then her own wake followed her, lifting her, to inch her further into the dense tangle of undergrowth.

From aloft there was a crack, and her tall fore-topmast gave way, spars, sails, and rigging falling onto the canopy, then, slowly subsiding as the mangroves gave way, onto her foredeck. Meanwhile the mainmast acquired the ethereal, greenish glow of St. Elmo's fire.

Slowly the squall passed, the sky cleared, and a terrible silence fell on the vessel as she lay under the moonlight. Kirton gave a short laugh. 'Well,' he remarked to no-one in particular but in a voice that most of the cowering crew could hear, 'the Spanish won't get us here!'

CHAPTER EIGHTEEN

The Lord of the Ship

LAMP-LIGHT FLOODED THE SALOON; IT WAS TWO HOURS BEFORE DAWN and Kirton had mustered his officers again. 'I take it the boat's crew found us?' he asked.

'Eventually,' said Jones, his voice tense and desperate.

'Good. Now at dawn Vee-Jay you and the entire ship's company will embark in the boat, work your way downstream and give yourselves up to the Spanish. You will tell them that we do not carry arms and you will stick to this story, after all, you never saw them loaded and you are the ship's chief mate. Moreover, you will tell the Spaniards that I insisted upon remaining behind, that I am in the grip of a fatal fever and not in my right mind. Avoid any hint that you have mutinied, which might give them grounds for arresting you and the crew. Throw all the blame on me; tell them the last thing you saw me doing was soaking the ship in paraffin . . .'

He looked round at their faces. They were all dog-tired, exhausted, yet incredulous, looking at each other, waiting for someone to protest, but no-one did. Was their habit of obedience so ingrained, Kirton asked himself? He smiled and went on. 'In an hour I shall have made up the crew's wages and apportioned adequate bonuses, to be paid by Messrs. Lee, Rodham & Co. No-one will go short. Now, when you meet the Spanish you can request passage under cartel to Jolo; I'll give you funds enough to buy a pearling schooner, or the like, outright; something to carry you all safely to Singapore where you can give my compliments to Lee and Rodham.'

'But sir,' Jones said at last, 'we cannot leave you here.' A murmur of agreement ran round the table.

Kirton shook his head. 'You can and will; it is my wish and command, the last I shall give you.' He looked round the table, fixing each of them with a smile—the older, apprehensive Anglo-Indian, the wiry, active Chinaman, and the tall, handsome Sikh. 'It has been a privilege to command you but, to use an English expression which I cannot translate, every dog has his day.' He stood up, leaning on the edge of the table, 'That is all, I wish you luck, now I think you must make your preparations . . .'

Tan and Pritam Singh withdrew with mumbled expressions of God knows what, but Jones tarried. 'Sir,' he said, his head waggling worse than usual, his deep brown eyes full of tears . . .'

'Go, Vee-Jay,' Kirton said, his own voice cracking with emotion. 'The men need you now. I am finished. The bones of my bad leg have been infected. I do not have long to live any way.' He stood up as the mate hesitated. 'Go, go!' Kirton insisted. 'The command of a brand new steamer awaits you.'

As Jones left the saloon Ah Chuan coughed at the pantry door. Kirton turned, but before he had a chance to tell his tiger to pack his belongings the steward said firmly, 'Ah Chuan stay with Captain Kirton.'

'No, no, Ah Chuan. You must go, go home with others, back to Singapore, back to your wife . . .'

'Ah Chuan's wife dead, *Tuan* . . .'

'I did not know . . .'

'Long time ago . . .'

'But your children . . .'

'No have childer . . .'

'It doesn't matter, Ah Chuan, you cannot stay. I am dying . . . my leg . . .'

'I savee, *Tuan*, I savee long-time, but Ah Chuan stay. Please . . . no wantchee go back Singapore-side.'

'You are certain? You may die in jungle . . .'

'Then I die . . .'

'But how will your bones rest with your ancestors?'

An Chuan smiled. 'I not know my family, *Tuan*. Come Singapore long-time before, when boy. Stowaway, clean boots, then catchee job as steward ... Now stay and die with Capt'n Kirton.'

The simple man's declaration almost broke Kirton's reserve and he held out his hand to the Chinaman. 'You my very good friend, Ah Chuan,' Kirton said, his voice thick with emotion. 'Absolute top-dollar ...' he managed.

'You must see missee now, *Tuan*. She stay too.'

'Where is she?'

'In your cabin, *Tuan*. Wait longtime. Velly flightened.'

Kirton went through to his cabin where Sharimah lay weeping on the double bunk. 'Oh Hari, please, I no go ...'

He stood looking at her, his heart full. Over their heads he could hear the stamp of feet as the crew assembled aft and prepared to embark in the boat. He was full of conflicting emotions and pragmatic thoughts. To have Ah Chuan by his side to carry out what was in his mind was one thing, to deprive Sharimah of her life seemed entirely different. He found it difficult to say anything at that moment, and in his turmoil he managed only: 'Very well. Now I have matters to deal with ...' and left her to her tears. At the back of his mind lay a plan to bundle her into the boat at the last moment.

Opening the ship's safe and collecting a large bag and some paper notes, he picked up two letters from his desk. Then he went back to the saloon and took a clean white table-cloth from the sideboard and carried it all on deck.

The after end of the poop was a hubbub of activity as the men lowered their bags of belongings down into the boat. As each of them went over the side down the Jacob's ladder, Kirton shook their hands and gave them some money and some *sycee* silver. The last men to go were Jones, Tan, and Pritam Singh.

When they were ready to cast off Kirton leaned over the side. He thanked them all for their service and handed Tan the table-cloth. 'Secure that to the boat-hook,' he said, 'and show it the instant you see the Spaniards. My guess is that you will meet them before you reach the river's mouth. Now, as to the Spencer rifles; make clear that there are none on board and never were; the ones Pritam and his *jagas* carried were simply replacements for the old Enfields. Leave the lie on my conscience. None of you were aboard when the guns were loaded, and I alone bear the responsibility. D'you all understand?'

The three men nodded.

'If you do meet them in their boats, warn them not to advance any further. Tell them that I have gone mad—*loco*, I think they call it, or say am an *amok*—and that I intend to burn the ship. She is mine, after all!' He waited for his words to sink in, then: 'Now finally, Vee-Jay, here is a letter for the commander of that corvette, and another for Mr Lee and Mr Rodham. In a minute I am going below to get Sharimah. Now you all get into the boat and I will cast you off when I have lowered her in.'

He waited until the three men had settled themselves in the over-crowded boat. Thank God they did not have to go far in her, he thought, for she was almost dangerously over-loaded. Fortunately the current would do most of the work for them. As Jones took the tiller Kirton called down: 'Mr Jones is your new *kurmudi*, your new *Tuan*. He will see you all get jobs in the new steam-boiler ship that soon come Singapore-side. Now, you wait, one more thing . . .'

He descended to the cabin and asked Sharimah to get out of bed. 'No, Hari, no!'

He grasped her round her waist, pinning her arms by her side and tried to drag her from the cabin, but she wriggled free and ran up the companionway. By the time Kirton reached the deck Sharimah had cast off the boat's painter and then sunk to her knees as the current caught the craft and, the men in it shoving aside the tangle of mangroves, drove it out into the full force of the river's stream.

'Sharimah!' Kirton wailed at her despairingly and at his cry most of the men in the boat turned to look at the two of them.

Then Jones stood up in the stern and waved, followed by the whole crew, setting the boat wobbling dangerously. 'God bless you, Captain!' Jones shouted and a sort of cheer rose up from the men sitting discon-solately about him.

And then they were carried off. Kirton stood staring after them for some time, then turned to Sharimah.

'Why . . . ?' he began, but she pressed her hand to his mouth.

'You lord of the ship,' she said simply.

Kirton coughed to clear his throat. 'You get some food, my lovely,' he said at last. 'Make nice *chow-chow* we all eat together, make happy. Ah Chuan and me very busy for maybe some time. You make plenty best *makanan*.'

Then, calling for Ah Chuan to come on deck with an oil-lamp, Kirton hobbled down onto the main deck and peeled back the hatch tarpaulin from one corner. With a great effort he lifted the first of four hatch-boards and began to half-carry, half-drag it onto the poop and aft to the counter. Ah Chuan joined him and while Kirton lowered the red ensign from the main-masthead, unrove the long halliard and began to loosely lash the four boards together, he sent the tiger off to gather together a number of items, including bedding from the mates' cabins, several cans of paraffin, and some tins of paint from the locker forward.

Once Ah Chuan had completed the pile of combustibles, the two men eased the extemporised raft over the counter, pulling its line so that it lay close beneath them. They carefully dropped onto the bobbing hatch-boards the heap of bedding, sousing it with paraffin and paint. Next Kirton went back to the hatch with the lantern and, scrambling over the coaming, clambered down into the hold and, finding an open case of Blakeslee cartridge boxes, he gathered up several and got them up on deck and then aft, to top off the pile of inflammable material piled on the raft over which he allowed the red ensign to fall.

'Nearly ready, Ah Chuan, but before we set fire, we need to make big bang.'

Beckoning for An Chuan to follow him, Kirton went to the ready-use lockers near the breech-loaders, extracting several cartridges and double-charging both cannon; then he showed Ah Chuan how to fire the port gun, telling him to stand-by to fire it.

'Now, you wait here,' he said, taking back aft the lantern and a single cartridge. Kneeling on the counter he pierced the cartridge and sprinkled the gun-powder over the combustibles. Finally he carefully dropped a handful of the Blakeslee boxes onto the black-powder.

Standing up he took a look at their handiwork before walking forward and hauling himself into the main shrouds. He ascended to the cross-trees from where, above the canopy of the mangroves, he could see *La Reina*, anchored just beyond the river's bar. He could also see, like water-beetles, the black shapes of several small craft and was able to make out the steam picket-launch and the *Tethys*'s own boat with her distinctive white hull and green gunwale. Matters must have fallen out as Kirton had predicted, though it was not hard to work out what the Spaniards would do. It had not taken long for the fierce current to carry the fugitives out to sea. Before descending, he cast a quick look round; there was no sign of the eagle, only a roiling pile of rain clouds spilling over the mountains and racing towards him. And from overhead a thickening overcast was already letting fall a thin and chilly rain.

Lest a deluge destroy his carefully prepared stratagem, Kirton swung onto a back stay and with the *éclat* he had once demonstrated in the old *Cormorant*, he slid to the deck, landing on his good leg. He was nevertheless breathing hard now as he returned to the extremity of the counter-stern.

Rain was beginning to pitter-patter onto the water; bending to the cleat where the flag halliard secured the raft, he paid out a few feet. The raft moved off until the line restrained it again, whereupon Kirton tossed the burning oil-lamp onto it and waited with bated breath. For a moment nothing appeared to happen, then the leaking oil from the reservoir caught fire and as soon as a few flames showed themselves, Kirton rapidly slackened the flag halliard.

The raft moved away, catching on some mangroves just as the fire got a grip. Kirton swore, and hauled the line back, giving it a jerk as thick black smoke began to rise and he wished that he had not added the cartridge boxes. As he let out a torrent of filthy language the raft was caught by an eddy and pulled clear of the outlying mangroves.

'Go, you bastard! Go!' he snarled desperately.

And then the river's current got a grip of it and Kirton threw the flag halliard after the raft. It snaked across the water as he hobbled forward as fast as he could to kneel at the starboard cannon.

'Fire, Ah Chuan, fire!' he bellowed.

The detonation of the two guns was not quite simultaneous, but it was close enough and Kirton stumbled aft to see what had happened to the raft. At first he could not see it, then he saw the wild flicker of the flames through the vegetation along with a rising pall of black smoke. It did not appear to be moving, but if they took shelter he did not think the exploding cartridges would do them any harm, so he motioned Ah Chuan to go below.

Sharimah met them at the saloon door, her face pale with the shock of the concussion of the guns.

'What happen, Hari?'

'I hope I have tricked the Spanish,' he said, forgetting she could not understand the full import of his remark, but she caught the triumph in his face, and the glee in the eyes of Ah Chuan, and so she smiled and he kissed her.

Teniente Miguel Espina stood on the forebridge of *La Reina* talking to his commander. He had met the *Tethys*'s boat as it crossed the bar, swept seawards as much by the out-flowing river as by any effort on the part of its occupants.

He had just handed his captain the letter Jones had given him and his captain had handed it back, ordering him to translate. Espina was in the process of reading the sentence denying the presence of any contraband arms on board when the rolling concussion of an explosion reached them, and they saw a cloud of smoke, thick and black, rise from the distant jungle, startling flocks of birds. Faint crackling detonations as of a fire in timber followed, borne seaward on a sudden wind that carried with it the first drops of rain.

After a moment the captain of *La Reina* remarked that the explosion was not ferocious enough to have been caused by a hold full of ammunition, no-one ran guns for profit without the ammunition for them, for the Love of God! His tone was full of reproach.

'There were no repeating rifles, were there, Teniente Espina? You let that boy fool you with his ridiculous "deduction." Moreover. you have wasted my time, brought dishonour on the ship and wasted coal! Get out of my sight!'

Chastened and humiliated, Espina did as he was bid, intent on revenging his hurt pride on Midshipman Bustamente.

La Reina's captain turned to his navigating officer and jerked his chin at the heavy clouds rolling up from the west. 'There will be more wind and much rain,' he said with a sigh. 'There is no point in our remaining here in Dutch waters. We'll take these Chinamen and their bastard officers to Jolo and I'll interview their chief mate once we are under way. Pass the word . . .'

After the order had been acknowledged and implemented, he went on, conversationally, 'I suppose the Englishman was mad? What do you think?'

'There is no sign of him or his woman in the boat, sir,' the navigating officer remarked.

His commander grunted. He was already formulating the *Report of Proceedings* he would have to make to his commodore once he returned to Jolo. At least he had the satisfaction of seeing the destruction of an impudent man and of his brigantine. As for the crew he would be delighted to off-load them at Jolo.

For some time Kirton remained on deck, watching the thick smoke slowly thin as the fire consumed the flammable material he had loaded on the raft. But by the time the rain had arrived in earnest, to hit the river's surface with such force as to hiss like a monstrous snake and raise a low kind of mist, Kirton and his two companions had secured themselves below. Here, after Ah Chuan had laid the saloon table, Sharimah served a sumptuous rice dish garnished with all the delicacies she could lay her hands upon. Coming in to the saloon Kirton noted that only two places had been laid up.

'Ah Chuan, you sit. Eat *chow-chow* with Missee and me.'

'No, *Tuan* . . .' Ah Chuan appeared horrified.

'Yes, Ah Chuan,' Kirton insisted. 'That is my order. There is no servant or master now, we are all on a journey . . .'

Reluctantly Ah Chuan drew out a chair and sat awkwardly, where-upon Sharimah rose, went into the pantry and brought him his chop-sticks. Kirton poured each of them a small tumbler of whisky. What he had in mind required a momentum that he must maintain and he made a great effort, despite the difficulties, to draw out of his tiger a full account of his early life, of how his family had been caught-up in a rebellious movement—perhaps the very same that occasioned old Cha to acquire all those rifles. The upheaval had caused the death of Ah Chuan's father by strangulation but his son had escaped from the imperial forces, making for Shanghai. Here he had stowed away on a Singapore-bound steamship. During Ah Chuan's story Kirton kept Ah Chuan's glass full until Kirton himself rose from the table.

He waved his hands at the clutter of dirty dishes and both Ah Chuan and Sharimah began to clear away, the former none-too-steadily. 'I have some ship's business to attend to,' Kirton said, withdrawing to his cabin. Here he gathered the ship's papers and carried them on deck and took them forward, walking without his stick. The rain had eased, though the chill in the air and the heavy overcast told of more to come. On the foredeck he struggled through the wreckage of the foremast and a dense mass of mangrove branches. A pair of *wa wa* gibbons made him jump as he pulled out pages of the ship's log, tore up the manifest, the account of the crew's wages, and a number of other documents. Going to the paint-locker he picked up a small paint-kettle, a quarter filled it with white spirit, and with a Vesta made a small fire. As it took hold he removed from his jacket's inner pocket his British Certificate of Competency as a master-mariner and threw it too onto the small fire which, after about ten minutes, burnt itself out. As the pile of paper reduced itself to mere glowing ash, Kirton kicked these about and regarded the charring of the teak deck.

He had thought of setting fire to the *Tethys* herself, but that promise to Ibrahim kept returning to him and several times he thought he saw the old man on deck. But by now he was running a high temperature and was sustained largely by determination and nervous energy. As he came aft again he picked up one of the Spencers, fired off the two shots remaining in the magazine and reloaded it.

Without hesitating, he descended the companionway. The saloon was empty and he heard Sharimah calling him from their cabin.

'Hari . . .'

Holding the rifle behind his back he opened the door. She lay on the double-bunk clad only in her *sarong*. Her face was drawn but she smiled that lovely enigmatic smile that had so beguiled him.

'Where's Ah Chuan?' he asked abruptly.

'Hari, come . . .' She held out her hand, but he repeated his question. 'Where's Ah Chuan?'

'In pantry,' she replied and Kirton turned away, closing the door behind him. Behind him she began to weep.

At the door of the saloon Kirton paused, then swallowed hard. No sound came from the pantry, the sliding door of which was closed. 'God forgive me,' he muttered, moving as fast as he could round the table to the sliding door, bringing the Spencer up to his hip. Taking a deep breath, he wrenched the pantry door aside.

But Ah Chuan had done his work for him. The faithful Chinaman lay slumped on the tiled deck in a pool of blood, some of which still oozed from the mess he had made of his left wrist with the razor-sharp carving knife from the saloon sideboard drawer. The set of the familiar moon face seemed almost as imperturbable in death as in life, except that the eyes registered the effects of pain and shock.

Kirton stood looking down at him, shaking with emotion, the tears coursing down his face. 'Oh, God, Ah Chuan, Oh, God, you could have gone in the boat . . .' Kirton knelt down and closed the dead man's eyes. 'May your soul fly to your ancestors my devoted tiger, even if your bones must lie here until the end of time,' he murmured.

For a long while Kirton remained where he was, then he got up somewhat unsteadily and backed out of the pantry, sliding the door closed behind him.

As he returned to his cabin he left the Spencer on the saloon table. He had no wish to frighten Sharimah more than was necessary. He found her as had left her, though tears now coursed down her cheeks.

'Ah Chuan *sudah mati*?' she asked through great sobs.

Kirton nodded. She made room for him on the bed and he lay down beside her. Her body was cool against the heat of the fever that was fast consuming his own. He wanted to tell her she should have gone in the boat, that there was no way through the mangroves, that the rains had come, that her fate was inextricably bound up with his, but she knew all that, had known it from the moment he had rescued her from the Bugis bully, even if he had not.

'No *merdeka*?' she asked, confronting him with the naked spectre of his failure.

'No, Sharimah, no *merdeka*. Your *Tuan* not so bloody clever after all.'

He heard her sigh, then she said, 'Kiss, me Hari.'

He noticed that she wore the sultan's pearl at her throat and as he touched her face she pressed his hand against her cheek. '*Saya sangat sayangkan awak*,' she said softly.

He was too moved to respond, but he took her in his arms and they began to make love.

Afterwards he lay on his back. The love-making and the unaccustomed whisky caused Sharimah to drift into a doze, then he heard her even breathing; she had fallen into a deep sleep. Having ensured she was indeed unconscious, he rose and went through into the saloon to pick-up the Spencer rifle. Helping himself to a large slug of whisky he returned to the cabin and levelled the gun directly at her naked breast.

As he pulled the trigger she woke; for an instant they stared at each other before her eyes clouded and he discharged the rifle again, and then again, after which he slumped down on the deck, his back to the chest of drawers upon which the bunk was constructed, feeling her warm blood seep through his jacket and shirt, his own body wracked by great spasms.

Eventually he dragged himself to his feet. 'That was too easy,' he muttered, 'too bloody easy . . .'

He groped his way into the chart-room, laid down the rifle, found a cigar, lit it and went on deck. It was pouring with rain now, the torrential deluge of the monsoon was upon them in all its elemental force. He had hoped to cover his approach to the island of Siasi under such a torrent of *hujan*.

'Best laid plans . . .' he murmured.

In a few seconds his cigar was extinguished and he was soaked to the skin. Down his white nankeen trousers and around his feet the rain washed out Sharimah's blood as he stood there, abject in his misery, his leg causing him tremendous pain, the fever thundering in his head. The idea of walking off the counter into the river occurred to him, but that was not what he had planned. If he had committed one murder and caused a second death, natural justice told him he must have the guts to take his own life, not let the river accomplish what he could not.

He went below again, recovered the Spencer from the chart-table, and returned to the cabin. Without closing the door behind him he leaned his back against the bulkhead and felt the strong timbers of the little ship, pressing into them with all the strength he could muster. Then he turned the rifle, opened his mouth, and felt the steel muzzle bitter on his palate. Stretching his arm, he reached for the trigger with an extended forefinger. He had to arch his spine and throw his head back, but after a struggle his finger tip felt the curve of the firing mechanism.

He pushed it away from him.

Part Three

The Rain Forest of Kalimantan (Indonesian Borneo), Summer 1964

Lieutenant Charles Kirton hardly slept that night. Despite the privations of their bivouac the platoon slumbered, as would he himself have done had the circumstances been normal. But they were far from normal and as the hours passed, counted by the change in the marine pickets charged with their guarding, he lay in the wet dampness and thought of the impossibility of his circumstances.

It all came flooding back to him as he lay there: the old family story which he knew to have been true because once, when he had been a small boy, he had been shown the letters that had changed his family's fortunes; the one from Gurney, Gurney & Jago with its embossed heading sent from their offices in Singapore—the very name of the Lion City had stirred him—and the other, handwritten in the elegant copper-plate script of the family's benefactor, his great-grandmother's brother which bore the address of the sender as: *'Brigantine "Tethys," At anchor, Tanjong Pagar, Singapore,'* with a date in the 1870s that he could no longer remember.

The significance of these two scraps of correspondence, it had been explained to him, were that his great-grandparents had been obliged to take his great-grandmother's maiden name in order for Messrs Gurney, Gurney & Jago to remit a considerable sum of money from a mysterious relative who, so the story ran, had disappeared at sea in somewhat disreputable circumstances.

While his great-grandmother was content to abandon her married name, her husband had been less so, until the sum of money was disclosed to him. Fortunately for his immediate family, he did not survive for long afterwards, allowing his widow to avoid the squandering of her brother's fortune. As for the young Charlie Kirton, he cared not a fig for any of this, considering it something of a privilege to have familial connections to a man widely regarded—or so the family myth ran—as some sort of a pirate. It certainly gave him a leg-up at school and he had been privately beguiled by the words *'Brigantine "Tethys," At anchor Tanjong Pagar.'*

But now, as he lay in his sodden sleeping bag, staring up at the distant stars through the mosquito netting and beyond that the canopy of mangroves, he was filled with a strange conflict and a good deal of apprehension. On the one hand it was ridiculous not to have led his men directly to the shelter of the abandoned wreck last night, and on the other he was seized by a visceral dread of having to dispose of the three bodies of which he had caught only a glimpse the previous evening. Perhaps there were more, perhaps not and if not, what had happened to the rest of the crew? Or was the *Tethys* abandoned in the mangroves because they had first abandoned their master and who else? His steward, perhaps, and another who had remained loyal; God alone knew.

In the end, after a fitful sleep, he got up just as the dawn was flushing the sky and, making a gesture to the sentry to keep quiet, he crawled across to where McGuigan lay. Placing his right forefinger on the sergeant's head, just beside his ear, he roused the Ulsterman from his dreams.

'Come, Sarn't,' he said. 'We've got work to do . . .'

McGuigan muttered an obscenity, then gathered himself together and slipped out of his sleeping bag to join his commanding officer.

'We don't need our weapons for this,' Kirton muttered as he picked up his torch. A moment later he led off through the tangle of vegetation.

When they reached the port side of the brigantine McGuigan whistled. 'Bloody hell, sir,' he said wonderingly, looking upwards at the vessel's topside. Over the last century the river had piled sediment against the port side, causing a slight list to starboard, but more importantly allowing an almost dry-shod approach. It took the two fit men no more than a moment to scramble aboard aided by the mangrove branches that embraced the hull.

On deck it was a shambles; fallen boughs, drifts of dead leaves, gibbon excrement, and bird-lime disfigured the decks and the order of the little merchantman's once neat fife- and pin-rails. Now only a few rotten coils of manila hemp showed where once a myriad of ropes had been neatly coiled down. Broken spars lay athwart the deck: the wreckage of the foremast. What remained of the worm-eaten mainmast still rose from its housing at the break of the poop. A cargo derrick swung from a goose-neck about six feet up the main mast.

'She must have been a lovely vessel in her prime,' Kirton said appreciatively.

'More yacht than merchantman,' McGuigan added.

The corner of the single hatch was open and when the two men stared down into it as they worked their way aft, their reflections stared back at them, just perceptible in the growing daylight.

'Full of bloody water,' McGuigan observed unnecessarily, but betraying his apprehension at the reason they were creeping about on their own.

'Yes, but look,' said Kirton pulling his torch out and sending its narrow beam into the stinking darkness. 'What the hell is a Blakeslee cartridge box?'

Beside him McGuigan shrugged. 'No idea, sir. Time to find out later,' he said, adding, 'I wonder if those tins of connie-onnie are still edible?'

'We can find that out later too . . . She must have been gun-running.' Kirton remarked, looking about the deck and pointing. 'There are chocks there for a boat.'

'But no boat.'

'I guess it took off the majority of the crew before . . . well, whatever happened here,' replied Kirton. 'Come on,' he said curtly, suddenly impatient to get their grisly task over and done with and leading the way aft. As they mounted the poop they both stopped and regarded the starboard breech-loading cannon.

'There's a museum-piece for you,' observed Kirton shortly, before continuing towards the stern.

At the sea-step of the companionway Kirton swung himself over and descended into the gloom below, beckoning McGuigan to follow.

'There are three of them as far as I can tell, Sarn't,' Kirton said, his voice stiff with formality and resolution. 'Come through . . .' He drew the sergeant into the saloon.

'Bloody hell, this must have been quite a cosy nook . . .' McGuigan stared round curiously.

Kirton said nothing, but brushed aside those cobwebs that he had failed to disturb on his quick reconnaissance of the previous evening and pointed inside the pantry. It was full of desiccated rat-droppings, bat-shit, and God alone knew what other detritus that a century had laid down. On the stone-coloured tiles of the deck lay the crumbled remains of a skeleton and a large carving knife.

'Get that lot over the starboard side, while I deal with the two in the after cabin.'

McGuigan swallowed hard. 'Very good, sir. Did himself in, by the look of it,' he gestured at the knife.

'Yes. Probably no choice.'

Kirton turned away and left the NCO to it, making his way into the master's cabin. He had left the door open the previous evening having done no more than take a cursory and revolted look inside. Now he braced himself and stepped over the threshold. He mastered the rising gorge in his throat and bent to his task. He was no expert but it was fairly obvious that the skeleton that lay on the bunk was that of a woman. Some long strands of dark hair remained stuck to the skull and lying on her vertebrae below on a gold chain that ran round her spine was a large and lustrous pearl.

Just inside the door, on the deck to the right of him lay a pile of bones, crowned by what remained of a skull, the top of which had been shattered. The bullet that had done the work of execution was embedded in the curling varnish of the bulkhead about four feet above the deck. An antique rifle lay across the heap of bones and a few shreds of blue cloth with six brass buttons clung to the collapsed rib-cage.

'So this,' he thought, staring down at the human remains, 'is my wicked great grand-uncle, or whatever he was . . .'

Kirton sighed and swallowed hard, deciding to work initially on the woman. Some remnant bedding enabled him to gather up the bones, but first he grasped the pearl and lifted it from its resting place.

'You must have been his *nyai*,' he muttered to himself. 'I wonder if you were beautiful?'

The chain pulled two vertebrae apart and the skull fell forward. With an oath, Kirton slipped the pearl in his pocket and began to quickly throw the bones onto the sheet he had spread out on the deck beside the remains of the man. He made three trips, for fear of tearing the fragile fabric, but after about a quarter of an hour he had finished. As he rolled the stained mattress up, he found first one and then two more slugs, just like the one in the bulkhead, that had embedded themselves beneath it.

'He shot you then,' he said to himself, then turned his attention to the man. Picking up a couple of the brass buttons he slipped them into the same pocket that contained the pearl.

'Come on, old fellow,' he murmured, wondering if the long dead man had been a practising Catholic and therefore guilty of a mortal sin. 'I don't blame you for ending it all in a hell-hole like this,' he muttered.

After that, he worked quickly, without thinking further, almost oblivious to the fact that McGuigan had finished disposing of the third skeleton and was completing the task by sweeping up the tiled deck of the pantry with a punctiliousness that Kirton found odd until he realised that McGuigan no more wanted a reminder of the corpses than any other man if they were going to operate from this strange gun emplacement.

Back in the master's cabin Kirton gathered up the last of the bones: a femur with a great gall on it and the ball of which was necrotic; and the man's pelvis, which showed similar signs of abnormality. He stared at the evidence of some form of disease, unconsciously pulling a face and muttering, 'poor bastard. That must have been bloody painful . . .'

When he came below after tossing the last remains of Captain Henry Kirton overboard with a suppressed shudder, he found McGuigan sitting at the saloon table on a dark heavy chair from which the stuffed cushion spewed horse-hair. He had wiped an area clear of dust and accumulated filth and had a bottle in front of him. He looked up as Kirton came in.

'I'm sorry sir, but I found this . . .' He indicated the bottle of Scotch whisky.

'Don't blame you, Sergeant, just this once. Taste okay?'

'Better than okay, sir, it's about the only thing that's improved aboard here in the last God knows how long.'

'Take another swig, then give me one. After that I'm afraid we'll have to ditch it and search out any others. We can't risk the men finding any booze.'

After a few moments, during which the whisky went some way to restoring their equanimity, Kirton remarked, 'you know Sergeant, I daresay you, like me, have seen some nasty sights during your service, but that was a most unpleasant task.'

'Aye, sir, and a most unceremonial burial,' McGuigan agreed. 'The rats must have had a fucking field-day.'

Kirton rose and slapped McGuigan on the shoulder, relieved of a great burden. 'Come on, let's go through the ship and see what we can make of her before we bring up the men.'

After they had reassured themselves that there were no more human remains, and where they might mess and accommodate the patrol, the two men returned to the bivouac for breakfast, making as sure as they possibly could not to make it obvious that they had tasted Scotch whisky. Before they moved out to occupy the *Tethys* Kirton took Bangau aside and told him in his fluent Malay what they had found aboard her.

'I think all the bad spirits have gone, Bangau, but if you wish not to come, I understand. You can stay here ...'

'You make a prayer, *Tuan*?' Bangau asked. The Iban Dayak's question chimed with McGuigan's remark that the disposal of the human remains had been utterly without ceremony. Kirton swallowed and lied.

'Yes, Bangau,' he said, compounding his untruth by adding, 'just a short one.'

'I come, *Tuan*,' the Ranger said decisively, whereupon a chastened Kirton smiled wanly.

'*Bagus*,' he said.

Shortly afterwards the Royal Marine patrol was on the move. As the hull of the *Tethys* suddenly loomed above them, they gave vent to their astonishment in a variety of expletives.

'Fucking hell,' remarked Snedding, watching Benjamin clamber up the ship's side. 'Just the job for you, you jungle-bunny,' he chuckled.

'Shut your fucking mouth you gob-shite,' riposted the Brummie, 'or I'll brain you with a coconut.'

Snedding followed Benjamin on deck. The two marines stood staring about them. 'Christ alive! Would you believe ... ?'

'Hey, bucket-mouth,' called Corporal Willis, who, with Bennett, was ready to pass up the heavy machine gun, 'give us a hand.'

They lugged the heavy gun, spare barrels, and ammunition over the side as Bangau slashed left and right with his *padang*, clearing the deck of mangroves as the rest of the patrol, led by Marine Meadows, clambered aboard. After a sentry had been posted, the next few hours were occupied by the majority of the patrol in cleaning those areas of the brigantine that they intended using and establishing the heavy machine gun on the long, elegant counter of the *Tethys*. While the men were thus engaged under the direction of the two NCOs, Kirton took a closer look round the brigantine. It was clear to him that they might hold out in such a position for some time, doing serious damage to the Indonesian supply lines. Food would be the main problem, he thought; perhaps they might make some use of that condensed milk in the hold after all. He wondered if the ship's pumps worked and they could get rid of the rain-water that had flooded the place; the stagnant pool was a too obvious attraction for mozzies.

Having shut off the master's cabin he decided to establish his own quarters in the chart-room where the old horse-hair settee offered him a better bed than he had enjoyed the previous night. Driven by the twin impulses of familial curiosity and that of a serious and accomplished yachtsman, he took a look round the space in which his piratical forebear must have spent many hours.

The chart-table drawers were full of old charts and in his poking about yielded a number of books, including a volume of old sailing directions and a set of nautical tables. The former—James Horsburgh's *The India Directory*—he cast aside after a cursory glance. He was about to do the same with the other but, for some reason, he opened it. Inside the cover on the fly-leaf, on an ornate label showing an old wooden-wall at anchor, he read:

T.S CANOPUS
Presented to Chief Cadet-Captain Henry Kirton,
for excellence in Navigation & Seamanship, June 1855.
Jno. Thos. Penney, Captain Superintendent.

Underneath the label was scrawled the adolescent signature of the man whose name Charlie Kirton now bore.

Somewhat reverentially he closed the book and pushed it to one side, his eyes falling upon the chart that had lain on the table for roughly a hundred years. It was covered in bat droppings—they had discovered that the *Tethys* was infested with bats, dead flies, and spiders. Interested, he compared it with what he recalled of the Dutch map, with its legend of *niet onderzocht,* he had been shown in Tawau. The coastline was delineated by the dotted lines that indicated a vague notion of the shore-line caused by the ever growing mangroves as determined by a running survey. But there, surrounded by a pencilled ring, lay the unmistakable words: *mouth of a river.*

Clearly, and for whatever reason, Captain Henry Kirton had brought his little ship into a refuge of his deliberate selection, for a course line, coming down from the north-east, led to the ringed words. Lieutenant Charles Kirton ran his right index finger lightly along the rhumb line, and followed the hurriedly made loop of the pencilled ring. A foot away lay the pencil with which the marks had been made. Kirton stared at it, but could not bring himself to pick it up.

At sunset Kirton assembled the entire patrol in the saloon for a briefing.

'Fucking hell,' remarked Snedding looking round him, 'the Borneo Hilton . . .' The other marines could scarce believe their eyes.

'It's like time-travelling,' Meadows remarked.

'Pipe-down lads,' McGuigan commanded as Kirton dropped down the companionway and entered the saloon.

'Bit of a crowd, eh?' Kirton remarked, pulling out the chair at the head of the table, which McGuigan had given a thorough cleaning after their tippling of that morning. 'Sit down men, those of you who can,' he said, 'the rest of you gather round . . .'

While he waited for the men to settle, Kirton realised that he must be sitting in the seat reserved for the master of the vessel. And, he noticed, there was a disfiguring groove that ran across the partially restored lustre of a once highly polished table-top. Idly he ran his finger along it.

'Pity about that, sir,' remarked McGuigan jestingly. 'I tried to get rid of it, but generally I thought we might get the mess silver out one night. There's a sideboard full of the stuff.'

'We might just do that, Sarn't,' Kirton replied with a lopsided smile. 'We may be here for some time.' Kirton looked about him. The men were now staring at him expectantly and he began passing his orders. When he had finished he asked if there were any questions. One man put up his hand.

'What is it, Snedding?'

'I get it that this is an old wreck, sir, but did you know it was here?' The question brought a smile to Kirton's face. If Snedding only knew . . . but he didn't and besides the matter was too odd to reveal to anyone, and certainly not the man his mates called 'bucket-mouth.'

'No, I didn't. Nor did Bungau here,' Kirton nodded in the Dayak's direction. 'Anything else?'

'Yeah, sir.'

'Go ahead, Benjamin.'

'Where exactly are we, sir?'

'We are *ulu*, Benjamin, which in Malay means up a river, a river in Borneo . . .'

Kirton dismissed his men to their allotted berths in the old crew accommodation.

As they filed up the companionway to make their way forward Snedding, scratching himself under the arm-pits, could be heard saying: '*Ulu! Ulu!*' to Benjamin.

'Cut that out, Snedding!' Kirton snapped, before turning to McGuigan and Willis. 'I don't want to hear any more of that crap, gentlemen.'

'No, sir,' said McGuigan, 'though Benjamin can look after himself.'

'I daresay he can, but we are not school-boys and I won't have any of that nonsense under my command, whatever they got away with in the *Llandaff*. Just squash it, or I'll have him up on a charge.'

Somewhat shamefacedly the two non-commissioned officers acknowledged the order.

'Now, then,' Kirton went on briskly, 'Changing the subject, we'll pipe down in ten minutes, but before that a few things to consider. We'll abolish differences of rank, gentlemen. This is no different from the jungle. The three of us will mess down aft here, taking one watch each. Now, we must assume that the enemy may move at any time from now on, so I want two men on watch . . .'

Half an hour later Kirton settled himself on the chart-room settee. As he lay composing himself to sleep and the events of that strange day passed before his mind's eye, he realised that he was strangely disquieted, not by the macabre task the day had begun with, but by the fact that, in his aversion from the task he and McGuigan had undertaken, he had not offered any prayer over the human remains. Both McGuigan and the Dyak Bangau had considered, in their differing ways, that he should have done and for a man of Kirton's deep religious sensibilities, he regarded the fact as a sin of omission. He had, moreover, lied about the matter to the Ranger. Getting down on his knees he made amends that evening in his prayers, by confessing his own fault and commending the souls of the long departed to God's infinite care.

Having, for the time being at least, salved his nagging conscience, he recalled the words on the chart not six feet away from him. 'Mouth of a river,' he murmured, smiling to himself in the darkness. The four words conjured up all those ridiculous boyhood presumptions he had made about his strange forebear's piratical doings. Now he knew that some at least of these had taken place in a river in Borneo, just as he had told Benjamin, and it was here, right here, that Captain Harry Kirton had ended-up.

Part Four

St Helena's Hospice, Colchester, England, December 2018

'HE HASN'T GOT LONG, FATHER,' THE NURSE SAID AS SHE ACCOMPANIED the Catholic priest to Colonel Charles Kirton's bed. 'But he is adamant he wishes to speak with you.'

'Of course.'

'Father Peter's here to see you, Colonel,' the nurse said, ushering-in the priest.

The emaciated figure in the bed stirred and held out his bony hand to the priest who drew up a chair and sat down. 'Good of you to come, Father Peter.'

'What is it, my son? I have heard your confession and administered extreme unction.'

A wan smile passed over Kirton's face. 'It takes even cancer rather longer to kill a Royal Marine than an ordinary fellow, Father,' he said, his faint chuckle turning into a violent cough.

When Kirton had regained his breath the priest asked: 'Tell me what is troubling you?'

'Many years ago, in Borneo,' Kirton said slowly and with a great effort, 'for reasons that . . . I need not explain, I was obliged to . . . er, dispose of three skeletons, the remains of three people who . . . well, never mind . . .' Kirton paused, gathering strength. Father Peter waited patiently. 'Point is, I did so without ceremony . . . without a thought . . .' and then with an effort: 'without committal . . .' He was silent for a moment before adding: 'Unpleasant job . . . thought about it later in the day . . . said a few words . . . for their souls . . . But now . . . it plays upon my conscience that I did nothing at the time of . . . of disposing of them . . .'

'And how did you do that?' the priest asked. 'Dispose of them, I mean.'

'We threw the bones in a river . . .'

'In Borneo . . .'

Kirton nodded.

'Were they all Christians?'

'One was born so . . . don't know about the others . . .'

'And you said prayers for their souls later?'

'That evening.' Kirton paused, then added, 'they had been dead a long time.'

'How long?'

'Perhaps a century.'

Father Peter concealed his astonishment. Then he put on his stole and laid his hand upon Kirton's forehead before making the sign of the cross. 'You have nothing with which to reproach yourself, my son . . .'

'Thank you Father . . .' Kirton drifted off, then, just as Father Peter rose to take his leave, he rallied. 'We stopped them . . .'

'Who?'

'The Indos . . . we commanded that river for three weeks . . . they didn't get a thing through before June the sixth . . . gave up afterwards . . .' Then there was a long pause before the dying man added: 'We blew her up before we left . . . hold full of . . . rifles . . . ammunition . . . sad end . . . but duty done.' Kirton's eyes were closed, but he was smiling. Only partially understanding this last rambling utterance, the priest made a final sign of the cross and quietly left the dying man. There were others awaiting his pastoral care.

Outside, just as he was taking leave of the nurse, Father Peter encountered the colonel's wife. Her face showed alarm when she saw him.

'Am I too late?' she asked, her face draining of colour.

'No, but I do not think he can last much longer, my dear.'

She was a handsome woman, Father Peter thought, noticing the lustrous pearl she wore about her neck. Under the circumstances, he thought, it hardly seemed suitable. She nodded at him, then hurried past to consult the nurse who then accompanied her to Kirton's bedside.

Kirton's eyes were closed but he sensed the presence of his wife and he turned his head and opened them to look at her. 'Julia, how good to see you . . .' He spoke with a sudden and surprising vigour that alarmed her, trying to heave himself up in the bed.

'Charlie, darling, please don't . . .' She sat and took his hand, as the effort proved too much for him and he sank back on the pillows.

After a pause he smiled wanly. 'And you are wearing the pearl . . . how lovely . . .'

Acknowledgements

No author functions in isolation and I wish to express my gratitude to a number of people for their help in the production of this novel. First my gratitude to George Jepson of McBooks for his long interest in my literary work and his enthusiasm to publish *A River in Borneo*; secondly my thanks to Lynn Zelem, production editor at Globe Pequot, and to Joshua Rosenberg for his assiduous copy-editing. A warm expression of appreciation must assuredly go to Geoffrey Huband both for his artistic and his imaginative skill in turning my rough brief into the splendid cover-art showing the *Tethys* off the coast of Borneo. Thanks are also due to my neighbour, friend and fellow former master-mariner Tony Boddy, whose knowledge of Sarawaki and Malay culture in the 1960s filled-in the considerable gaps in my own; also to former Royal Marine Ray Kay for details of that Corps during the period of 'Confrontation.' Grateful thanks are also due to Victoria Pryor and Barbara Levy, my agents in the United States and United Kingdom respectively, whilst my long-standing debt to my wife, Chris, remains fathomless.

R.W.